# Captured in Frame

# Captured in Frame

by

## Laura Thomas

Captured in Frame
Published by Mountain Brook Ink
White Salmon, WA U.S.A.



The website addresses shown in this book are not intended in any way to be or imply an endorsement on the part of Mountain Brook Ink, nor do we vouch for their content.

This story is a work of fiction. All characters and events are the product of the author's imagination. Any resemblance to any person, living or dead, is coincidental.

All Scripture quotations taken from THE MESSAGE, copyright © 1993, 2002, 2018 by Eugene H. Peterson. Used by permission of NavPress. All rights reserved.


ISBN 9781-953957-43-6

The Team: Miralee Ferrell, Tim Pietz, Kristen Johnson, Cindy Jackson
Cover Design: Indie Cover Design, Lynnette Bonner Designer

*Mountain Brook Ink is an inspirational publisher offering fiction you can believe in.*
Printed in the United States of America

# Dedication

For Heidi—my beautiful sister, my brave inspiration, and my best friend.

# Acknowledgments

I am absolutely thrilled to be able to share *Captured in Frame*, the first story in my "Bite of Betrayal" series! This is my eleventh published book, but it's extra special as I was able to go back to my British roots with an English setting—plus, I have the honor of working with a new publisher, Mountain Brook Ink. My heartfelt thanks go out to:

Mountain Brook Ink—to Miralee Ferrell and her wonderful team for inviting me into this publishing family. I'm beyond excited for us to work together with these books!

Karen Neumair at Credo Communications—my fantastic literary agent, who found the perfect publishing home for this Christian romantic suspense series.

Blossom Turner—my talented critique partner who is not afraid to tell me the truth (which I desperately need, especially in those early drafts)… I so appreciate you!

Charlotte, Jameson, and Jacob—my amazing grown children, for always bringing so much joy to your old mom's heart!

Lyndon—my husband who joined me on a crazy adventure several decades ago, that swept us across the world and planted us in a new country. Here's to our beautiful Canadian life, along with precious memories of the UK. I love it all with you by my side.

My heavenly Father—for giving me light and life and words.

# Chapter One

Georgia's eyes flew open—someone else was in the cottage.

*Breathe.*

A noise from downstairs. A thud. Muffled. Muted. Perhaps it was a dream or more likely, a nightmare. Wouldn't be the first time for Georgia Brooks. Sleep was an elusive companion these days…

Another thump from the kitchen below.

*What on earth?* She sat bolt upright in the unfamiliar bed, swallowed hard, and rolled over to the nightstand.

5:44 AM

Still dark, and she was alone. Very much alone. Pulling the phone from its charger, she clutched it in both hands and stared at the screen for several seconds.

Call her sister? Call the police? It could be nothing. This was her first night in England in a strange house. One she hadn't slept in since childhood. An ancient country cottage would make peculiar sounds, right? Creaky floorboards. Leaky pipes… but thuds?

Only one way to find out.

Georgia yanked the crisp, white sheet aside. She crawled to the end of the bed, phone in hand, and set bare feet on weathered floorboards. The bedroom door was ajar and the warm glow of a nightlight in the upstairs hallway guided her footsteps through the space.

At the doorway, she paused.

Silence.

Nothing, after all.

*Just a sweet, quirky cottage telling me a new day is dawning.*

Georgia leaned one pajama-clad hip against the door jamb and closed her eyes. A feisty imagination and jet lag. Maybe one too many sleeping pills. Plus, a plethora of emotional issues. Deep breath in through the nose, and slow release out from the mouth. Again. And again.

She opened her eyes and checked the time on her phone. It had been two long minutes and no more disturbing sounds. She should go downstairs and take a quick look around to put her mind at ease. Maybe make a cup of tea—wasn't that the English way? Take a nap until it was a civil enough hour to call Harriet. Her sister would be a voice of reason.

She grabbed her silky robe from the hook on the back of the bedroom door and wrapped it around her trembling body. Yes, tea would help calm her nerves.

With the first tentative step onto the hall landing, her nostrils tingled.

Burning. Something was burning.

*NO. Oh please, no.*

Her knees buckled and she collapsed to the floor. Dark spots danced before her eyes and she struggled to gasp for air. Could it be a nightmare, after all? She would wake up soon. A pinch to the skin on her lower arm confirmed this was no dream. A successful sharp inhale of something singed was enough to propel her into dialing mode.

Harriet picked up on the third ring.

"Georgia?" A two-syllabled croak, fresh from sleep.

"There's a fire, Harriet." Her voice was a whisper. "And… I think there's someone downstairs."

"What?"

Georgia heard her murmur something to Leo.

"You have to get out of the cottage, okay? Where exactly are you now?"

"I just woke up. I'm outside my bedroom door. I-I don't know if anyone's still down there. I heard some noises…."

"Can you see the fire? Can you hear it?"

The dancing spots dissipated from her vision as she pulled herself up and took three cautious steps down the hallway, clutching the wall. "No. No, I can't. I smell it though. I smell burning." She cringed at the hint of hysteria in her voice. *I'm the one who's always in control.* Responsible big sister.

"We're on our way. We'll literally be five minutes. Are you sure it's a fire? I don't want you to put yourself in danger, but can you see down the stairs? I'll stay on the line with you." More mumbling with her husband.

Georgia stumbled to the top of the staircase and craned her neck to peer down toward the living area. No orange glow. No crackling. No smoke. *Weird.* She sniffed again to make sure she wasn't imagining things.

"I don't see smoke, but I still smell it. I'm heading down the staircase now." She stood on each tread for several beats, waiting for someone below to hear the creaking. Her stomach clenched.

"Georgia, please be careful. We're in the car now. Leo phoned it in so you should hear a siren any minute coming from the village."

Pre-dawn light filtered in through a sliver of a gap between the ivory living room curtains. Georgia squinted and lowered her whisper. "I'm downstairs. Everything seems fine." She glanced around the corner down the hallway to the entrance. "The front door looks as if it's still locked."

"What about the fire?"

"No smoke, but I still smell it…" *Must be in the kitchen.*

"You need to head straight out the front door. Please don't take any chances."

Georgia bit her bottom lip. "I think I need to start taking chances, sis."

"Not with fire." Harriet's voice quivered.

They had their own horrific childhood memories from a house fire, one that changed their family forever.

"I'm not going to do anything crazy, but I'm not going to let Bramble Cottage burn to the ground."

A flicker of courage ignited her belly. A forgotten sensation she needed to embrace. Wasn't this three-month stay in England all about facing the future with fortitude? Finding healing from a broken heart and maybe even hope again?

Harriet broke into her moment of reverie. "For heaven's sake, we're two minutes away. *Please* will you get out of there through the front door?"

The kitchen. As Georgia pivoted toward the back of the house, a strip of light glowed along the base of the kitchen door. *I turned it off last night. I know I did.* Her mouth went dry. The room beckoned and Georgia followed with slow, steady steps.

The smell was stronger as she neared the door and resolve began to crumble as vivid memories surfaced from long ago. Lash of angry flames. Intensity of searing heat. Devastation of desperate screams. Her five-year-old self running outside and gulping the sweetest fresh air before her childhood came crashing down around her.

She shook her head and blinked moisture from her eyes. This was different. She was no helpless five-year-old. With the phone still at her ear, she could hear Harriet reassure Lucy everything was fine—her three-year-old niece must have been woken and bundled into the car, too. Georgia winced as she thought of her little sisters, Harriet and Sophie, as two-year-old twins when the house fire happened. Not much younger than Lucy was now…

"Hello? Are you still in the cottage? Tell me you're outside."

*Focus.* "I'm about to open the kitchen door."

"Please, wait." Harriet's voice rose an octave. "We're almost there."

The smooth, iron doorknob turned in Georgia's hand as she rotated it with care. She took a deep breath and thrust the wooden door wide open.

# Chapter Two

GEORGIA'S LIMBS REFUSED TO MOVE AS a gust of fresh morning air rushed at her from the open back door. Bracing herself for an attack of some sort, she tensed every muscle until she got her bearings. It was a decent-sized kitchen with a couple of possible places to wait in hiding. She scanned the room with precision—as a photographer, she was nothing if not observant:

Muddy footprints on the tiled gray floor.

The backdoor key placed on top of the stove.

The stainless-steel toaster on the counter had been used. Two slices of charred bread mocked her from their slots.

A groan broke free.

Sirens sounded—either from her sister's phone or outside down the country lane.

"Georgia? Will you say something?"

"I'm here. I'm fine. There's no fire." She changed the phone to her other ear and stepped toward the toaster. She reached out and touched it. Still warm. "I guess the fire truck was overkill."

"We're pulling up outside and the fire engine's here, too. Plus, the police."

Georgia's shoulders slumped. Way to make an entrance into the sleepy village of Bramble Downs. Could this get any worse? She hung up and slid the phone into her robe pocket.

A commotion at the front door coincided with a tall, uniformed police officer appearing at the back entrance.

"Ma'am?"

Georgia felt the blood rush from her face and collapsed onto a wooden kitchen chair. "Come on in. I think he's gone."

"He?" The policeman took three strides to reach her. "I'm Officer Parker. Do you need medical attention?" He held his phone at the ready.

"No. No, thanks. I'm just a little shaken up." She closed her robe tighter over the tank top she wore with cotton pajama shorts.

He raised a brow. "American?"

"Canadian."

"What's your name, Miss?" She couldn't help but notice how his oversized ears seemed to hold his peaked black hat in place.

"Georgia Brooks."

"Anyone else here with you?"

She glanced down at the bare fingers on her left hand. "No." *I'm all alone.*

"This is your home?"

He was no local. Everyone in this tiny village knew who lived where, with whom, and why. "Yes, it belongs to me. I only arrived yesterday. It's kind of a long story…"

Satisfied and uninterested in said long story, he nodded and disappeared in the direction of the front door.

Georgia ran her fingers through her tangled hair and exhaled. She was safe. Why the burnt toast? The only person who knew what her reaction would be to that particular smell was *him*. Why on earth would he do that? A shiver ran through her body.

"There she is." Harriet hurried into the kitchen and enveloped her sister in a warm hug. "Thank goodness you're okay. You scared the life out of me. What's going on? Is everything all right?" Her eyes flickered around the kitchen and she sniffed. "Burnt toast?"

Georgia sighed. "It seems someone came in here while I was sleeping and burnt two slices."

"What?" Harriet blinked in confusion. "Why? Who would be so cruel? Who else even knows about…"

"Please, don't ask me to explain. Honestly, I've no idea." Georgia turned around. "Is Lucy here, too? I'm sorry to wake you all for nothing."

"It's fine. She's in the car with Leo. I wasn't sure what we might be walking into." She clasped Georgia's hands. "I'm so glad it wasn't a fire."

Georgia bit her lip. "Me, too. At least the fire truck can go home."

"It's leaving." Officer Parker's sudden reappearance caused her to flinch. "Don't worry, it's better to be safe than sorry. Has anything been stolen, Miss Brooks?"

"Not as far as I can tell. My camera equipment and all my personal things were with me upstairs. I'm a photographer."

"That's something, at least. We'll get this area fingerprinted and I'll write up a report. If you could both refrain from touching anything, we'd appreciate it." He followed Harriet's gaze over to the toaster and sniffed. "Burnt toast?"

"Yes." Georgia's voice was a mere whisper. "Someone was in here—the toaster was warm when I touched it. He made sure it was burnt."

"You suspected it was a fire?" His dark bushy brows met in the middle.

Harriet stood and straightened the sweater she wore over silky pajamas. "It was an honest mistake, Officer. There was a dreadful house fire when we were kids and the smell of burnt toast is a trigger for her."

Georgia met the officer's kind eyes. "I'm aware of how wacky that sounds."

"Not at all." He pulled out a notebook and a pen. "Do you think someone was sending you a message today with this burnt toast? A coincidence seems highly unlikely."

*How could he? Surely not.*

"I have no clue. Other than Harriet, nobody living here would know anything about my past."

Officer Parker inspected the kitchen window. "It doesn't look like either of the doors were compromised. We'll check all the windows though."

Georgia pointed a trembling finger toward the stove. "No need. I guess he used that key."

Harriet tilted her head to one side. "Someone else had a key and then left it here?"

Officer Parker cleared his throat. "Could you both go into the living room for a few minutes while we process the kitchen?"

Georgia's head pounded. "Come on." She clutched her sister's hand and headed to the floral sofa where they both flopped down and were swallowed by soft cushions.

"Hello? Doctor Hughes here." A deep male voice floated in from the front hallway.

*What now?* "Doctor?" Georgia mouthed to Harriet and whipped her head around. Some guy in navy scrubs stood in the entrance with a medical bag and a serious scowl.

"Will?" Harriet stood and walked over to him. "Good to see you—why are you here though?"

Scrubs-guy ran a hand through a shock of light brown hair and furrowed his brow. "I finished my shift at the hospital and was on my way home. Saw the flashing lights and wanted to see if I could help. Leo said to come on in. Is everyone okay?"

"Yes, thankfully." Harriet lifted one slim arm out toward the sofa. "This is Georgia. She literally flew in from Canada yesterday and some creep broke into the cottage. She's not hurt."

*Not physically at least.* Georgia plastered on a smile. "Hi." That one syllable was all she could manage at this point. She attempted to smooth the bird's nest in the back of her wavy hair.

"Nice to meet you." He dipped his head. "Terrible circumstances though."

"Right? I can't believe it." Harriet folded her arms across her chest. "I don't know when we last had any trouble like this in the village. Our Grandma would turn in her grave if she knew someone had broken into Bramble Cottage."

"I'm sure. Well, if there's nothing I can do here, I'll be on my way. See you at church on Sunday. Cheerio." He waved in Georgia's direction.

"Sure, and thanks for stopping by. That was kind of you." Harriet spoke for them both, and then plodded back to the sofa, stretching her arms above her head.

"A friend of yours?" Georgia concentrated on a broken thumbnail.

"He's Leo's good buddy, and also our local surgeon. Salt of the earth kind of guy, too. Everyone in Bramble Downs refers to him as the dreamy doc."

"Dreamy?"

Harriet pursed her lips. "How can you have missed all that handsome? You *must* be overtired."

"I have a lot on my mind, sis." Like an intruder. Although she had noticed signs of exhaustion in his deep green eyes. Yes, she could identify with exhaustion. "You know, I'm about ready to fall asleep here, which is not the best idea with these men wandering around. I need to trick my body into believing it really is morning."

"Want me to pull the curtains? Let some daylight in?" Harriet stifled a yawn. "Not that the sun's up quite yet."

Georgia cringed. "Sorry. This is the absolute worst start to my stay here, isn't it? I'll get the curtains."

"Hey, quit being so hard on yourself. The break-in was hardly your fault."

Georgia stood and padded over to the window. "I'd feel better if you would go on home with your sweet family and catch up on some sleep. I'll watch for the sunrise while the police do their thing and then I'll head back to bed."

"I don't think I should leave you…"

"I'm a big girl, you know." She swished the full-length linen drapes to one side.

A strangled cry escaped her lips.

# Chapter Three

GEORGIA COULDN'T PULL HER EYES away from the postcard taped in the middle of the window. A shiver rippled up her spine as she absorbed the sinister scene of a dead body crumpled on the ground. A middle-aged man, a forehead marred by a bullet hole, a neck twisted to an unnatural angle. Her empty stomach heaved at the sight of so much dark blood pooled around the body.

"What is it?" Harriet was at Georgia's side in an instant, followed by Officer Parker and the younger policeman. They all stood and stared at the monstrosity.

"What happened?" The good doctor jogged back into the room and joined them by the window.

"I thought you left." Harriet's voice was monotone as she stood transfixed by the awful image.

"I started talking to Leo outside and heard a scream. Told Leo to stay with Lucy. What is this?" He'd homed in on the postcard. "Good grief. I can handle my fair share of blood, but this is… graphic."

"It's disgusting." Georgia pulled her robe tighter in an attempt to stave off a sudden chill that had nothing to do with the gust of crisp morning air Will brought in with him.

"Perhaps you should sit, Georgia. You're trembling." He took her elbow and guided her back to the sofa.

"I feel like I might pass out…" She leaned over her knees and took in a deep breath as darkness threatened to eclipse her vision.

"Mind if I take your pulse?"

"Go ahead." Her mouth felt full of cotton balls as she sensed him lifting her left wrist.

Harriet settled onto the sofa and rubbed her back. "I'll text Leo—he must be worried sick out there not knowing what's going on."

"I'm fine, guys. Really." The sensation passed and her head cleared enough for her to watch the meticulous actions of Officer Parker.

He took a step closer to the postcard and cocked his head. "Taped to the inside of the window. Not good. Someone took their time in here."

Georgia nodded and tried not to be distracted by Will's featherlight touch on her wrist.

"I presume the postcard wasn't here yesterday?"

*Seriously?* "I can assure you it wasn't there when I closed the curtains last night." She bit her bottom lip and glanced back at the image. "Someone came in here and taped it to the window while I was asleep." She swallowed the lump in her throat.

Harriet reached for her sister's right hand and gave it a squeeze. Did Harriet remember the postcards he used to send?

*Please don't say anything.* Georgia reciprocated the squeeze hoping she would get the message. They couldn't risk making eye contact with each other while these two police officers watched their every move.

"You're fine now." Will crouched down in front of Georgia. "I'm afraid I have to leave, but please don't hesitate to give me a call if you have any health concerns later. Harriet has my number."

"Thanks."

He attempted a smile and stood. "Bye for now. I'll see myself out."

Harriet pulled a soft throw from the arm of the sofa and

wrapped it around Georgia's shoulders. "I'll be two seconds. I'm going to tell Leo to go on home with Lucy while I stay with you."

"There's no need for you to stay. You should go—"

"I'm not arguing." Harriet jumped up and hurried off toward the foyer. Stubborn. A born caretaker.

"Miss Brooks?" Officer Parker had asked her a question.

"Sorry, what did you say?"

"Any idea who would do this? Who would want to spook you or send some sort of message?"

*Cool. Play it cool. At least, until you figure out why he's doing this.* "No clue. Like I said, I only arrived yesterday."

The twitch of his eyebrow said he wasn't convinced. "Let's see if there's anything written on the back, shall we? Then we can get it checked for fingerprints." He nodded to his fellow officer.

Why the postcard? Why here and why now? The image made her skin crawl as her mind raced with possible scenarios.

Harriet returned and cuddled up next to her. Like the old days when they would all huddle on the couch together watching a movie and eating chocolate on a Friday night. Three sisters and Mom. Good memories.

They both watched in silence as the postcard was dusted for fingerprints and then peeled with care from the pane of glass. The young, stocky policeman turned it over and showed it to Officer Parker. His expression gave nothing away.

"What does it say?" Georgia bit on her thumbnail.

"There's only one word." He paused for effect. "*GONE.*"

Gone? "May I see the handwriting?"

Officer Parker lowered it in front of her face in his gloved hand. "Block capitals. Pretty generic. Does it look familiar?"

She squinted. "No. Not at all." Weird. Not his usual slanted scrawl.

"Gone?" Harriet whispered. "Does it mean you've gone from Canada?"

Georgia glanced from Harriet to the stoic policemen. "I'm sorry, but I can't tell you what I don't know. All I *do* know is someone was obviously in my cottage and they tried to freak me out." Tears blurred her vision. "And succeeded."

"Oh, sweetie." Harriet put a protective arm around Georgia's shoulders. "Officers, if you've finished with her for now, do you think I could get my sister settled upstairs? She's had a nasty shock and she's in desperate need of sleep. I'll stay with her and you can finish up down here. Is that okay?"

Without waiting for confirmation, they stood and Harriet steered her toward the staircase.

"Miss Brooks."

Georgia turned her head.

"I'll leave my card on the kitchen counter. Please call if you think of anything else. Anything at all. I'll let you rest and we'll talk later. I'll need your fingerprints to eliminate them from our findings here."

"Yes, of course. Thank you." These guys were thorough. Georgia wiped a stray tear from her cheek and plodded up the stairs, followed by Harriet.

As Georgia reached the cozy bedroom, a wave of exhaustion hit her full on. Nauseous, she climbed into bed, cocooned the duvet around her, and sat propped up against the white leather headboard.

Harriet opened the window behind the drawn curtains. "The burning smell's gone up here, but we might as well get some fresh air circulating." She perched on the edge of the bed. "Want to tell me what's going on?" She squeezed Georgia's toes through the bedding. "This doesn't feel good. The postcard must be from Daniel, don't you think?"

"But I can't for the life of me imagine why." Georgia pulled at a thread on the snowy white cover. "I haven't seen him in six months. Our only correspondence has been through email. Trust me, the divorce got ugly very quickly." She reached for the pillow next to her and hugged it to her chest. "And why send such a hideous picture? A dead guy shot in the head? If it was him, he must have reached an all-time low."

"Do you suppose he's mad that you got the cottage after the divorce?"

"He made a fuss at the time, but he knew deep down I was going to want it. It's been in our family for years and means the world to me."

Harriet groaned. "I'm sorry it all turned out badly between you two. You kept it hidden from us so well. I thought you were living the dream. My perfect sister and her perfect man."

"So did I. This was supposed to be our actual dream cottage. We were going to spend our summers and maybe even retire here one day. Like Grandma and Grandpa did."

"I know. We have so many memories from our vacations in Bramble Downs as kids. How could Daniel possibly imagine you would part with the cottage? I'm glad you fought to keep it."

Georgia admired the wooden exposed beam running down the length of her bedroom ceiling. The completed renovations were exquisite. "Me, too. I guess I'll have to enjoy it on my own now."

Harriet's eyes narrowed. "Daniel's the biggest jerk out there and he's made a huge mistake, but I can't get my head around why he would be here stalking you with the toast and the postcard. It doesn't add up. Besides, I thought he shacked up with that other woman and moved on."

"He did. He moved in with her as soon as he packed his

things and left our townhouse." Georgia tasted bile. "And he'll do anything for her, apparently. It's like she has this weird hold over him. I was lucky to end up with Bramble Cottage. Apparently, she was pushing for us to put it up for sale and split the proceeds. There was no way I was going to let that happen. She's taken enough from me."

"But the postcard?" Harriet ran her fingers through her chic, bobbed hair. "That was his trademark. The special thing he always did when he went on one of his assignments, wasn't it?"

Georgia let out a sigh and closed her eyes. "I knew you'd remember that."

"I used to be so jealous you'd found such a romantic man."

"He was. I had a stack of postcards from all over the world. He'd send one from every city he visited."

"I hope you threw them all out when he left."

"You better believe it. If I wasn't so averse to the smell of burning, I would've lit a big old bonfire and held a ceremony to get rid of every last memory."

Harriet scowled. "I can't believe the way he treated you. Although why would he leave you a postcard now? He's got his new life. Even if it *is* him, what would he mean by 'gone'? I'm guessing he knew you were coming to England."

"That's just it—I didn't tell him the date I was coming, although it wouldn't have been hard to find out. The thing is, I'm sure the word *gone* wasn't written by him. He's a leftie with a distinct slant to his handwriting. Besides, he's a journalist—he could never write only one word. Back in the day, he would cram words into every square inch on his postcards." Her chest ached at the memory of his charming prose. "Plus, we had a secret code."

"You did?"

She tucked a strand of hair behind one ear. "Yes. Postcards aren't exactly private. It wasn't rocket science, but he could be as romantic as he wanted…"

"Without piquing your mailman's curiosity?"

"Exactly. Before he decided his romance was better served elsewhere." Her face heated as she swallowed down rage and shame.

Harriet tapped her fingers on the bedcover. "Maybe he changed his mind and wants back in on the cottage. Had second thoughts and likes the idea of an investment property in England. He's definitely not sentimental about Bramble Cottage like you are. Could his new woman be pushing him again into getting you to change your mind?"

Georgia jutted her chin. "He knows there's no way I'm giving up this place. It belonged to Grandma and she wanted me to have it. Remember how cheaply she sold it to me? Besides, I paid him out for his share in it. We're done."

"Unless he got greedy afterwards." Harriet stood and paced along the wide-planked floor. "Tell me about the burnt toast. Daniel must have known that would upset you."

Georgia's heart squeezed. This hurt more than anything. "He knew. Of course, I told him about the house fire years ago— it was one of the first things we talked about when we started dating in college. I remember he was curious about how Dad died."

"Such a nightmare."

"For us all. Daniel was aware that the smell of anything burning sent my heart racing. He used to be protective about that. Kind and considerate. Until the end."

Harriet stopped. "Why? What happened?"

Georgia took a moment. "Before we broke up, when he was

already in a relationship with the other woman, things got intense. We both said words we shouldn't have and pressed each other's buttons. The day I could take no more was when he locked me in our bedroom and went down to the kitchen." She studied the ceiling. "It sounds so pathetic, but he knew exactly how to drive me crazy. He turned the toaster on high and burnt an entire loaf, slice after slice. He deactivated the smoke alarm and everything."

"What?" Harriet's eyes flashed and she sank back down onto the bed. "That's so cruel."

Georgia dug her fingernails into her palms. "I know. It sounds even more ridiculous when I say it out loud, but I honestly thought I was losing my mind. The burning smell got stronger and stronger. All my little-girl memories of our house burning down and of losing Dad smothered me."

"Of course."

"I cried until I had no voice. It was the cruelest thing he could have dreamed up. So, I let Daniel go after loving him for over a dozen years." She squeezed the pillow tight. "The marriage was over. This experimental stay in the cottage is supposed to be about me finally moving on. Seeing if England might be a good fit for me—if I can do it alone."

"I'm sorry." Harriet's brown eyes shone with unshed tears. "I can't believe you didn't tell me. I had no idea things got so bad between you guys. Does Mom or Sophie know about all this?"

Georgia shook her head. "A couple of my close friends knew. Sophie's busy in Paris and you have your own little family to look after—I guess I was waiting to have some heart-to-heart conversations with you both while I was here. I'd rather you didn't tell Sophie anything yet."

"Of course. This is your news to share."

"Thanks. Mom… well, I didn't want to burden her with my

worries. She probably would've insisted I move back home with her or something. I was trying to get through it all on my own. Prove to myself I wasn't a complete wreck."

Harriet clutched her sister's hand. "I think Mom would have respected that. I wish you'd shared with me though. You've been on my heart so much. I've been praying for you."

"I know. I'm grateful for your prayers. Your perseverance paid off. I guess it wasn't until I was well and truly in the pit that I realized my actual need for God." She shrugged. "I've been the classic prodigal daughter."

"Well, we're all glad you found your way back home."

The sound of the backdoor closing downstairs made both girls flinch. Harriet stood. "I suppose they've finished up. How about I make you a nice cup of tea before you get some rest?"

"Tea? How English you've become." Georgia gave a weak smile. "Thanks, that would be lovely. And thanks for being here."

"I'll always be here for you." Harriet disappeared downstairs and left Georgia alone.

She lay her head back and closed her eyes. In the stillness of morning, the dawn chorus started up outside the bedroom window. She pictured the backyard, bordered by trees and bushes, not huge but large enough to provide shade and privacy. She would take a better look around today, get her bearings and maybe even meet some neighbors. In a village this size, no doubt her excitement with the police and fire brigade would be major news and a dramatic start to her stay here. *Exactly what I didn't want.*

A muffled shrill sounded from her pocket. She'd forgotten her phone was still buried in her robe. Who would be calling this early?

She dug it out and checked the screen. Mom calling from Canada?

"Hey, Mom, how are you?"

"Georgia, I'm fine. Did I wake you?"

*I wish.* "No, I was awake. You know, jet lag and all. Are you heading to bed?"

"Not exactly. I received a phone call." She cleared her throat. "It's very bad news I'm afraid."

Every hair on Georgia's head stood on end. "What is it? Is it Sophie?" She was the only one not accounted for.

"No, Sophie's fine. She's got her flight booked to be there with you in a couple of weeks."

*Thank goodness.* "What is it then?"

"There's been an accident, honey. It's Daniel."

*Daniel?* She clutched the bedding in her free hand. "Just tell me, Mom."

"I'm so sorry, sweetheart, but there's no easy way to say this. Daniel is dead."

# Chapter Four

DOCTOR WILL HUGHES DROVE PAST THE roadside "For Sale" sign and pulled his SUV into his circular driveway, second guessing himself yet again about selling the place. He killed the engine and leaned back into the headrest and allowed his weary eyes to shut. Every muscle ached. Heart included.

The decision to sell was excruciating. He tilted his head to one side and then the other. *A massage would be perfect about now.* Memories of happier times blazed behind his eyelids. *Don't go there.* He buried that thought and rubbed the stubble on his chin. Perhaps he could creep in without waking Rachel and Jack. Breakfast could wait—sleep was priority number one.

He grabbed his leather messenger bag from the floor of the vehicle and stepped out onto the gravel. His medical bag securely stowed in the trunk, he closed the car door and locked it with as little noise as possible and then plodded toward the front door, each step crunching like cereal underfoot.

Before inserting the key into the lock, Will turned to catch the first hint of sunrise, his favorite part of the day—even after an exhausting night shift dealing with emergency surgeries and sick kids.

He let out a contented sigh as a crack of light broke into the purple darkness and spread across the horizon, rich with the promise of a warm, late summer's day. How could anyone doubt there was a Creator with such extravagant masterpieces on display? Still, silent, spectacular moments like this never failed to stir his heart.

Yet all was not still and silent in other parts of the village. A muscle in his cheek twitched as he thought of Georgia. Harriet's sister from Canada. How frightening to have a break-in at Bramble Cottage on her first night here. That was one grisly postcard on her window. He shuddered at the memory.

What was her story? He seemed to recall she had a divorce of some magnitude. Then Leo arranged for her to do some photography work here in England for a while. Will's curiosity was stirred. They didn't have many visitors in the village, especially from abroad. He would've preferred to meet under more pleasant circumstances. A nice conversation and a cup of tea. One glimpse confirmed she was as beautiful as Harriet claimed, even first thing in the morning.

He hitched the bag further onto his shoulder.

Poor Georgia. Welcome to England. No wonder she seemed shaken up. Most likely in shock. Maybe Harriet would bring her to church on Sunday and he could check on her. For professional reasons. That was all.

He shook his head in an attempt to unscramble his thoughts. A night shift always left him a little discombobulated. One deep breath of fresh country air, and serenity enveloped him like a comforting blanket. Then his chest squeezed. How many times had he and his wife enjoyed beautiful moments like this together watching the patchwork of fields light up and ease into a new morning?

The blanket of comfort felt heavy now, a burden too much for him to bear alone. *God, it's going to be one of those days. I need You. I also need sleep.*

Leaving the dawn to unfold behind him, Will pivoted, unlocked the door, and crept into the spacious hallway. He shed his shoes and dumped his bag onto the hardwood floor. Light shone from upstairs, but all was quiet. The usual note from Rachel was on the hall table beneath the mirror. She was grabbing a few hours of sleep in the guest room, but she'd had a good night babysitting Jack. Everything was fine. No need for Will to worry. Maybe he would manage to nap for an hour or two before Jack awoke. Ignoring sudden pangs of hunger, he climbed the spiral staircase and chanced a quick peek into his son's nursery.

Will pushed the door open and a creak sounded. He grimaced and then crept over to the huge crib where his blond-haired boy slept clutching the silky trim of his yellow blanket in one pudgy hand. At almost two years old, Jack took up every square inch of the crib. When were babies supposed to move into big-boy beds anyway?

Will leaned against the slatted footboard and blew out a steady stream of air as he considered the upheaval they both had ahead of them. Graduating from crib to bed was nothing compared to selling the house and moving.

He vacillated back and forth almost on a daily basis as to whether he should sell. He had a spreadsheet of pros and cons on his laptop. Should he rip Jack away from the only home he'd ever known? Would he even care at his age? He rounded the crib and touched Jack's downy cheek.

They'd put so much love and attention into every detail of this house. He would never find a place like this again. Yet along with the precious memories of their time here as a couple and then bringing a newborn baby into this home, it was filled to the rafters with grief. Sometimes so thick he could almost taste it in the air. Suffocating.

Jack stirred and Will froze. *Please sleep a bit longer, little man. Let Daddy grab a nap.* He watched the rise and fall of his son's chest beneath his racing car onesie until it was slow and even again, his own lids becoming heavier by the second.

Rather than confront the master bedroom, Will stumbled to the other side of the nursery and collapsed into the glider rocking chair. He adjusted the pillow behind his head and reached for the lop-eared stuffed bunny strewn on the carpet next to him. The soft brown toy he bought when they discovered they were having a baby.

Will invited sleep as he rocked slowly back and forth. With bunny clutched against him, a solitary tear escaped and fell down his stubbled cheek onto his navy scrubs. Would this ever get any easier?

And would he ever have the courage to admit the whole truth to anyone?

# Chapter Five

"DEAD?" HARRIET DROPPED THE TRAY ONTO the window seat and rushed to Georgia's side. "What? Daniel is *dead?*"

Georgia swiped at her wet cheeks. "I can't believe it."

"What did Mom say exactly?" Harriet sank onto the bed and clasped her sister's hand. "How? I mean, did she have details?"

"Only that it was a hit-and-run in downtown Vancouver. Near Canada Place. Sometime early last night, I think. No one's been charged yet. The police are looking into everything—that's how Uncle Pete found out and then phoned Mom."

Harriet shuddered. "He would've recognized Daniel's name straight away. Everyone in the family knows him." She winced. "Knew him."

Georgia's head spun and she squeezed her eyes shut. The postcard. The wretched toast. What was going on? Her ex-husband was gone forever. Her head knew Daniel had moved on and he was no longer hers to mourn, yet they'd shared so much. Twelve years of marriage, most of them happy. Deep down, *really* deep down, a part of her would always love him. Even when another part hated him. More warm tears leaked down her cheeks.

Harriet found a tissue box on the bedside table and passed it to Georgia. "I'm so sorry. This is a lot to process."

"Mom sounded pretty shaken up. She said it reminded her of when Dad died. The shock and the grief and everything." Georgia rubbed her chest-bone as a fresh layer of pain settled upon her.

"Poor Mom. She'll want to fly out and be with you, you know that."

*This is too much.* "I know. She wanted me to fly back to Vancouver tonight. Then she threatened to come here. I told her she doesn't need to do that. It's not like Daniel and I were still together. I dealt with the loss months ago. It's a shock, that's all." Who was she trying to fool? Her chin wobbled and Harriet drew her in for a hug.

"It's okay to be sad." Harriet squeezed tighter. "He was in your life for a really long time, sis, and your *husband* until recently. You need to give yourself the chance to grieve."

Georgia managed a nod. Her family had been nothing but gracious when she eloped with Daniel. They were surprised but had loved on him and been kind and generous to them both as they navigated college. She knew her family prayed for him—and for her. He swept her off her feet and she chose to put him and everything else before her once-precious faith. How had she lost her way so quickly? *I fell head-over-heels for Daniel and nothing else mattered.*

She clung to Harriet as sobs racked her body and a myriad of memories replayed through her mind.

After several minutes, Harriet pulled back. "Ready for the tea yet?"

A pathetic sniffle. "Please."

"It's probably getting cold." She retrieved a cup and saucer for each of them and handed one to Georgia.

"Thanks." She set the saucer on her lap and lifted the bone china teacup to her lips with trembling fingers. The warmth and sweetness felt like a hug. She took another sip and allowed it to calm her churning insides as dappled sunlight filtered through the dove-gray bedroom curtains.

Harriet sat on the end of the bed and drained her own cup. "Sorry. It's pretty tepid." She scrunched her nose and then glanced at her phone on the bedcover as the screen lit up. "Text from Mom." She picked it up and scrolled. "She's telling me to make sure you're not left alone. She wants to fly over to be with you if you won't go back home."

Georgia finished her tea. "Please, can you persuade Mom I'm okay? She'll be here for your birthday party soon enough. This is horrible, but I'll get through it. Besides, if some lunatic is breaking into Bramble Cottage, I don't want to put Mom in danger."

"You think whoever left the postcard will come back?" Harriet's eyes widened. "I can't believe all this is happening."

Georgia set her cup and saucer on the bedside table and hugged her knees to her chest. "I hope not, but I don't know what to think."

Harriet chewed on her lower lip for a moment while she stared at her sister. "Hear me out. If there was any thought it might be Daniel messing with your head by burning the toast and leaving the postcard early this morning…"

"I've already gone there in my scrambled brain. It couldn't have been him. I figured that out anyway. The postcard wasn't written by Daniel. I'm positive."

"So, if it wasn't Daniel, then *who*?"

"I honestly don't know." In the recesses of her muddled mind she couldn't shake the notion that Daniel may have dabbled in something less than legal in the last couple of years. The mysterious padded envelope in Paris last summer. Something she had no desire to ever ask him about. Had she stumbled into the thick of it now? Her head throbbed from lack of sleep, stress, and the torrent of tears.

Harriet tapped her chin and stared across the room with a faraway look in her eyes. "Well, let's think about this logically. Your intruder was someone who knew about your fear of fire *and* about the postcards Daniel used to send to you."

"That narrows it down to a small circle. He didn't have many close friends." *I used to be his best friend.* "That leaves his immediate family, and his new woman. Vanessa." She said the name through gritted teeth.

"But why? Why would anyone want to travel halfway around the world in order to freak you out?"

Georgia rubbed her grainy eyes. She wasn't thinking straight. "This is all too much. I need to get some sleep. Clear my head."

Harriet stood and returned the cups to the tray. "I can stay downstairs while you rest."

"No, you've been amazing, but you need to get back to your family. I'll probably sleep most of today anyway. Try to process all this. Unpack my suitcase later."

Harriet's brow furrowed. "Wouldn't you feel better having someone with you? You've had the worst morning imaginable and Leo's working from home and is perfectly capable of keeping Lucy amused. Or you can come home with me…"

Darling Lucy. Georgia ached to see her niece but not when she was in this frame of mind. "You're so sweet, but, no. I need some alone-time and don't want Lucy to see her aunty as a blubbering mess." She rubbed her warm cheeks with the palms of her hands. "I have some serious thinking to do."

"Anything I can help with? If you decide to fly back to Vancouver for a while, I can make arrangements…"

Georgia shook her head. "No, I have no intention of getting back on a plane anytime soon. I guess there'll be a funeral at some point, but I'm his ex-wife now. Besides, I planned on giving myself at least three months to experience English life as a single woman. I need to do this. Get to know the new and improved Bramble Cottage." She gazed toward the open window. "Maybe I'll even grab my camera and take some shots of the garden later today if the weather cooperates, keep my mind occupied."

"If you're sure. Don't forget to call that police officer. I can run you down to the station if necessary." Harriet raised a brow. "And I'll try my best to keep Mom at bay."

"I'll let you know if I get sick of my own company. Promise."

Harriet rested the tray on the bed while she tucked the sheets around Georgia. She was such a mother. "Call me if you're nervous tonight. If you don't want to stay in our guest room, I could even come back here for a sleepover." She shrugged. "It'll be like the old days."

"Thanks. I know you're trying to help but I need to do this on my own." She gripped the sheet with clenched fingers. "I won't be scared away from my own cottage. I've been planning this for months."

"I get it. I do." Harriet's eyes brimmed. "But I still can't believe Daniel's gone. It's such a shock. His poor family. You need to give yourself grace to come to terms with it, too."

Georgia massaged her temples. "It's going to take a while to sink in. That's why I need to carry on with my plans. Stay busy. Because I think the reality is going to sneak up on me when I least expect it."

"True. Maybe tomorrow you could rest and finish settling in, then come to church with us on Sunday?" Harriet smoothed the bedcover as she spoke. "I know Lucy will want to introduce you to her little friends. We can go to the village pub for lunch afterwards. They do the best roast beef."

As numbness made its way through Georgia's body, neither food nor church sounded appealing. Only sleep. She gave a noncommittal grunt. She hadn't set foot in a church for so long—the thought of facing anyone at her old church in Vancouver was too much. Her rekindled faith was fragile, like everything else in her life at the moment. *Perhaps I could manage a new church where no one knows me…*

"Will's going to be there, by the way." Harriet retrieved the tray.

"Hmm?"

"Our dreamy doc. I know he'll want to check on you. He's a sweetheart like that." Harriet's eyes blinked way too fast. She was hopeless at trying to play it cool. "No pressure though."

Good grief, was her sister trying to set her up? At church? So inappropriate. "Go home and get some rest, Harriet. I think you need it as much as I do."

Harriet let out an exaggerated sigh. "Okay, fine. I still have a key, so I'll lock the door on my way out. Love you."

"Love you, too."

Georgia leaned over to her bedside table and slid open the top drawer. Sleeping pills were her only chance for some shut-eye now. Convincing herself it was a new day and therefore acceptable to begin again with the dosage, she took two and washed them down with a swig from her water bottle. Closing heavy eyelids, she listened as Harriet checked the backdoor and then left through the front entrance and turned the lock. She exhaled and rolled onto her side. Silence filled the air. *Please let me sleep without nightmares.* She pushed thoughts of fires and flames to one side, but then images of her ex-husband being hit by a speeding car screamed through her mind.

He might have treated her like dirt at the end of their

marriage, but no one deserved to die in a senseless accident like that. He was really gone.

*GONE.* The message on the postcard. Georgia's skin prickled. Her breath caught in her throat.

*Oh Lord...*

Was Daniel's death an accident?

# Chapter Six

WILL CHECKED HIS WATCH AND GROUND his teeth. The Sunday morning church service started in ten minutes, and there was no way he was going to be late. Pet peeves prevailed. He pulled his SUV into a parking spot and checked the rearview mirror.

"You okay, little man?"

Jack craned his neck to watch through his backseat window as the trickle of congregation members ambled toward the entrance of Saint Pete's. "Go?"

Will felt the tips of his son's running shoes dig into the back of the driver's seat. "Yes, let's go. We don't want to be late." He jumped out of the car, grabbed Jack's bag, and picked up the treasured stuffed toy from the floor. "Mustn't forget Bunny Rabbit."

"Bunny Wabbit."

Jack's sweet voice caused Will's throat to constrict. His vocabulary was expanding every week. He hardly seemed like a baby anymore.

"Go?"

"Yes. Let's get you out of this car seat."

Will slung the bag over his shoulder and carried a wriggling Jack toward the huge wooden doors. Organ music floated out on the fresh morning air and within seconds the tension eased in his neck. *I need this, Lord.*

"Morning, Will. Morning, Jack." The kind vicar's wife

greeted them as he walked into the cool of the foyer. "How are you both doing today?"

"We're doing well, thanks for asking." Will offered his best smile.

"Really?" Her hushed voice held so much compassion, he nearly wept on the spot.

"Really." He swiveled so Jack could see one of his favorite babysitters. "Jack brought Bunny to see you today."

Jack held out the toy and then pulled it back to his chest. "Mine."

Will winced. "Sorry. We're not very good at sharing yet."

She lay a cool hand on his arm. "All in good time, dear. He's doing so well. You both are. Do you need me to watch him this Wednesday?"

"Thanks, but my parents want him for a sleepover midweek. Although I may need to ask Rachel if she could cover my Thursday night shift again."

"I'm sure she'll be glad to. You're her best babysitting job. You spoil that daughter of mine, you know."

Will ruffled his son's fine, blond hair. "If she's willing to stay and watch Jack overnight while I'm at the hospital, I figure the least I can do is let her friend come along so they can both stay in the guest suite."

"But the pizza allowance?" She broke into a grin.

"Trust me, it's worth it for my own peace of mind. Rachel's great with Jack." Will glanced at his watch. "I should get moving here and settle him into the Tiny Tots room. See you later." He avoided eye contact with everyone else as he made a beeline to Jack's nursery class.

Will spotted Rachel at the entrance of the room and waved.

"Here he is—and with Bunny, too." Rachel held out her

arms and Jack leaned toward her. "He's so good with being left, Doctor Hughes. All the others make such a fuss when their parents go into the service."

*He's used to being with sitters.* Will cleared his throat and set Jack's bag inside the room. "He knows you well, Rachel. I think that helps." He kissed the top of Jack's head. "See you later, buddy. Have fun and be good."

"Bye-bye." Jack's turquoise eyes disappeared into happy slits as he grinned and waved the hand that wasn't holding Bunny.

The church bells rang out their cheery welcome and Will sighed as he headed back to the foyer alone. It didn't get any easier. If possible, he would duck into the sanctuary without having to interact with anyone else. Slip into the back row. As usual. However, when he rounded the corner, he stopped in his tracks and stared. It was her. Harriet's sister.

As if framed in a picture, Georgia stood in the doorway, perfectly poised. Shafts of hazy light glowed behind her silhouette and caught coppery tones in her long, brown hair.

Will closed his gaping mouth.

Dressed in stilettos, a black skirt that hugged her to perfection, and a matching top, she oozed class and style. When she removed her oversized sunglasses, he caught a heaviness in her eyes. Pain. Was she still shaken from the break-in at her cottage?

She took one wary step farther inside the foyer and bit her lower lip. A Canadian beauty with a camera over one shoulder and the weight of the world on the other—what was her story? He was captivated. Intrigued. For the first time in well over a year, something stirred in his heart.

"Morning, doctor."

The moment was broken as the local young vet brushed past

him on her way into the service. She looked back and batted her eyelashes. Really? In church? He couldn't even bring himself to respond.

"Will?" Harriet rushed toward him holding little Lucy's hand. "Morning. We're running super late, as usual. I'm going to drop Lucy in Tiny Tots while Leo parks the car. Would you mind taking Georgia inside the sanctuary and maybe sit with her in the back somewhere?" She lowered her voice. "She's pretty upset. I'll explain later."

"Of course." *No hardship whatsoever.*

"I'll try not to be long. You know how Lucy can be sometimes when I leave."

The little girl grinned at them, a dimple appearing in each cheek.

"This sweet angel?"

Will turned at the sound of Georgia's voice.

She crouched in front of her niece. "Have fun, Lucy. We'll play together later, okay?"

Lucy beamed.

Harriet lifted her daughter and balanced her on one hip. "Come on, darling, we better get you into your class. Mister Will is going to look after Aunty Georgia for us." She scurried away with a soft chuckle.

Georgia straightened and flashed her brown eyes at Will. "I'm sorry about Harriet. I don't need babysitting. You'd think *she* was the bossy, big sister." Her Canadian accent drew attention from several regulars filing into the service.

"It's not a problem." Will attempted a casual smile and a shrug. "Up to you. I sit at the back in case Jack needs me."

"Jack?"

"My son."

Her cheeks flushed. "You have a son? Well, yes, of course. The back suits me just fine."

Will gestured toward the sanctuary with his left hand and noticed her quick inspection of his naked ring finger. "Shall we?"

"Sure." She slipped her camera from her shoulder and carried it in her hand.

"Planning to take some shots?" He nodded at the camera.

"I was thinking I might take some of the grounds and the outside of the church after the service. It's so pretty here."

"Perfect morning. For taking pictures, I mean. With the weather and everything." *What?* Why was he getting so flustered?

One of the greeters presented them both with a hearty handshake and an order of service bulletin.

Will led the way and slid into the empty back row and Georgia followed, leaving a sizable gap between them as they sat on the cushioned pew. *She's keeping her distance then. Fair enough. She doesn't know me from Adam.* He was a complete stranger and so far, England hadn't exactly welcomed her with open arms. Should he ask if the police had any joy finding the prowler? See if she was feeling okay physically? *Why am I acting like a blithering idiot?*

At that moment, the organ music changed, and everyone stood as the service began. He tried not to be distracted as subtle hints of her floral perfume wafted in his direction. From his peripheral vision, it was obvious she was uncomfortable. Maybe nervous. She wrung her hands and glanced about the sanctuary. Perhaps old churches freaked her out. It took him a while to get used to the ancient vibe in Saint Pete's.

Harriet appeared at the end of the row along with Leo, and Will shuffled further down the pew to make room. Georgia maintained an oversized space between them. *Cautious.*

The choir began singing the first hymn and the congregation

stood and joined in. Will was silent as he allowed the truths in the words of "Holy, Holy, Holy" to wash over him. Interesting how he'd recently found such peace in the hymns of old.

Out of curiosity, he inclined his ear in a subtle attempt to hear Georgia's singing voice but only caught hints of her sister's melodic soprano from the other side. Maybe Georgia didn't know the tune—they might sing other variations over the pond. Then he detected a sniffle. *Is she crying?* He turned his head in her direction.

Tears streaked her cheeks. As she brushed at them, she met his gaze. Raw pain. Fresh grief. He saw it in that split second. Recognized it. His heart lurched.

She averted her eyes and lifted her chin. Should he say something? If he were closer, he could whisper and see if she was feeling okay. As a concerned doctor. Maybe a new friend.

The hymn finished and everyone sat in unison as the vicar gave a welcome from the front. Will took that moment to slide along the pew closer to her. Georgia frowned at him, her eyes still watery.

"Are you okay?" His whisper was barely audible.

"Fine, thank you." She sniffed and Harriet whispered something in her other ear. She shook her head and looked back at Will. "Thanks for your concern, but I can assure you, I'm all right." She gestured with one hand. "You can move back along to make room."

"Make room?"

The first Bible reading allowed them to continue their whisperings.

"Yes. Surely your *wife* will want to sit next to you?" There was a challenge in Georgia's tone and a fire in her eyes.

Will's mouth dropped open and he lowered his head.

It was obvious she had no clue.

# Chapter Seven



*Jerk.*

Georgia knew she was being hard on the charming doctor—who, upon closer inspection, was indeed dreamy. Whichever way you cut it, he was a jerk. He had a son? So, he was a family man, even though she noticed he wore no wedding ring. Perhaps it was a surgeon thing. Anyway, while he was leaning in nice and close to Georgia with his gorgeous green eyes so full of concern, where was his poor wife? Caring for their boy or out at work or at home making Will's lunch ready for when he decided to grace her with his presence. She fumed. He was selfish. *He's like Daniel.* She still felt the bite from her ex-husband's wandering eye.

Her harsh reply did the trick. He scooted back along the pew without another word. Eating a hefty slice of humble pie. Good. *Just because he's handsome and smart, and probably filthy rich, that doesn't give him permission to befriend, flirt, and home in on someone who is obviously in distress.*

Maybe *flirt* was too strong a word. He'd hit a nerve and she hadn't imagined the tenderness in his voice or the tiny spark between them that needed dousing. Her stupid tears hadn't helped.

*What's with me anyway?* She'd cried for most of Friday and in sporadic bursts yesterday. Cried for Daniel's death and rehashed the death of their relationship. She hadn't loved the notion of coming to church today. Another rest day would've been nice, but she didn't want to disappoint Harriet. Her sister was the caretaker of the family and would do anything in her power to ensure everyone was okay.

As Georgia crossed her legs and bounced one foot at a rapid rate, her eyes were drawn upward to the stained-glass windows situated on both sides of the church. They were breathtaking. Morning light filtered through colored glass, brightening the space with a glorious glow.

*Beauty in the broken.*

The phrase filled her mind as she recognized familiar Bible stories brought to life in each window. The beauty was evident in the broken shards when crafted into a masterpiece.

Broken shards. *That's how my life feels about now.*

She tuned in to the words being read by a middle-aged woman dressed head-to-toe in purple. Something about a broken spirit, a broken and contrite heart. Familiar verses she never stopped to consider before.

Was God still able to shine His glorious Light through the fragments of her brokenness?

She took a breath and held it for a moment. Her perfectionist tendencies had been blown out of the water when she discovered she was unable to conceive. Again, when her marriage dissolved. Finally, when her friends retreated, not knowing how to react to her life's implosion.

*But You're still with me, aren't you, God?*

She exhaled and felt the gentlest whisper of peace in His assurance.

Her whole adult life she attempted to capture beauty through the lens of her camera. Nature, weddings, cities, babies. Even in fragile imperfections. It filled her with joy. Maybe God found joy in the beauty of her brokenness.

However, the hymn at the beginning of the service was her

undoing. There was something about singing "Holy, Holy, Holy" and being in this ancient sanctuary. Her memories of having a close relationship with God came flooding back and gave her major chills. *I know I'm loved but will I ever feel worthy?*

She rubbed the goosebumps on her bare arms, chilled on the outside as well as within. Heat from the morning sunshine had no way of penetrating these thick stone walls. How old was this church? She would have to do her homework and include it in the photography project she was working on. Yes, history, architecture, faith through the generations—it would be a fascinating slant and she could include some shots of those stunning stained-glass windows.

Georgia inhaled the musty air and focused on the glass stories again while the vicar went through a list of announcements. Bursts of tangerine, crimson, and indigo reflected onto the worn, wooden floor at the front of the church. Rainbows of light. It warmed her heart.

Will cleared his throat, breaking her moment of awe, and she glanced in his direction. His head was bowed, eyes closed. She checked to see if she'd missed a prayer being said, but the vicar was talking about an upcoming harvest festival. *I guess at least Will's a praying man.* Another peek. His rolled-up sleeves revealed tanned, muscular forearms and strong, clasped hands. Surgeon fingers. Didn't Harriet say his specialty was pediatrics? *I wonder how many lives those hands have saved...*

Just like that, an image of other hands flooded her mind. Hands that had broken into her cottage. Burnt the toast. Taped the postcard. Had that person crept up her stairs first? Watched her sleep? A shiver rippled through her body as she studied the congregation from her perspective in the back row. Mainly gray-haired folk. Several young families sat together. A smattering of men and women her age. Her intruder could be in this church. She dug her fingernails into her crossed arms.

Whoever it was, he was good. The police found nothing—no prints on the postcard. Must have worn gloves. They'd promised to schedule a regular police drive-by at Bramble Cottage over the weekend to make sure the prowler didn't come back. Yesterday had been uneventful. Harriet tried to persuade Georgia to stay at her place until they figured out who the culprit was, but she refused again. She was done with cowering in the shadows of her happily-ever-after dreams. She had her recently renewed faith and her supportive family. She would not be chased off by someone who didn't even have the guts to show his face. *If only I could figure out who he is...*

A sudden commotion to Georgia's left caught her attention. She snapped her head toward her sister who stood, her eyes wide.

Before Georgia could ask what was going on, Harriet leaned across and grabbed Will's shoulder. "Come, quickly."

He didn't even question her. Georgia shifted her knees to one side, allowing Will to scramble along the pew and chase after Harriet. Leo had already disappeared. Several of the congregation members turned, genuine concern etched their faces, but the next moment everyone rose from their seats for another hymn.

Something was wrong.

Georgia picked up her camera and purse and fled the pew in search of the others.

By the front door, a lone elderly gentleman wearing a tweed suit sat in a wheelchair. "They went that way, dear." He pointed to her left and she sped down the corridor as fast as her high heels would allow, following a hum of voices.

"Georgia." Leo, her usually-cool brother-in-law strode out of a room. He raked both hands through his wavy dark hair.

"What's happened? Is it Lucy?"

"Oui." Leo's native French gave away his fear.

She joined him at the doorway and peered into the nursery. Lucy sat on Harriet's lap and Will crouched in front of them, his back to her. Lucy's face was snow-white, and sobs heaved her tiny body.

"I don't understand what happened." Leo shook his head. "Will thinks she's broken her arm. I have to wait outside for the ambulance and the police."

"Police?"

He shrugged. "Something about a woman being here who shouldn't have been… I don't know…"

Two flustered teenaged girls barged past them as they led a trail of toddlers from the room toward the church entrance in whispered urgency.

Georgia's stomach tightened. "You go on in and be with your family. I'll wait outside for the ambulance. I'll bring them straight in."

"You sure?"

"Absolutely. Any idea how long they'll be?"

"A few minutes. They were on a home call close by. Merci, Georgia." Leo hurried back into the room and Georgia's heart broke as she watched her young niece in obvious pain. She turned back and made her way to the church entrance to wait outside.

The air was warm and scented with honeysuckle as she paced across the gravel pathway. Poor little Lucy. The police were involved? Who was this woman Leo mentioned? Georgia spotted the girls and toddlers who vacated the nursery. They waited on a grassy patch along with a few adults. Georgia waved and the older-looking girl waved back. *I have to find out what happened.* She beckoned her over to the church entrance.

The teen walked toward Georgia carrying a blond little boy in her arms, who was almost asleep. "How's Lucy? You must be her aunt from Canada."

Did all of Bramble Downs know she was coming? "Yes, I'm Georgia. I'm afraid I don't know how she's doing. I said I'd wait out here for the ambulance. They think she may have broken her arm."

The girl gasped and tears filled her eyes. "Oh, no."

Georgia reached out and touched her arm. "Hey, accidents happen. I'm sure it wasn't anyone's fault. What's your name, honey?"

"Rachel."

"Okay, Rachel. Listen, the police are on their way, too. Lucy's dad mentioned something about a strange woman being in there. Can you tell me what happened?"

Rachel blew wayward strands of auburn hair from her face. "Not really. I didn't even notice the lady come in. We were setting out the craft supplies on the tables. The kids were all playing with the big toys. It's their free time when they first arrive. One minute, Lucy was dancing in the middle of the room—she always dances—and the next she let out a shriek. I turned and saw the back of a woman literally sprinting from the room."

"You didn't recognize her?"

Rachel shook her head. "Although I think maybe she tried to *take* Lucy."

"What?"

"One of the other little girls said the lady lifted Lucy up but she wriggled from her grip and that must've been when she screamed, and we all turned to see what was going on."

"Lucy fell?"

"Yes, I think she must have landed awkwardly on her arm."

She glanced back at the church entrance. "I hope it's not broken. Who would do something like that?"

Georgia bit her lip. Was danger following her everywhere? She scanned the parking lot and the quiet street in case anyone was watching her.

"What did this woman look like, Rachel? Do you remember?"

Her forehead wrinkled. "Long blonde hair. Black workout clothes. I only got a quick glimpse of the back of her."

"Of course." She gave her head a shake and focused on the traumatized girl in front of her. "You mustn't worry. This wasn't your fault. The ambulance will soon be here."

"Ab-lance?" The boy in Rachel's arms whipped his head around. His startling turquoise eyes almost took Georgia's breath away.

"Hello, handsome. What's your name?" Georgia stroked his light blond hair and he rewarded her with a cheeky grin.

"This is Jack. I'll have to hang on to him for a while. His dad is the doctor."

"This is Will's son?" He was adorable.

"Yeah. I babysit for Jack, so he knows me pretty well. My mum does, too. We all try to help out."

*Curious.* Perhaps Will's wife also had a demanding career. Must be difficult with a little one.

"Well, you have the most gorgeous eyes I've ever seen, Jack."

"They're amazing, aren't they?" Rachel kissed his head. "The color of the Caribbean Ocean. Not that I've ever been. Emma, his mummy, had the exact same shade."

*Wait.* "Did you say *had*?"

Rachel nodded. "She was so lovely. We all miss her."

A knot formed in Georgia's stomach. "Can I ask what happened?" Maybe she moved away…

"She died in a car accident. It was awful. Jack was such a tiny baby."

Georgia's mouth fell open as the ambulance pulled up. Rachel was still talking, the paramedics were walking her way, but all she could think about was how her hasty assumptions resulted in hurling such callous words in the face of a kind doctor.

Who was also a widower.

# Chapter Eight

"SHE'LL BE FINE." GEORGIA PUT AN arm around her sister and gave a reassuring squeeze. It was her turn to offer comfort as they sat together in the sterile hospital waiting room. "I wish this hadn't happened to Lucy, but I'm sure the police will follow up on it." *Please let this be some awful random event.*

"I know. I hope they catch the woman as soon as possible. Who has the nerve to walk in and try to take a child?"

"Especially in church."

Harriet dabbed her cheeks with a tissue. "That's what gets me. You want to feel safe in a church. I wonder what pushed this woman to do something like that."

"Maybe she wants a child of her own and can't for some reason. Got desperate. It happens." Georgia closed her eyes. She felt that pain more than her family understood.

Harriet put a hand on Georgia's bare arm. "I'm sorry. I didn't mean to…"

"Oh, no. You don't get to feel sorry for me while your girl's in surgery."

"I can't help it." Harriet wiped away what was left of her mascara and let out a sigh. "At least Will was there for us. I feel better knowing he's operating. He's got a reputation for being the best orthopedic surgeon in pediatrics around here. Rachel is used to babysitting little Jack so…"

Georgia let out a groan.

"What is it?"

"Nothing." *Now is not the time to share this particular nugget.*

Harriet swung around to face her. "Please. I need a little distraction, so spill the reason for that dramatic groan."

Georgia slumped back in the plastic orange chair, the distinct hospital smell of sanitizer and sickness unsettling her stomach. "I may have upset him."

"Will? When?"

"In church." Somehow, that made it sound even worse. "But it wasn't altogether my fault. I had no idea."

Harriet narrowed her eyes. "I can't imagine Will getting easily offended. Are you sure you're not overreacting?"

"I thought he was acting kind of flirty."

"Flirty?"

"In hindsight, it was more like kindness. I had no clue his wife is… dead." Georgia focused on a large black ink spot on the gray floor.

"Oh, no." Harriet's voice fell flat.

"Yes. You know how I react when I get a mere whiff of a married man flirting—after what happened with Daniel and me. I imagined his poor wife being at home while he was scooting up to sit close to me on the pew with those mesmerizing green eyes of his… and I shot him down. Asked him if his wife was coming to sit with him." Georgia swallowed. "And I may have been snarky."

Harriet's mouth fell open. "That's not good. In all fairness, I don't think I mentioned he was a widower, did I?"

"No." Her eyes flashed. "It might have been useful information, don't you think?"

Harriet covered her smirk. "Sorry, but do you honestly believe I would've left you in the careful and oh-so-talented hands of a married man?"

"I was a little rattled about that. Now I need to apologize to him. Especially as he's in there fixing my niece."

"My poor little girl." Harriet glanced at her watch for the hundredth time. "He should be finished soon, shouldn't he? I mean, unless there are complications."

"There won't be. Kids her age heal super quickly. Although you might want to make an appointment with a children's counselor. I hope she didn't realize what this woman's intentions were, but you never know how trauma like this can play out later on." She dragged her fingers through her long hair. "Trust me, I know these things." *If only I'd gone for counseling after the fire when I was a kid.*

"You're right. I will. We'll pray she has healing in every area."

"You're an amazing mommy, you know that, don't you? Talking of which, do you want me to call Mom? She'll want to know." Georgia plucked her phone from her bag. No new messages.

"Yes, and she'll be desperate to fly out here and help." Harriet fiddled with her earring. "It was hard enough persuading her to sit tight after your news on Friday when I spoke with her. I don't know how much more she can take being so far away."

"It'll be a tough sell."

"I know. So, yes, if you don't mind, could you do that sooner rather than later? Leo will be back any minute. Try to convince Mom not to change her plane tickets. She'll be here in a couple of weeks for our birthday party anyway and then she can coddle us all as much as she wants."

Georgia stood and stretched her legs. If she didn't move around soon, jet lag was sure to get the better of her. "I'll give it my best shot. There's a courtyard we passed on our way in, and I could use some air. I'll call from there and then grab us some coffee from the vending machine on my way back."

"Need the caffeine?"

"Do I ever." She looked down at her little sister, pale and anxious. Harriet was always a bundle of energy, the optimist in the family. "Hang in there."

"Give Mom my love and tell her not to worry. I'll text Sophie quick and fill her in."

"Will do. Sophie probably already knows something's up… you guys and your twin thing." She shouldered her camera and picked up her purse.

Harriet chuckled. Because it was true.

"Can you tell Sophie I'll call her later tonight? She was busy yesterday, so I left her a message. You know, about Daniel and everything." Saying his name made her chest ache. *He's actually dead.*

"Of course. She'll be desperate to talk with you."

"Thanks. Won't be long." Georgia's stiletto heels clicked on the shiny floor as she followed the signs to the courtyard. High heels seemed such a good idea when she thought she would be doing church and then having lunch at the cozy pub in the village. Major regrets at this point but she couldn't exactly slip them off and go barefoot in a hospital.

The courtyard was deserted and afforded her privacy while she shared details with her mom of Lucy's accident. She sat on a wooden bench and crossed her legs.

"No, Mom, Harriet says not to change your flight. I'm here and I can help out."

A pause before her mother spoke. "But you've had a horrible shock yourself, sweetie. I can't bear being this far from my girls when you're all going through these trials. I should be there with you."

"You will be, Mom. In two weeks." Georgia bit her lower lip. "I was wondering, do you have more info on what happened to Daniel?"

"Not yet. I'm sorry. I haven't spoken to your uncle since he called with the news. I'll text or give you a shout as soon as I hear anything." A loud sigh. "I know he wasn't your husband anymore, but you were married for a long time. You need to give yourself opportunity to grieve properly, Georgia. Don't try to bottle everything up."

*She knows me too well.* "Sure, Mom. I know. My head's in a bit of a daze at the moment. So much has happened since I got here."

"I'm praying for you. For all of you."

"Thanks." Her mother's daily prayers sustained her through the years, even when she didn't care one way or another. "I should go and check on the family. Lucy will be out from surgery soon."

"You give my precious granddaughter a kiss for me."

"Promise. Love you, Mom."

"I love you, too. Call me anytime."

Georgia slid her phone back in her purse and stared into space. The muggy late-summer air was a slight improvement on being inside the stuffy hospital. She hated hospitals. Her hands clasped the camera on her lap. She'd endured so many tests, with prodding and poking. So much disappointment.

"Georgia?" Leo did a double-take and held the door open for her to come back inside. "I thought that was you. Are you okay? Where's Harriet?"

She joined him and they hurried along the corridor. "She asked me to call Mom. I was getting some coffee, too. Want some?"

"No thanks. I'm anxious to see if there's any news from surgery."

Georgia lifted a brow. "I think Harriet would've told you if there was any news." It was no mean feat keeping up with his long strides. "You carry on, and I'll be there in a couple of minutes."

"Yes. Yes. Of course."

Georgia stopped at the vending machine and extracted two cappuccinos. Fancy for a hospital. Shame there were no lids. Somehow, she needed to juggle two steaming cups, her purse, and a camera. *I've got this.*

With the greatest of care, she navigated a set of double doors and was turning the corner to reach the waiting room when someone in a huge rush powered straight into her.

*NO.* She jumped back to avoid the splashes of hot coffee and dropped her purse in an attempt to save her beloved camera. "I'm so sorry—"

Another apologetic voice joined hers and she glanced up to see Will. Seriously?

"My fault." He bent down to retrieve her purse contents— including a container of sleeping pills, her wallet, and a runaway tube of lipstick. "I shouldn't have been coming so fast around the corner." He stood. "Did you manage to avoid the spillage?"

Thankful no one else was around to witness her klutziness, she set the coffees down on a side table between the chairs lining the hall. "I'm fine."

He held out her items and as their fingers touched for a moment, a spike of awareness shot up her arm. She pulled away as if burned. *Haven't felt anything like that in a while.*

"Are you sure?"

"Yes, thanks." Georgia grabbed the pills and stuffed them in the side compartment of her purse and zipped it tight, and then dropped everything else in with a flourish. "I'm really regretting there were no lids for the cups now." She eyed his navy-blue scrubs and winced. "I think you're wearing half my coffee. Sorry. I hope it didn't burn you."

"No harm done. Let me help you back to the waiting room. I'm guessing that's where you were heading." He carried the half-empty coffees and led the way. As seconds passed, the awkward silence reminded Georgia of their last conversation in the church.

She cleared her throat. "How was the surgery?"

"Went like clockwork. It was very straightforward."

"Thank goodness." She turned to him as they walked side-by-side. "And thank you."

He continued to stare ahead. "My pleasure."

Frosty and a little too professional. *Argh.* She needed to apologize for earlier.

They arrived at the waiting room where Leo and Harriet stood side-by-side at the entrance.

Georgia gestured toward Will. "Here's your coffee. Sorry it's only half-full. We had a slight accident."

Harriet accepted a cup from Will. "Thanks. How's our girl?"

"Lucy's doing well. It was the most straightforward elbow fracture, and she did marvelously through the surgery. She'll be out for a while, but I know Mum and Dad will want to be there when she wakes up."

Harriet looked a lesser shade of pale. "You bet we will. Thanks so much."

Leo blew out a long breath. "What a relief. Yes, *merci.*"

"Of course. I'm glad I was there to help." Will handed the other cup to Georgia.

She smiled her thanks and turned to Harriet. "Anything else you guys need? Food?"

"We're fine, thanks." Harriet nodded toward an overnight bag on the floor. "Leo brought enough supplies to last us all night.

Although we should be able to take her home later this evening, right, Will?"

He nodded. "I don't foresee any complications. She's pretty young, and it's been a traumatic day, so you might want to sleep close by her at home tonight. The cast may be uncomfortable at first but it's bright pink, so I think that should help."

Leo chuckled. "Her favorite color."

"Lucky guess."

"Thanks again, man." Leo shook Will's hand. "You probably need to get back to Jack on your day off. Am I right?"

"I often get called in on emergency, it's not a problem."

Now that Georgia was convinced Lucy was okay, she needed to talk with Will. "Are you heading home?"

"Yes, unless anyone has any more questions. I'll check in with the nurse later but feel free to call me anytime." He put a hand on Harriet's shoulder. "She's going to be right as rain before you know it."

"Thanks." Harriet leaned against Leo. "It's been a bit much for my mommy-heart."

Georgia swallowed the lump in her throat and looked up at Will. "I should go back to the cottage and make some calls. Could I walk you out?"

He furrowed his brow. Did he suspect more tongue-lashing?

"Of course." He ran a hand around the back of his neck. "I can give you a ride home, if you like."

Brave guy. "There's no need. I can call a cab."

He offered a half-smile. "I think you'll find taxis in this neck of the woods on a Sunday are rather scarce. Trust me, it's no problem. I have to drive past your place on the way."

She glanced at her sister, who was trying not to grin. "Okay, great. Thanks. I'll call you guys later."

Harriet hugged Georgia, careful to avoid spilling more coffee. "I'm sorry about all this. Not quite what I had in mind for today. Maybe you'll be able to catch up on some sleep." She gave her an extra squeeze. "And please, if you're nervous tonight, call us."

"Thanks. I'm sure I'll be fine. Give Lucy my love and tell her I'll see her tomorrow."

Georgia followed Will from the waiting room and tried to keep up as they passed a group of nurses and several visitors. She sipped her cappuccino, the rich aroma promising a strong shot of caffeine. It tasted creamy and bold, not bad at all for a hospital vending machine.

How was she going to attempt an apology without causing further upset by bringing up Will's deceased wife? With every step in her stilettos, another layer of stress and sadness fell heavy on her heart. Will's grief. The intruder's gall. The postcard's message. Lucy's accident. Daniel's death... he was actually dead. A gasp leaked from her lips.

"Are you worried about Lucy?"

Georgia blinked. "A little."

He touched her arm. This time she didn't pull away from the tingle. "She's going to be absolutely fine."

If only that was her sole concern. A tear snaked down her cheek. He didn't miss it.

"Hey, everything's going to be all right, Georgia."

His caring hand on her arm and his forest green eyes so filled with genuine concern was her undoing. The floodgates opened there in the hospital hallway and there was nothing she could do to stop them.

# Chapter Nine

Will slowed his steps. *Not what I expected.* "Let's sit for a moment, shall we? There's no one else out here." He steered Georgia from the hospital corridor out to the little courtyard so she could gather herself. They sat side-by-side on one of the wooden slatted benches and he held her coffee cup and let her cry. Sobs worked their way through her slender body, and he felt the urge to wrap her in his arms.

He refrained. This was something deeper than her niece breaking an arm. Tears had coursed down her lovely cheeks in church this morning, too. The break-in at her cottage could have upset her more than he thought, and Lucy's incident pushed her over the edge. He couldn't help noticing the sleeping pills that rolled onto the floor earlier. She was carrying a lot.

"I'm so sorry." She dug in her purse and pulled out a tissue. "I'm not usually this much of a wreck." She dabbed at her eyes and mopped the moisture from her cheeks. "Ugly-crying is something I save for my alone-time."

"Please don't apologize." Good grief, she was beautiful— even after an ugly-cry.

"Are you for real?" Her brown eyes widened. "I have every reason to apologize to you."

*Ah.* She found out about Emma. "There's no need…"

"Yes." She touched his hand and ignited a spark. "I was out of line this morning. I had no idea… I'm so sorry. For your loss and for my erroneous assumptions. You've been nothing but kind and friendly." She sniffed.

Deep breath. "I accept your apology. You had no way of knowing I was a widower. Actually, if I came off as friendly, that's a miracle in itself."

She tilted her head. "How so?"

Confession time. "According to those who know me best, I'm a hermit—which is a fair assessment—and I'm way too serious. Although I was intentionally making an effort to loosen up a bit this morning. Maybe I went too far. Imagine that."

Her eyes crinkled when she smiled. Cute. "Too serious? You had me fooled." She bit her lip. "But I understand why you might be serious. Losing your wife. Raising your little boy on your own. I met him at church—he's adorable."

Will swallowed down his emotion. "Thank you. I don't know if I'll ever get over losing her. My focus is on Jack now. He's the light of my life but it's not easy. I won't pretend otherwise." *Carrying the burden of the truth makes it all the more unbearable.*

She let out a deep sigh. "Admittedly, I'm overtired, and jet lag isn't helping my emotional stability, but there's a reason for my tears. I don't know if Harriet mentioned anything to you yet, but I found out on Friday my ex-husband was killed in a car accident." She stared at her camera as she spoke. Was it her security blanket of sorts?

"Georgia, I'm so sorry."

"That's why I was a little upset in the service. Then when I assumed you were married and you were so… friendly, my mind shot to him. How he broke my heart when he decided I wasn't enough, and he found a new model. Smarter. Prettier. Younger."

He clenched his fists in his lap. How could anyone hurt this woman?

Her eyes found his. "He left me. Our divorce was finalized

six months ago. Now he's… dead. Honestly, my emotions are all over the map. One moment I hate him for what he did to us, and the next I can't believe he's gone."

Will shook his head. "That's awful. This happened only on Friday?"

"Thursday evening in Canada. I'm having trouble processing it."

"Of course. It's still so fresh." He understood grief better than most. "Listen, I'll grab my bag from my locker and let's get you home. You've had a grueling few days, to say the least."

She stood and smoothed her pencil skirt. "Thanks for understanding. You're a good listener."

He handed her the cup. "Any time." And he meant it.

Georgia relaxed into the supple leather of the passenger seat and allowed Will to drive her home. They settled into a comfortable silence and she watched the world go by. A quiet Sunday late-afternoon for most in this sleepy neck of the woods. Once they left the modern hospital behind, they were once again surrounded by fields bordered with hedgerows. With the windows open, the scent of freshly mowed grass wafted in and revived her.

"Have you always lived here?" He gave the impression of being more of a city slicker than country bumpkin, and now she was curious.

Will glanced at her from behind his designer shades before returning his attention to the winding road ahead. "No. We moved here from London about five years ago."

"With work?"

"Yes. A change of pace. We both had demanding professions—Emma was a nurse and I wanted to specialize in pediatric surgery. It made sense to move here. Start a family." A muscle popped in his jaw.

Emma. The wife. Pretty name. "You like village life?"

"I do. It's not for everyone, but there's something wholesome and good about being in the countryside. The fresh air. The close-knit community. I'm a private person, but I appreciate how the villagers watch out for one another. It's been good for Jack. How about you? Are you a city girl?"

She looked down at her stilettos. "How did you guess? Yes, I love the heartbeat of the city. It's always suited my photography business well. I thrive on its energy and love being close to the arts and entertainment culture downtown in Vancouver. At least, I used to." Something shifted when Daniel left. It didn't hold the same charm anymore. "But I felt it was time to mix things up a bit, so I'm here for three months. Maybe more, depending on how everything goes."

"Here you are, your home-sweet-home." Will pulled up outside Bramble Cottage. "It's lovely. Am I correct in saying it's been in your family for a while?"

A warmth filled her insides at the thought of her late grandparents. "You are indeed. It belonged to my grandma and grandad. They lived here for as long as I can remember. I have the best memories of staying with them as a child. Did you ever meet Grandma? Your paths may have crossed in your first couple of years here."

He turned to face her. "No, I'm afraid I didn't. To be honest, I was so immersed in my new job for the first year or two, I wasn't very good at working on relationships outside the hospital. I didn't meet Leo and Harriet until after we had Jack. We got to know them in the church nursery and became friends in no time." He nodded at the cottage. "So, you inherited it then?"

She raised a shoulder. "Sort of. Grandma desperately wanted it to stay in the family and I always adored it, so before she passed away, she sold it at a ridiculously low price to Daniel and me." She stumbled over his name as if it were a foreign language. "That was about three years ago."

He peered back at the property. "It's in great shape."

She saw it with fresh eyes and nodded. She had always adored the perfect pale pink cottage with its thatched roof and abundance of roses. "Thanks. It needed a ton of modernizing and maintenance, so I made a trip out here to set up all the renos and managed it as best I could from Canada."

He whistled. "That must have been a nightmare. It's hard enough when you live here."

"It wasn't so bad. It was a labor of love, and we were in no rush to get it finished. Work schedules kept us in Canada most of the time." *Not to mention our dream to get pregnant.* "We had a few hiccups with the thatched roof, and I sent Harriet in to speak sternly with the workers once in a while, but it worked out beautifully. She was a fabulous project manager. I'm so pleased to finally be living in it. Even if I got off to a rocky start this weekend."

His eyebrows met with concern. "Do you want me to come inside and check things out for you? I don't want to overstep, but I still can't believe your place was broken into. It rarely happens in this village. Like I said, people watch out for each other."

No way was she going to hint at the fact it was not a random intrusion. He really would think she was crazy. "It's fine. It's still light, and I think it was a one-off. Hopefully, the police scared him away."

"He didn't steal anything?"

"No." *Only my peace of mind. Maybe my sanity.* "Anyway, I should let you get home and back to your son. Thanks so much for the ride." She grabbed her purse and camera from the floor before he could ask any more questions.

"I'll wait here until you open the front door. Leo would want me to make sure you're safely inside." He picked up his phone from the center console. "Actually, if you're comfortable, can I give you my number?"

Her eyes widened.

He blushed. "Purely in case you have an emergency. Not that you will. I…I'm sure you're completely fine here. If Leo and Harriet are at the hospital and you need anything…"

Will was gushing. He looked so serious, it was charming. "Of course." She grabbed her phone and navigated to her contacts list. "Here."

Their fingers brushed as he took the phone and entered his details. Georgia felt her cheeks heat. Preposterous. He wasn't searching for a relationship and neither was she. Her quest to be a strong, independent woman didn't include a crush on some delightful surgeon.

"There you go." He handed it back and she avoided his fingers. "Please don't hesitate to ring me. I'm only ten minutes away—other than when I'm on shift at the hospital."

"Will you be seeing Lucy again?"

"I'm not due at work until Tuesday, unless your sister needs me to check on her. My colleague will be doing the rounds tonight, and I'm confident Lucy will be sent home. I'll try to pop over to her house tomorrow for an unofficial check-up. Perhaps I'll see you there?"

"Perhaps you will."

"Here, let me help you."

Will jumped out and jogged around to hold her door open while she half-slid from the SUV to the gravel with as much grace as possible in a pencil skirt. "Thanks again."

"My pleasure."

Such a gentleman. Were all Englishmen this courteous? Daniel was sweet back in the day, but more recent venomous behavior sullied those early memories. Could she ever trust a man again? Not any time soon.

She unlatched the wooden gate and retrieved her key from her bag as she teetered on the uneven pathway in high heels. Note to self—try to wear more countrified footwear. Like Wellington boots. Aware Will's car engine was still purring by the side of the road, she turned the key and stepped inside the entrance. A quick peer into the living area and she exhaled. Nothing seemed amiss.

Georgia waved at Will and he waved back before driving off and leaving her in the empty cottage. She closed the front door and made sure it was locked. The heady scent of the roses she picked from the garden yesterday wafted throughout. She sighed. Yes, this was her home-sweet-home, for the next little while at least.

Kicking off her shoes, she set her bag and camera on the entry table and padded to the kitchen. A cup of tea was in order. So much had happened in the past couple of days. She would attempt to put together some dinner with her meagre supplies, and then check on Lucy's progress.

A quick inventory of fridge contents proved disappointing. Too bad that roast beef lunch at the pub hadn't panned out. Tomorrow she'd have to hit the supermarket after arranging a car rental. For tonight, it would be cheese and crackers and a random bar of chocolate. Pretty much what she survived on at home since going solo. Daniel was the cook in their marriage. Her stomach sank. How could he be dead?

With a heavy heart, she filled the kettle with water. Her eyes gravitated to the toaster. She could almost smell the burnt toast with the fear locked in her imagination. Who was in here on Friday morning? What did they want?

Last night, she'd tossed and turned again for hours. The heaviness of fresh grief overshadowed thoughts of the intruder. Try as she might, she couldn't come up with any logical reason why someone would break in here, burn toast, tape a postcard to the window, and leave. Not steal. Not inflict physical harm. Just scare the living daylights out of her. Who would want to do that? It had to be connected to Daniel somehow.

The warm air in the kitchen was stifling. The forecast threatened heavy storms for that evening, and the humidity caused Georgia's blouse to stick to her back. While the kettle boiled, she dumped a tea bag in a white china mug. *I have to get out of these church clothes and into a T-shirt and shorts.*

She admired the pink roses as she passed the coffee table and jogged up the stairs where it was even warmer. Too bad air conditioning wasn't a thing in quaint English cottages. She would have to get into the habit of opening the windows in the morning until this unusually hot spell was over. At least she remembered to close her bedroom curtains before she left for church to keep the sun from turning her sleeping area into a sauna.

She took two steps into the bedroom and knew something was off. The space was bright and hot. The curtains were wide open. Her hackles raised.

She stumbled backward onto the bed.

Was she paranoid or had someone been in her room?

*And what if he's still inside the cottage?*

# Chapter Ten

GEORGIA SUCKED IN A BREATH AND waited for several heartbeats. Complete silence filled her home. Standing on shaky legs, she peered through the bedroom window, half expecting to see someone in her backyard stalking her.

She lifted her chin and scanned the trees and shrubs to the deserted alley behind her property. Dirty gray clouds eclipsed the light as the promised storm rolled in over the village. Dotted around the patchwork of fields beyond, docile black and white cows chewed their cud like any other regular late-summer evening. Only it didn't feel regular.

Her phone burst into song from the foyer and Georgia's whole body jumped. She raced downstairs and grabbed it from her bag. Sophie.

"Sophie?"

"Yeah—you okay? You sound out of breath."

Slow exhale. "I think so."

"What's going on?"

Georgia scanned the living area. Nothing was amiss. "It sounds silly, but I know I closed my bedroom curtains this morning."

"Okay, you may need to fill me in here. I was calling to send my love. Harriet told me about Daniel… I'm so sorry."

She paced over to the kitchen. The back door was locked. "It was a shock, to say the least."

"How are you holding up? Why are you talking about curtains?"

"I'm hanging in there. It's been a long day at the hospital and everything, but I felt sure I pulled my bedroom curtains shut this morning when I left for church. Now they're open."

"Oh, hon. Are you worried someone's been in your cottage again?"

She wiped a trickle of sweat from her forehead. "Harriet told you about the postcard? I don't know. Maybe I'm going crazy. I haven't slept well since I arrived."

"Understandable. Want to go around and check all your rooms while I'm here with you?"

"Yeah." She started back up the stairs. "Not that you can do anything from Paris…"

"I'm your moral support. Keep talking and walking. Tell me how you're really doing."

"Honestly, I'm a hot mess. Daniel's death is only part of it. Friday was surreal and then today with Lucy…" She poked her head in the bathroom and promised herself a soak in the clawfoot tub later.

"Hey, you need to give yourself a break. I know you're usually the one who has everything running smoothly, but you couldn't have seen any of this coming. Is Lucy okay? Harriet texted me when they were still waiting for her to come out of surgery. I can't believe all this is happening to our family."

"Lucy's fine. The surgery went perfectly well, and they're hoping to be home tonight."

A sigh of relief. "That's good news. Poor sweet girl. I tried to call Harriet just now, but the line was busy. She's probably talking with Mom."

"Mom's itching to fly over this minute." Georgia checked the spare bedroom. Nothing.

"So am I, I'm not going to lie. It's tough not being together at times like this. Say the word, and I can change my flights and be there this week rather than next."

The third bedroom, her converted darkroom was also untouched. "Thanks, I'll let you know. It's been way too long, sis."

"And you've had such a sucky year. I thought you guys were going to make it, you know?"

Georgia perched on the top stair and closed her tired eyes. "You did? I got the impression you suspected Daniel was hiding something when we were in Paris with you last summer."

"Maybe…"

"It's okay. We tried to avoid talking about our marriage problems. I was so determined we would work things out."

Sophie groaned. "I know. My heart breaks for you. You didn't deserve to be disrespected and disregarded like that. He used to be so sweet. It was like he flipped a switch. I couldn't believe how different he was when you were here. Shifty. Almost angry. Weird, considering he was the one who arranged the trip."

Georgia wound a ringlet of hair around her fingers and opened her eyes. Rain now pounded every window. "Anyway, enough of that. I'm so looking forward to having you stay with me. It's going to be like old times."

Sophie chuckled. "I loved staying at Bramble Cottage with Grandma and Grandad when we were young. I have to see what you've done with the place. Harriet says it's gorgeous."

"She's been an absolute gem overseeing the work." Georgia's stomach let out a low rumble, a reminder she hadn't eaten since breakfast. "And you're more than welcome to make yourself at home in my kitchen."

"You mean cook for you."

"You know it's a better option than letting me loose in the kitchen."

"True."

"Speaking of which, I need to make myself something to eat and then I'll check back with Harriet. I'll text you with any news. Promise."

"Sure. Are you still nervous about being in the cottage?"

"Not really. I looked in all the rooms. I guess I was mistaken about closing the curtains, after all."

"Jet lag can be brutal." The sound of running water gushed from a faucet in Sophie's kitchen.

Georgia stood and paced back to her bedroom. "Sounds like you're making dinner, too. Only I'll bet *you're* not dining on cheese and crackers."

"Clearly, I need to get there as soon as possible."

"Definitely. On your own tonight?"

"Yep."

"Look at us. A couple of sad sisters eating solo." Georgia attempted a laugh. "I can't wait to see you."

"Me, too. I know I wasn't Daniel's number one fan toward the end, but I'm shocked he's… gone. We can talk as much as you want when I get there."

"I appreciate that, Soph."

"Listen, I'm going to need your shoulder to cry on as much you need mine."

Georgia closed the curtains. "Turning thirty's not so bad, you know."

"Mom thinks I'm going to be a spinster." A muffled clang of saucepans sounded in the background.

"I'm an even older one."

"Poor us. You'll be careful, won't you? Call me anytime. Plus, you know Harriet would do literally anything to help. She'll be more than happy to let you stay at her place. That's what family's for."

"I know. Also, if I don't want to add to Harriet's stress, there's someone else close by I can call on." An image of Will filled her mind and a warmth spread in her belly. He was safe and kind… and attractive.

"You do? That's great. Who?" Sophie waited for an answer.

"A new friend. He's from Harriet's church."

"He? I thought we were both doing the spinster-sister thing? Tell me more."

Georgia's mouth curved. "His name's Will, he's a surgeon, and a very sweet man who offered to help me out."

"I think I've met him before, and by the smile in your voice I think I'm going to meet him again."

"Don't get excited, we're just friends." *Which is why my cheeks are burning.* "Now I'm hanging up before you grill me. Love you."

"Love you, too."

"*Au revoir.*"

Georgia ended the call and stared at the curtains.

*I know I closed them this morning.*

# Chapter Eleven

WILL LEANED OVER INTO THE BACKSEAT of the car, his leather jacket soaking wet already. A torrential rainstorm on a dreary Monday morning meant one thing—the day could only get better.

"Come on, buddy." He pulled up the hood of Jack's raincoat and unlatched the car seat. "We're going to see how Lucy's getting on."

"Out?"

"Yes, let's get you out. Your friend has an owie on her arm. Remember we have to be very gentle, okay?"

"Okay." Jack scrunched his nose as Will pulled him into the downpour and tucked him tight against his chest.

"Let's run."

Jack giggled at the game as Will slammed the car door and sprinted across the puddled road to Leo and Harriet's house. He knocked on the cherry-red front door, grateful to shelter beneath the generous overhang.

Leo answered. "Will, Jack. Come in. You're drenched."

"Morning. We certainly are." They piled into the entrance hall and Will set Jack and the bag on the tiled floor. "Hey little man, let's take off our shoes and coats and then we can check on Lucy." He looked up at Leo while he worked on removing his wriggling son's shoes. "How's she doing?"

Leo took their wet jackets and hung them on an iron coat rack. "Not too bad. She slept in our bed with Harriet last night— although I don't think Harriet got much sleep. She was so worried about our girl."

"Of course."

"But the doctor who discharged us didn't foresee any problems. We have some pain meds for her when she needs them."

"Good. They'll make her drowsy, too."

"She'll be pleased to see her friend." Leo leaned down and gave Jack a high-five.

Jack's chuckle made Will's heart melt. A day off work with his boy was precisely what he needed. He placed a gift bag in Jack's hands. "Remember, this is for Lucy."

Jack eyed the gift and nodded.

They followed Leo into the living area where a fire was blazing in the grate. Not altogether unusual on an unpredictable summer's day in England. The warmth enveloped them like a hug and added to the cozy ambiance. Candles flickered on the mantel as Harriet tucked a fuzzy blanket around Lucy's tiny form on the sofa. Her arm lay on top, complete with a shocking-pink cast.

"Hi, guys." Harriet's eyes hinted at a less than great night's sleep.

"Morning." Will raised a brow. "Did you manage to get any shut-eye at all?"

She shrugged her shoulders and chuckled. "A little. Lucy slept pretty well, but I was scared she might roll on her arm or fall out of our bed—I basically watched her sleep. I'm going to be next to useless today, but I can put the kettle on." She plodded over to the kitchen area of the open-plan room while Leo sat on the end of the sofa cradling his daughter's feet.

"Hi there, Lucy." Will focused on the patient and held Jack's hand in case he decided to jump on the sofa with his injured friend. "How's our brave little girl?"

Lucy's face was pale, but two dimples appeared when she

managed a smile. "Good." Her little-girl voice was barely above a whisper. She pointed at her arm. "I got a booze."

Will feigned shock. "A bruise?"

He knelt beside her and Jack clung to him, wide eyes pinned on the bright pink cast.

"Is it sore?"

She shook her head and dark curls bounced on her shoulders.

"Well, that's excellent news." He placed a hand on her forehead. *Good, no fever.* "Jack brought you something special." He squeezed his son's leg. "Can you give the present to Lucy now?"

Jack looked at the small package in his hand and raised his fair eyebrows.

"Did you forget you were even carrying it?"

Jack thrust the bag toward Lucy and then set it on her lap with the greatest of care.

"Good boy."

"What do you say, Lucy?" Harriet came back in and settled into the armchair, stifling a yawn. "Don't forget your manners, sweetie."

"Thank-oo."

"You're welcome." Will pulled Jack onto his lap as they sat on the floor. "We thought it may keep you company while you're resting."

"Want me to help, Lucy?" Leo leaned over and pulled the shiny bag apart so she could stick her good hand inside.

She pulled out the gift and squealed. "A bunny." The lop-eared stuffed rabbit was soon covered in kisses.

"Mine?" Jack's pudgy fingers wriggled.

Will anticipated this reaction. *Lucky I brought his own bunny along.* "No, this one is for Lucy. Yours is in your bag. Want me to get it?"

Jack nodded.

"All right. You help Mister Leo take care of Lucy."

Will jumped up and headed to the entrance. He was rummaging through Jack's bag when the doorbell chimed. "Want me to get that, Leo?"

"Please."

Will grabbed Jack's well-loved bunny and opened the front door. The sight of Georgia made his pulse race. Her long hair was pulled into a bun on top of her head and damp strands curled around her cheeks. He couldn't help notice her red lips matched a red polka dot umbrella. Black skinny jeans, black jacket, black boots. Was she one of those women who always looked good? He suspected so.

"Georgia. Come in, come in. It's raining cats and dogs out there."

"Hi. I saw your car across the street." She shook out her umbrella and stepped inside.

"Can I take your jacket?"

"Thanks. I'm used to rain in Vancouver, but I can't believe how chilly it is out there this morning." She dumped the umbrella and her purse on the floor before handing him her damp jacket.

He tried not to react to the jolt that went through him as their fingers brushed. "Don't worry, your sister has a fire roaring."

"Hey, Georgia." Harriet called from the living room. "Come on in. I'd get up but I'm down to my last ounce of energy."

Georgia picked up her purse and joined the others. Will inhaled a hint of something sweet and sophisticated as he followed close behind.

"How's my favorite niece?" She rushed over to Lucy's side and squatted next to her.

"Aunty." Lucy's face beamed and she put out her good arm for a hug, knocking her rabbit to the floor.

"Is this a new bunny? She's very cute." Georgia retrieved it and tucked the rabbit under the blanket next to Lucy.

Lucy nodded and gave her bunny a kiss.

"I heard you were such a brave girl, and wow—your cast is our favorite color."

"Pink." Lucy blinked twice, batting her long dark lashes. She was fighting to stay awake.

"I have something else pink for you." Georgia delved into her large purse and plucked out a hot pink book with a unicorn on the front. "Maybe we can read it together later?"

"Thank-oo." Lucy succumbed to her pain medication and closed her eyes.

Leo stood and stretched his arms above his head. "Tea for everyone?"

"Thanks, babe." Harriet gave a thumbs-up. "The kettle just flicked off."

"Please," Georgia and Will said in unison.

Leo whistled along to the jazz music playing in the background as he sauntered over to the open kitchen area.

"I see Lucy has a friend visiting today." Georgia winked at Jack, who was now snuggling his own bunny.

"Right. This is Jack. My son." Will lifted his boy into his arms, gave him a tickle, and was rewarded with a baby chuckle.

"We already met at church, didn't we, Jack?"

Jack buried his head in Will's shoulder.

"He gets shy."

"It's fine. So do I sometimes." Georgia sniffed the air as she padded over to Harriet's armchair and gave her a hug, too. "The vanilla candles smell delicious, sis."

"Thanks. I have a lavender one for you. I'm in love with this new candle store in the village, I'll take you there eventually. I'm sorry I couldn't give you a ride to the car rental place today. Did you get your errands done?"

"Don't even think about it—you had enough going on this morning. I called a taxi. He was super friendly and has a brother who's a locksmith and will rekey my locks for me tomorrow. I can't believe how nice everyone is here. Well, most people, at least."

Will noticed a shadow pass over her face. He glanced over at Harriet.

She'd seen it, too. She tilted her head. "Is everything okay at Bramble Cottage?"

Georgia paused before pasting on a smile. "Of course. I'm a bit skittish after what happened on Friday, that's all. I'll get over it."

Was Georgia hiding something? Will caught her gaze before she darted off toward the kitchen island.

"So, Leo, have you taken today off work?" Her voice was a little too peppy.

*Nice change of subject.*

"I brought some work home from the office. I can do it later when my two beauties are having a good nap."

"Well, what can I do to help?" Georgia was already setting mugs on a tray. "I'm free to do whatever you like."

"I can help, too." Will sank into another armchair with Jack on his lap. "I'm off work today and we have no big plans. Other than nap time." Impressive. Could he sound any more pathetic?

Harriet leaned forward, her hands clasped. "You could do me a massive favor, Will. Keep my sister occupied this afternoon as I'm going to be incredibly busy napping. I've been a disastrous hostess so far."

Will's heart warmed at the thought of spending time with

Georgia. He could get to know her better and maybe probe to see if she'd run into more problems at the cottage.

Georgia huffed and placed one hand on her hip. "I don't need babysitting and I don't need a host. This is now my home-away-from-home, remember? I've visited often enough to be able to get my bearings. I'm very capable of finding something to do if you don't need me here."

"Like what?" Harriet arched an eyebrow and crept over to where Lucy was now sleeping. She stroked her daughter's fine hair away from her face and settled at the other end of the sofa.

Jack jumped down from Will's lap, discovered the basket of toys in the corner of the room, and picked up a rag book.

Georgia leaned against the kitchen island. "For a start, I could plan where I'm going to take my photo shoots."

"What's the project exactly?" Will asked. "It's for Leo's mom, isn't it?"

She nodded. "Madame Duval was kind enough to give me a feature in her French magazine. I'm doing a lifestyle spread on a typical English country village. Bramble Downs is perfect. She thought I would have a fresh approach as a Canadian who also owns a property here."

"Plus, Mamère loves your work." Leo raised his hands in the air. "She raves about your photography every time I show her your latest shoots."

"That's so kind, Leo." Georgia's cheeks glowed. "Thankfully, we have another sister who's fluent in French and a brilliant writer. She can be my personal editor and translator."

"Yay for Sophie." Harriet accepted a steaming mug from her husband. "Thanks, hon."

"Sounds like the perfect plan." Will took his tea and set it on a side table. "So much artistic talent in one family." He stared at the framed painting of Harriet on stage when she was a professional ballerina. The Brooks sisters certainly had the arts covered.

Georgia turned to Will. "I guess you've met Sophie."

"The Parisian baker? Yes, briefly at church when she visited Harriet. The first time she came they both had long hair and I honestly couldn't tell the twins apart."

"Don't feel bad. Even I struggled and I'm their sister." Georgia nodded toward Harriet. "It was a huge deal when this one chopped her hair into a bob. I think everyone was secretly relieved they finally looked different."

Harriet raised her mug. "You're welcome."

Will chuckled. "Sophie's a writer as well as a baker?"

"Yes. She's excellent at both." Georgia took a sip of her tea. "I can't wait for her to work her magic in my kitchen. Her baking's out of this world."

Harriet held one finger in the air. "But back to you, Georgia. I just had a brilliant idea, though I say so myself. You should totally go over to Will's place—if that's good with you, Will." She implored Georgia with wide eyes. "Hear me out. He's got the most amazing house. It's completely unexpected."

"Thanks a lot." Will rubbed his forehead.

"No, what I mean is it's unexpected in a village like ours. It would be such a fabulous contrast for the feature. In fact, it's the complete opposite to your sweet country cottage."

"Way to go with making your friend feel obligated." Georgia perched on the deep window seat and turned to Will. "I'm so sorry. You'll have to excuse her. She really needs some sleep."

"Although she has a good point..." Leo shrugged and hurried back to the kitchen, away from any line of fire.

Will cleared his throat. He hadn't hosted a woman in his place since Emma died, other than the babysitters for Jack, his mom, and the cleaning lady. Perhaps it wouldn't be so bad…

"You're more than welcome." His words were sincere. He could do this. "Jack will be having his nap when I get back home, so I could show you around and you could take some shots of the place, if you want to collect your camera en route."

Georgia eyed her oversized purse. "I don't go anywhere without it…"

"Perfect." Harriet looked a little too excited about this, but he trusted she knew what was best for Georgia—as well as for him. Maybe they both needed a distraction. Both were dealing with a tsunami of grief. Some companionship wouldn't hurt. Platonic with no pressure. A fun friendship. She was only here for a few months, after all.

One thing was certain—neither were ready for a romantic relationship.

# Chapter Twelve

GEORGIA AGREED TO GO TO WILL'S place on the condition she follow in her yellow rental car—that way she had a method of escape if the afternoon proved to be awkward. As she pulled up behind Will and Jack onto their gravel driveway, she was also grateful he couldn't see the way her mouth gaped wide open. Their home was stunning. It was also For Sale. *Interesting.*

Like nothing else she had seen in the quintessential English village of Bramble Downs, this house oozed contemporary flair with not a hint of thatched roof nor rose trellis. Whitewashed smooth walls, angular lines, and overgenerous expanses of glass windows—yes, this seemed well suited to a surgeon. Precise. Pristine. Polished. Although warmth exuded from soft gray pillars and stonework preventing a clinical or cold appearance. The double doors were a caramel-colored wood, flanked by luscious greenery in huge white pots. This property was crying out to be photographed.

She closed her mouth and exited the car. "Your home is gorgeous." Understatement of the year. She shouldered her purse and took Jack's bag from Will, who carried a very sleepy toddler.

"Thanks. I know it's not your typical Bramble Downs home, but we fell in love with it immediately." He gazed out across the view of rolling hills washed a vivid shade of green by the rainstorm. "It was our dream home."

Georgia felt a sharp pain in her chest. She knew all about planning to live with the love of your life in a dream home. Bramble Cottage was Daniel and hers.

"Now, I think Jack and I might be ready to move on. We'll see."

Poor Will. How was she supposed to hang out here when he was clearly still grieving and uncomfortable talking about his life? His wife? Did he even have visitors here or was it still a sanctuary for father and son? *I'll bet that's why he's trying to sell it. Move on.*

He propped the front door open for her with one shoulder. "Come on in."

"Are you sure about this?"

That cute crease appeared between Will's eyebrows. "Of course. I'll put the kettle on and then you're welcome to take some photos, if you like. The rain stopped at long last so you might want to check out the back garden later."

"Yes. Thank you." *Pull yourself together, girl.* She stepped into the tiled foyer.

"You make yourself comfortable while I settle this little sleepyhead in his bedroom. I won't be long."

"No rush."

Will slipped off his boots and carried Jack up the winding staircase, whispering as he went. He looked good in jeans. Not that she noticed.

*Yeah, right.* Her power of observation and attention to detail were part of her very fabric. Made her a successful photographer. She slipped out of her jacket and ankle boots and grabbed the camera from her purse. Curious to see any hints of his late wife, she wandered into the great room.

The interior continued the clean lines from the shell of the house—all white walls as far as she could see, blond hardwood floors, with pops of colorful area rugs and tasteful art on the walls. She detected the faint aroma of furniture polish as she walked toward the fireplace, where a mantle of chunky barn wood stood proud in the center of the room. Over in one corner, a basket overflowing with colorful toys made her smile. Jack.

She turned back to the mantle and couldn't resist inspecting several framed photographs—Jack as a beautiful pink-cheeked baby, Will with Jack on a sandy beach maybe a year ago, and a wedding shot of Will and Emma. She was a gorgeous bride— long, loose ringlets the exact shade of Jack's blond hair, and a fitted strapless bridal gown in a shimmering white satin. Startling turquoise eyes. Will, handsome in top hat and tails was leaning in mere inches from kissing her lips. A perfect shot. They had a good photographer, that much was obvious.

"Ah, you found our wedding photo, I see." Will came up behind her and they both stared at the image.

"She was beautiful. How long were you married?"

"Not long enough." He paused. "Almost seven years. How about you?"

She closed her eyes. "Twelve years. Maybe a little too long."

Several seconds of silence passed until Georgia spun around. "Hey, I know this is kind of uncomfortable. Harriet is very well-meaning, but she doesn't get it."

"Get what?"

*Oh no, now what have I said? Insinuating my sister has set us up, when he obviously doesn't feel the same…*

"Well, what I mean is… I'm licking my wounds after a particularly nasty divorce as well as trying to come to terms with Daniel's sudden death. It's a lot."

"Sadly, I understand." A muscle twitched in his cheek.

"That's just it. You're still working through your own grief—a love story cut short." She could feel the heat rush to her face. Why was she blabbering? "At least Daniel wasn't a part of my life when he died, but you…" She looked up into his sorrowful green eyes and sighed. "It isn't fair that her life was snatched away from you and Jack. I'm so sorry for you both."

He cleared his throat and stuffed both hands in his pockets, a sheen of moisture clouding his eyes.

*Great. Now I've upset him even more.*

"It's not that simple." His voice was a whisper.

"What do you mean?" Georgia reached out and touched his sleeve, then pulled away. "I apologize, I've no right to ask. I probably shouldn't be here. Maybe I should head back to Bramble Cottage…"

"No." His tone was urgent. "No, there's no need to run off. It seems we've both had our fair share of pain, and I've read it's healthy to talk about it. When you're ready, that is."

"You've read about it?" She narrowed her eyes.

He shrugged. "What can I say? I'm a books guy. I like to go deep with research."

"Makes sense. What else does Doctor Will Hughes like to do?" She perched on the arm of a buttery leather sofa, intrigued.

"I like to run. It's my release. There are some fantastic trails nearby. I'm also a decent bowler in cricket. I also like to cook."

"You cook?" Was there anything more attractive than a man in the kitchen?

He nodded. "With opera music blaring."

Georgia craned her neck to take in the state-of-the art kitchen. "Renaissance man. Nice."

"And my faith is really important to me. Always has been but I think since Emma died, I've experienced a fresh appreciation for who God is and what He means to me."

She fiddled with her camera strap as she spoke. "I'm kind of on my own faith journey, too."

"Is that something recent?"

"Let's say it took a turn for the worse when I was in college and met Daniel. We both decided we didn't need God in our lives." She scowled. "How self-righteous were we? I feel so foolish saying that now."

"We all have our stories. Not many are easy and light."

Georgia tucked a strand of hair behind one ear. "True. Although I feel like I'm finding my feet again. Being in church yesterday was a big step for me. As you may have noticed."

Will raised his brows. "Hey, no judgement here."

"Thanks. Anyway, I'm realizing now how grateful I am for my faith-filled childhood. The truths I learned back in the day. It was all still there. Just needed reviving."

"I like that." Will glanced over his shoulder. "And what about your kitchen skills?"

"I'm afraid Sophie inherited all the cooking genes. Harriet's not bad, actually. I'm what you would call a very basic cook."

"Like frozen and take-out basic?"

She grimaced. "Guilty, but I love *eating* good food and I'll listen to opera music anytime someone wants to cook for me."

"Is that so?" Will leaned against the white wall and gave a half-smile.

"Yes. My mom loves it, so I cut my teeth listening to Callas and Pavarotti."

"I like your mom already."

"I'm sure you'll get to meet her when she comes here for the twins' thirtieth birthday party. She'll be staying a while." Georgia slid down onto the sofa and set her camera on the cushion beside her. "There's nothing I love more than going for a long drive in my convertible with opera blaring and wind in my hair."

Will's face fell. "Excuse me a moment, while I go and put the kettle on for tea. Unless you prefer coffee?"

"Thanks. Tea would be lovely." What had she said? This guy was hard to read. Relaxed one minute, a brick wall the next. *Although who am I to judge when he's being so gracious with me?*

He retreated to the kitchen while Georgia twirled a strand of hair around her fingers. *Is this a mistake? Perhaps I should snap a few pictures and go home.*

"It won't be long." He reappeared and sank into the love seat opposite her. "You'll have to excuse me and my awkwardness. Put me in an operating room and I'm a take-charge kind of guy with the steadiest hand you could imagine. Put me in a room with a beautiful woman and I'm a blithering idiot."

"You're most definitely not any kind of idiot." *Also, did you call me beautiful?* Her cheeks heated at the compliment and something fluttered within her chest. How long had it been since she received a compliment from a man?

His eyes met hers. "The thing is, I'm not used to having… company."

"There's nothing wrong with knowing your social limits. Give me a night in over a big party any day of the week."

"For real?" He leaned forward, his hands clasped.

"Absolutely. We used to party and live on the edge in our early twenties but looking back that was more Daniel. I went along with all of it for him. I'm getting more comfortable in my own skin these days."

He nodded. "That's a good sign. I'm a self-confessed loner. Emma was always the one who pushed me to live a little. So now I'm trying my best but I'm afraid I have a lot of work to do in the socializing department."

Georgia fought the sudden urge to hug him. "Hey, it's all good. We take it one day at a time. Remember the way I broke down at the hospital yesterday? That was a tidal wave of grief, right there."

"It's been a stressful weekend for you."

She slid her bare feet up beside her. "I know. You must think I'm unhinged. I can assure you, I'm not normally a wreck."

"Tell me who you normally are." He raised a brow. "Back in Canada."

She thrust her chin in the air. "Let's see. A professional photographer who usually has more work than she can fit into her schedule. I'm confident—in my work, at least. Responsible—that comes with being the eldest of three girls. A perfectionist. I'm loyal to a fault." Her chin dropped. "Probably not the vibes I've been giving so far. Let's say you haven't exactly seen me at my best."

"I know for a fact you're a talented photographer."

She met his gaze.

"I've seen some of your work. Harriet's immensely proud of you." He gestured around the room. "I'd be honored if you choose to photograph my home for your project."

This man was charming. "You're kind."

"And as for the events of this weekend, you're allowed to have an emotional moment after everything that's happened. I still can't believe someone broke into your place."

*If only it was as simple as that.* Her hands trembled as they rested on her camera.

"Georgia, I know Harriet asked earlier but I have to ask you straight up—have you had any more trouble at the cottage since early Friday?"

Her stomach clenched. "Not really. It's complicated."

"I do 'complicated' quite well." He stood. "I don't know about you, but I could use a friend who doesn't have all their boxes checked. Someone who might understand a little of my pain."

The warmth in his emerald eyes was almost her undoing. "That might be nice."

"I was hoping you'd say that. Why don't I make us tea and you can tell me everything, or as much as you're comfortable sharing? I even have cake."

"Thanks, Will." He was right. With Harriet busy tending to Lucy at the moment, having someone else to talk to in-person might be helpful. Lovely even. *In a platonic, I'm-ignoring-your-delicious-aftershave-and-the-biceps-under-your-shirt kind of way.*

Forty minutes, a couple of slices of lemon pound cake, and a large pot of tea later, Will jogged up the staircase to retrieve a shouting Jack from his crib. He wasn't much of a crying baby—thankfully—he tended to yell his frustration instead.

"I'm here, buddy." While Will plucked Jack from his blanket and lowered his squirming body to the floor for a nappy change, he mulled over the details Georgia shared with him. It was all very cryptic. The ominous postcard and her ex-husband's death couldn't be a coincidence. No way.

"Good boy, Jack. You hold bunny while I finish up here and I'll take you to see Miss Georgia."

"Shawsha?"

"Close enough, little man. I think you're going to like her." *I think I like her, too.*

After the initial awkward moment seeing pictures of Emma, and then Georgia trusting him with her story, they'd clicked and conversation flowed easily. Although something told him he was only scratching the surface. There was more she was not saying, but he was in no position to accuse her of having secrets when his own had been eating him alive for months.

"Shawsha?" Jack opened his eyes wide and Will pinched his chubby cheek.

"Yes. Let's go see Shawsha, shall we?"

Will checked his reflection in the hallway mirror before heading downstairs. He looked tired. He *was* tired. Although a ripple ran through his belly and for the first time in what felt like forever, he was excited about spending time with someone other than Jack. Someone with captivating chocolate-brown eyes and a smile that lit up a room.

And maybe even his heart.

## Chapter Thirteen

FOR THE FIRST TIME SINCE HER rude awakening in the early hours of Friday, Georgia felt peace in the most tender parts of her heart. Granted, she hadn't been able to disclose everything to Will during their conversation, but at least she could vent about the postcard and the burnt toast. A little about her marriage and her family. He was so kind, so patient, so doctorly. She felt safe here. Unlike at Bramble Cottage.

With a frustrated sigh, she picked up her camera and walked back to the foyer to collect her boots. Before he went up to see Jack, Will opened the sliding glass doors in case she wanted to check out the backyard. The freshness of outdoors beckoned and she followed.

The post-rainstorm air was all earth and moss as Georgia inhaled the childhood memories of English summers past. She held the viewfinder of the camera to her eye and took several shots of various layers of green in manicured lawn, shaped hedges, and exotic plants. Stepping stones led to a tree-swing, which hung lazily from a gigantic Weeping Willow. She captured the idyllic scene, illuminated by an unexpected afternoon sunbeam. *Perfect.*

Grateful for the opportunity to survey the property without Will watching, she took tentative steps on the slick gray concrete and meandered around the fire pit and outdoor furniture, paying close attention to detail. Was this all Emma, or did Will have impeccable taste?

He'd given her free rein to shoot inside and out, with the proviso that his name and address weren't included, of course. He was a private man. With the magazine being published in France, he had little to worry about with regard to his safety… unlike Georgia. The gruesome postcard invaded her thoughts. She folded her arms across her chest to ward off an unwelcome chill.

"Jack wanted to come and see you." Will's deep voice sounded from the open doors.

Georgia spun around and grinned. "Hi, Jack." She took two steps toward them and lost her footing with the slippery sole of her boot. Her feet came from under her and she landed on her backside on the slick concrete. Will was there in a flash. He crouched down next to her and stood Jack up beside him.

"Georgia, are you hurt?"

She caught her breath and looked up into two concerned pairs of eyes—one as green as the forest behind them and the other as turquoise as the ocean. She wanted to cry out in pain and sheer embarrassment knowing her rear end would be black and blue within hours, but attempted to put on a brave face, for Jack's sake as well as her own pride.

"I'm fine." Both words were clipped as she grimaced.

Jack's creased forehead mirrored his father's.

"Really, all good here. I even saved my camera." She raised it with one hand. Her natural instinct was always to protect her equipment. Thank goodness she had the neck strap on.

Jack thrust his well-loved bunny toward her. "Better?"

Her heart melted as his anxious face urged her to take the bunny.

"Thank you, Jack. That's so sweet of you." She accepted the bunny and sat cross-legged on the damp patio, the toy in her lap.

"Wow." Will wiped his chin with his fingers. "That's the

first time he's ever voluntarily given Bunny to someone."

"I clearly need all the help I can get. Even from Bunny. Right, Jack?"

He pursed his lips and nodded. "Right."

That was it. Georgia erupted into a fit of giggles. Jack joined in with his darling toddler-chuckle and then Will's laugh caused her to almost tear up again. It was the first time she'd heard him laugh out loud and it was higher pitched than she imagined. Infectious. Adorable. The three of them let it all out until Georgia's phone sounded a text notification from her pocket.

"I guess I didn't break my phone. That's a bonus." She swiveled to her knees and pulled her cell from her jeans. "It's probably Harriet—she'll be horrified when I tell her how clumsy I've been. She's definitely the only dainty ballerina in our family."

"Let me help you up and perhaps we should go back inside." Will offered his hand and Georgia willed her face not to flush at the touch of his warm fingers. She stood and met his gaze. For a moment she didn't dare breathe. Didn't retrieve her hand. It fit so perfectly in his...

When was the last time she experienced butterflies dancing in her belly? *I'm not ready for this.* As seconds stretched, her mouth ran dry as she searched for something sensible to say. *This is ridiculous. I have to get out of here before I make an even bigger fool of myself.*

"Bunny?" Reality beckoned along with a blond-haired toddler at their feet. The little guy was concerned about his beloved toy.

"Yes, yes. Thanks, Jack." She broke eye contact with Will and handed the toy back. "Your bunny made me feel much better, but I have to go."

With a pathetic apology for her abrupt exit and a promise to call Will if she needed anything at all, Georgia fled to her car and started the engine. She checked her text message—it was Sophie making sure she was okay. *Other than flustered, I'm fine.* She waved at Will and Jack as they stood together in the doorway with matching furrowed brows, before maneuvering her vehicle in the ample space on the driveway and out of sight.

Her foot fell heavier on the accelerator and the compact hatchback hugged each curve on the winding road. She opened all the windows, pulled the elastic from her hair, and allowed the brisk afternoon breeze to whip her long locks about her head. The danger in her cottage and the flutter in her heart were both unexpected intrusions on what she planned for her time in England. *I need to think.*

At home in Canada, she would take to the wide, open highway, with beautiful British Columbia presenting the most magnificent vistas of mountain, ocean, and trees. It was her release. Once upon a time, Daniel would sit in the passenger seat beside her, hands in the air, shades on, dark blond hair rushing in the wind. Life was so much fun before her dreams disintegrated one by one. Until her life looked nothing like the perfect plan she envisioned.

*But God, you have a plan for my life, don't You? Better than anything I dreamed up. It has to be…*

Learning to loosen her grip on life was easier said than done. Some days she didn't recognize the angry woman staring back at her in the mirror. The past year, she buried herself in more work than she was able to keep up with in an attempt to numb the pain. She put off dealing with the tough issues that tugged at her heartstrings begging for attention. Like forgiveness…

What was that noise? A huddle of donkeys braying in the

adjacent field caused her to lose concentration for a split second and when she refocused, a silver sports car sped toward her head-on. With a shriek, she pulled sharp left, slammed on the brakes, and swerved into the hedgerow. She froze, eyes squeezed shut. *What just happened?*

When Georgia's pulse slowed to near-normal, she cracked her eyes open and glanced in the rearview mirror. The sports car pulled over, but the driver made no attempt to exit the vehicle. Male, black baseball cap, shades. He watched her in his mirror. Revved his engine. As the seconds ticked by, Georgia couldn't move. Was this some kind of weird stand-off? Why wasn't he coming to at least check on her? How could he not have seen her in this vehicle the color of sunshine?

As if satisfied she wasn't mangled on the side of the road, he raised his hand with an obscene gesture and sped off down the lane.

Blowing a long breath through pursed lips, Georgia released her death-grip on the steering wheel, rolled her tight shoulders, and took a moment to evaluate her physical condition. No injuries. Although her nerves were frayed and she'd feel tension in her neck later.

A sudden desire to flee the scene flooded her being. Was the car still drivable? Her nonexistent knowledge of vehicle maintenance prompted a mental note to rectify that at some point in the future. There hadn't been an obvious bump when she veered into the hedge, but it was a rental car and should be inspected for scratches. *I'm an excellent rule-follower if nothing else.*

Georgia grabbed her camera and got out of the car. It wouldn't hurt to document the incident in case the rental place kicked up a fuss. She inspected the front. No dents. *Phew.* She ran a hand across the front left bumper where a few scratches mani-fested. Focus the lens. *Click. Click.* Honesty was always the best policy.

The sound of another vehicle approaching from behind on the quiet stretch of road caused every muscle to tense. Was the crazy driver coming back? She pivoted on the spot and exhaled when she realized it was a police car. *I hope he noticed the speeding silver bullet.* She tucked her windswept hair behind her ears and waited for the driver to approach. It was the officer who came to her cottage for the break-in on Friday. What was his name? Parker.

His face registered recognition. "Hello again, Miss. Are we having some car trouble?" He eyed her vehicle.

"No. I don't think so. I swerved off the road and was worried I might have damaged it, but there are only a few tiny scratches. Unfortunately, it's a rental."

He folded his arms across his chest. "They may ding you for that. Wise to take a photo. Was it a donkey?"

"I'm sorry, what?"

"A donkey. Is that why you swerved into the hedge? They rule the road in these parts. Blinking nuisance."

Village life. "Ah, no. It was a silver sports car actually. You must have passed him. He was coming straight for me. I know some of these lanes are narrow but there's no reason for him to be over on my side of the road." As she spoke, she suspected the officer might wonder whether she reverted back to her North American driving habits. She straightened her shoulders. "Of course, I was driving on the left, as I should be."

Officer Parker removed his peaked cap and scratched his thatch of salt-and-pepper hair. "Strange. I didn't pass anyone. Must have turned off at Bluebonnet Lane. He didn't stop then?"

"Only long enough to see I wasn't injured."

"I see." He returned the cap to his head and squinted. "You've been most unfortunate since you arrived."

*No kidding.* "Yes, yes I suppose I have."

"Did you want to report it?" His hand was in his pocket ready to document the incident.

Georgia shook her head. "No. That's not necessary. I want to get home, that's all."

"You don't mind driving on the other side of the road then?"

"No. It doesn't bother me. I've done it a fair bit over the years." She took a step back, hoping to get behind the wheel. She was in no mood for chit-chat.

"Right you are, then." He cocked his head to one side. "Everything in order at the cottage? No other trouble, I hope." He glanced behind him at the empty road.

For a moment, Georgia hesitated. Officer Parker had a kindness about him and reminded her of Uncle Pete back in Vancouver. "I'm fine, for the most part, but I wonder if I could request a favor?"

"I'll try my best." He raised both bushy eyebrows.

"I know we mentioned it for over the weekend, but could you have someone drive by Bramble Cottage for a few more nights? After what happened on Friday, I guess I'm a little nervous. An extra pair of eyes would be much appreciated."

He nodded and pulled out a notebook from his uniform pocket. "I think we can manage that. Miss Brooks, isn't it?"

"Georgia. And thank you, officer."

"You're welcome." He shook his head. "We have very few break-ins in Bramble Downs. That postcard of yours was exceedingly strange. Bad luck for it to happen on your first night in the country. Jolly bad luck."

"Right. Well, thanks again. I should go." Georgia lifted her hand and offered her best smile.

"Drive safe, now."

Officer Parker made no attempt to move as she jumped into the car and took off—in cautious mode—until she could no longer see him in her rearview mirror.

Desperate to hunker down and find rest in her new home, she prayed Bramble Cottage would be the glorious haven she hoped for, and not the dangerous hazard it was shaping up to be.

# Chapter Fourteen

GEORGIA GROANED AND TUGGED THE THROW blanket over her head. The crowing of a persistent cockerel from a neighboring yard persuaded her it was time to get up. She reached for her phone on the coffee table and pulled it under the blanket to check.

6:00 AM

There was no falling back to sleep now that her body knew it was morning.

After spending a restful and blissfully regular couple of days puttering around the cottage, it was starting to feel like home. She'd finished unpacking, caught up on emails, started a WWII romance novel, and picked more soft pink roses from the front yard, which now perfumed the air in the living room. The lock guy had come and changed everything in a matter of minutes, giving her an extra measure of comfort. The postcard-and-toast scare from Friday still smarted, but on the whole, her screaming nerves calmed to a low-grade thrum.

So much so, she fell asleep sometime around midnight cuddled up on the sofa watching a soothing documentary about English country gardens. *Maybe I've conquered jet lag.* That would be a blessing. Although with her stress-induced insomnia over the past months, she was in no hurry to flush away the sleeping pills quite yet.

Emerging from the blanket with reluctance, she stretched her arms above her head, and plodded barefoot to the kitchen.

*Need caffeine.*

She switched the kettle on, measured out the precise quota of ground coffee, and added it to the French press.

A quick scan of her phone showed two messages; one from Harriet and one from her mom. Nothing from Will yet today. A deflated sigh passed through her lips and took her by surprise. Why was she checking for messages from a man she had known a few short days? Although his caring texts yesterday were welcome. It was kind of him to check on her between his shifts. *I guess I'm enjoying his friendship. That's all.*

She kept scrolling. Harriet wanted to meet for a cream tea at lunchtime—Lucy was up bright and early and already asking if they could go to Brambles and Berries, her favorite tea room.

Georgia grinned. That was good news if her niece was feeling up to an outing. Plus, how was this little tea-loving princess only three years old?

She asked if Lucy would please bring her new bunny along for scones.

The response was a smiley face and a noon meet-up time. Setting the phone down on the kitchen table, a black folder caught her eye. *Argh, I need to make a start on this village life photography project for Leo's mom at some point.* After a terrifying start to her stay in Bramble Downs, it was challenging to get her head in a creative space for capturing the charm of village life.

The tearoom. She could take some shots at lunchtime.

The kettle flicked off and she poured boiling water onto the grinds and gave it a stir before fixing the lid on top. She reached for her phone and checked her mom's message. It was a long one. No surprise there. *Poor Mom. She must be frantic with Daniel's accident and then Lucy's arm.* At the end of the text, she almost knocked over the French press as she processed the words.

The message said Daniel's hit-and-run was now being treated as a homicide. *What?* She'd known in the pit of her stomach something was off. The message on her postcard, for one thing. Why did the authorities suspect foul play? A prickle of fear worked its way through her body as she read on. Uncle Pete would keep them informed but a witness had come forward.

*God, what is going on? How much danger am I in here?*

She dialed her mom as her thoughts ran wild.

"Mom, it's me. I got your text."

"Georgia? Just a second, sweetheart, let me get the light."

"You're in bed already? Sorry, but I need to know what's going on with Daniel's accident."

"I hated to send a text, but I guessed you would be asleep over there when I got the news from Uncle Pete."

Georgia sank onto the kitchen chair. "What did he say exactly?"

"He said it's not a regular hit-and-run scenario like they thought at first. Uncle Pete promised to keep me in the loop as much as he's allowed. I don't understand it though. Daniel wasn't into anything shady, was he?"

Georgia snagged her fingers through a tangle in her hair. "I don't know what he's been up to, Mom. I literally haven't seen him since March. You'll have to check with his girlfriend." Her foot tapped on the floor double-time as familiar bitterness clawed at her chest. "I'm sure she's busy consoling Daniel's parents right now." Bitterness was replaced by envy. She loved Mr. and Mrs. Price like family and part of her longed to comfort them. It wasn't their fault their son ruined her life. "They must still be in shock."

"Daniel's mother definitely is. She called me earlier today to see if you were in town. She misses you. After all those years, you were like a daughter to her, sweetheart."

Georgia squeezed her eyes shut. "I know. Daniel destroyed more than one relationship. Anyway, she has Vanessa now."

"Well, that's it. Apparently, Daniel and Vanessa broke up over a week ago. She's heard nothing from her. In fact, she doesn't know for sure if Vanessa is aware of Daniel's death. Isn't that bizarre?"

*What?* "Wait, I don't understand. Daniel and Vanessa were living together…"

"I know. I didn't like to ask details, she's so upset after losing her boy. Now to think maybe it wasn't a random accident." Georgia's mom sucked in a breath. "I'm worried about you all alone over there."

"Mom, I'm fine." *If only you knew.* "And you'll be here for the party mothering us all to death before you know it."

"But I'm sure Harriet needs help with Lucy now, too. I'm more than happy to catch an earlier flight—"

"There's no need. Really. Sophie offered to come earlier if necessary. Besides, don't you have work commitments up until you leave?" The comforting aroma of brewing coffee wafted over to her side of the kitchen.

"I'm an event planner, sweetheart, not a brain surgeon. I have people who can take over my work without it causing a fuss. It wouldn't be a problem."

Georgia ran her fingers over the distressed wood of the table again and again. "Mom, can we stick with the plan, please? Lucy's healing nicely. Harriet has plenty of help. Sophie can hop on a flight and be here in hours, and I really need to find my feet here. Let the dust settle. Why not stay in Vancouver and represent our family at Daniel's funeral service? If you're comfortable. I know it would mean a lot to his parents."

"You don't mind if I go?"

*Lord, help me release the bitterness. People are grieving.* "Of course not. I think it would be a nice thing to do. The Price family were always kind to me and they've suffered a horrible loss."

"I'm so proud of you." Georgia heard a smile in her mom's voice. "You're healing. You know I'm praying for you every day."

"And I appreciate it." *I need it more than you know.* "I should head off now though. I need to take a shower and get on with my day, but I'll speak to you soon. Please text me if you find out anything more on Daniel's… passing."

"Of course. Are you seeing that nice surgeon today?"

Georgia arched a brow. "Have you been talking to Harriet?"

"She said he was taking care of you."

Her foot stopped tapping. "He's a friend, that's all." *Then why is my face flaming hot?*

"Well, I'm excited to meet your *friend* at the twins' birthday party. He will be there, I hope?"

"He knows Leo and Harriet pretty well, so maybe, but please don't put the heavies on me, Mom. I'm not looking for another relationship anytime soon. I'm too busy licking my wounds and I've only been here a few days."

"I know. I want you to be happy.."

"I don't need a man to make me happy. Trust me, it doesn't work that way." She stood and stretched again. *What I wouldn't do for a massage about now.*

"I totally agree. I'm still looking forward to meeting your surgeon."

Georgia moaned. "Love you, Mom. Bye."

"I love you, too. Take care."

She puffed out her cheeks, set the phone on the counter, and selected a white mug from the open shelf. A headache was starting to throb after absorbing such disturbing information this early in the morning. *Coffee.*

The rich brew permeated the air as she poured. So, Daniel broke up with Vanessa? Or was it the other way around?

A dollop of cream. A quick stir.

And now his death was a possible homicide. Her suspicions were on track. He'd got himself into something dangerous. Dragged her into his mess. *I didn't ask for any of this.* She clenched her fingers around the handle of the mug as anger pulsed through her veins. Was she a terrible person to feel this much anger toward someone who was dead?

*God, give me grace to get through this one step at a time.*

She took a long sip and leaned against the fridge.

Her mind detoured from Daniel to more pleasant thoughts of Doctor Will Hughes. Could they be any more different? *Will.* Her heart skipped a beat. Devoted father, skilled surgeon, man of faith. It didn't hurt that he was devastatingly handsome. There was chemistry there, for sure, but it was too complicated. Too soon. Probably for the best he was working today and she could concentrate on other things.

Like who would want to kill her ex-husband.

# Chapter Fifteen

With ten minutes to spare, Georgia pulled into a vacant parking spot outside Brambles and Berries tearoom. It was charming—Lucy had impeccable taste. Her stomach grumbled a reminder to pick up groceries on her way home. Anxiety killed her appetite of late, but her pantry was still depleted, and she needed to take care of herself.

Checking her bright pink lipstick in the rearview mirror, she took a second glance down the street. The unnerving news from her mother this morning heightened her already-fraught stress levels. *Get a grip, girl.*

She picked up her camera from the passenger seat and slung her bag over one shoulder. She could make a start on the village photo spread for Leo's mom. There was time to snap a few outside shots of the tearoom in the sunshine. She locked the car door and crossed the road to get a better view of the exterior.

Deep green ivy climbed a haphazard route up creamy stone walls, ancient and worn. The window box from the second story overflowed with purple Lobelia and Petunias and drew the eye to a wrought iron "Brambles and Berries" sign. A plethora of red flowers cascaded from tall black planters either side of the welcoming wooden door beckoning passers-by to rest a while with a cup of tea.

Georgia focused her lens. The notion of sitting and resting and allowing her worries and fears to melt away was delightful—albeit delusional. Not much chance of that happening but she did need to eat and wanted to see how Lucy was doing.

She snapped several full height shots of the tearoom and marveled at the slow pace of this village. The lunchtime rush consisted of an elderly couple ambling along arm-in-arm and a young mom pushing a double-stroller with twins. She offered an encouraging smile to the mom, crossed the road, and made a beeline for Brambles and Berries.

A bell jingled above her head, welcoming her with a waft of warm cinnamon buns as she closed the door behind her.

"Hello, dear." A gray-haired lady with excellent posture greeted her at the entrance. "Table for one?"

Ouch. That was her new normal. "No, my sister made a reservation for three. Harriet Duval."

"Harriet? Yes, of course. Please, let's sit you by the window, shall we?"

Georgia scouted the room and a moment of panic quickened her pulse. "If you don't mind, do you think we could have a booth?"

The woman raised her brows and then broke into a smile. "I think Lucy would love a booth."

"You know Lucy?"

"She's my favorite customer but don't tell the others." With a wink, she led Georgia to a dark pink velvet booth with rosebud cushions.

"Lucy will love this." She slid into the center with her back against the wall and a perfect view of everything—and everyone. "This is great. Thank you. I can wait on ordering until they arrive."

With a nod, the spry older woman returned to her duties straightening place settings and checking on the other customers. Within minutes, Georgia's neck and shoulders relaxed as she enjoyed the soft strains of big band music playing in the background amidst the clink of china teacups on saucers. Other than a middle-aged couple engrossed in conversation at a table for two by the window, there were only ladies lunching here today. No suspicious men flaunting postcards in sight.

She skimmed her fingers across the smooth white linen tablecloth and thought of her grandmother. Grandma loved to go out for a cream tea. Fresh scones, strawberry jam, clotted cream. Georgia noticed the couple at the window were sharing one and for a moment she was tempted. No, she already knew she had to have a cinnamon bun with the first whiff upon entering. A quick glance at the glass cake plate by the cash register confirmed her decision, with its display of gigantic swirls of sugary goodness oozing with frosting. How could she resist? Her mouth watered.

The bell jingled over the door and Harriet and Lucy appeared, both in pastel summer dresses. Georgia waved and they spotted her.

"Aunty." Lucy's face lit up as she led her mom straight to the booth and pointed at her injured arm. "Aunty, see my cast?"

Georgia kissed her cheek. "I sure do. It's the prettiest pink cast I've ever seen. It even matches your swirly, twirl-y dress."

Lucy turned a full circle, lifting her cast as high as she could. "I'm very careful." She furrowed her dark brows.

"You are, sweetheart." Harriet helped Lucy into the booth and settled her bunny on the seat next to her. "You're being very careful with that arm. It'll be all better before you know it." She leaned over and gave Georgia a hug. "How are you doing today?"

"Pretty good. All things considered, you know. I feel like I'll be a whole lot better after I devour one of those cinnamon buns."

"Right? They smell fantastic. I could do with a little comfort food myself. I think I'll join you." She slid a laminated menu in front of Lucy. "You take a look and let me know what you want."

Georgia couldn't help grinning as Lucy scanned the items, running her pointy finger across each one. "Is she actually reading that? It's very convincing."

"She always has chocolate milk and chocolate cake, but she likes to keep her options open."

The server returned with a notebook and took their order, and then gave Lucy a coloring sheet and some crayons. "For my favorite chocolate cake customer."

Lucy grinned and got to work on her coloring. In hushed tones, Georgia shared the news of Daniel's death investigation, knowing Harriet was sure to find out from their mother at some point.

"Seriously?" Harriet leaned closer. "I don't even know what to say."

"Me neither. I feel numb about the whole thing, if I'm going to be honest."

"It's surreal. Daniel?"

They sat in silence for several moments.

"I have some *good* news," Harriet continued in a whisper. "Well, as good as it possibly could be, I suppose. That woman at church on Sunday?" She glanced down at her daughter. "It really was a totally random abduction attempt."

"It was?" Georgia exhaled. It was nothing to do with her, after all. Still horrific, but one less thing she had to feel guilty about. "How do you know?"

"I got a call from the police station this morning. It's awful. This woman had a breakdown and drove all the way from Cornwall searching for her baby. She doesn't actually have a child, but I guess something snapped and she decided a church would be a good place to find one. After she ran from Saint Pete's, she kept driving and her family reported her missing."

"That's heartbreaking."

"I know. She's been found and is in care now. We're not pressing charges as long as she's properly looked after and gets help."

"I'm glad she was found."

Lucy peered up from her coloring with big, brown eyes. "Pretty dress, Aunty."

Georgia smoothed the cream fabric of her fitted shift dress. "Thank you, Lucy. I thought I should wear something nice for our tea party."

"You look fabulous." Harriet gave a nod of approval. "Although I hate to sound like Mom, but I think you've lost a little weight even in the few days you've been here."

"Do you think maybe I've been a tad stressed?" She raised a brow.

"Good point. Although I may have to borrow that dress for a date night with Leo."

Georgia's shoulders fell. "You know, I struggled with putting it on today."

"How come?"

"I've been wearing black since the news about Daniel. Not by some conscious choice but I guess it felt right. Matched my mood. Wearing this was a weird stretch for me today."

Harriet grasped her hand. "Hey, one day at a time. If you feel sad and want to wear black, that's normal. If you feel like washing your hair and wearing a cream dress, that's perfectly fine, too. Don't be hard on yourself."

The pot of Earl Grey tea, giant cinnamon buns, and Lucy's chocolate fix, arrived. Georgia chuckled. "Well, this should take care of my weight loss."

As they sipped tea from bone china cups and nibbled on

delicious pastries, the sisters reminisced on their childhood vacations spent in Bramble Downs until Georgia changed the subject.

"Can I ask you something about Will's wife?" She bit her bottom lip. "He's started to open up a little but I'm curious. What was she like?"

Harriet tilted her head. "Sweet. Pretty. Kind. Everyone said Emma was a great nurse."

"How well did you know her? I don't remember you ever mentioning her name."

"We hung out a couple of times. It wasn't until after she died that we got to know Will better. I think Emma had a rough time delivering Jack and we didn't see much of her after that... and then there was the accident."

Georgia shook her head. "It's devastating. A driving accident, wasn't it?"

Harriet put an arm around Lucy. "The worst. It was such a shock to everyone in the village. I think you've been good for him."

"With my issues? Are you joking?" *How can I possibly be good for this man who has already been through so much?*

"Let's just say I haven't seen him look this *alive* in a very long time."

Georgia wiped her mouth with a white linen napkin. "That's sweet, but don't read too much into it."

"Can't blame a girl for trying."

Georgia reached over and squeezed Harriet's hand. "Thanks."

"For what?"

"For being here for me. For this. Coming out with you two today was exactly what I needed." She tried to put sinister notions about Daniel's death and her home-intrusion to one side and focus on the joy in front of her. "I'm glad you invited me."

"Our pleasure. I knew you'd love it here. I've rented it out for the birthday party. I'm sending you home with a pot of their home-made blackberry jam, too. It reminds me of the stuff Grandma used to make."

"With her scones, warm from the oven."

"Yes." Harriet closed her eyes and sniffed. "I can almost smell them now. She was such an amazing baker. I guess that's where Sophie gets it from."

Georgia shrugged. "One of us had to inherit it." She tapped her fingertips on her chin. "Although I think I might try making jam now that I'm in an English village. It seems like a country-living thing to do."

Harriet almost choked on her tea. "I never thought of you as a jam-maker but, yes. You should do it. You could document it for your photography project of village life."

"I could." Her wheels started turning. "I have blackberry bushes in my back garden. Maybe Grandma even planted them there."

"We could come and help you pick berries on Monday if you like?" Harriet turned to Lucy. "Do you think you could pick some yummy blackberries for Aunty with your good hand next week, sweetheart?"

Lucy nodded with her mouth full of chocolate cake.

*Wait. Will mentioned Monday was his day off and maybe getting together…*

Georgia pursed her lips. "Actually, I may take a raincheck on that, if you don't mind."

Harriet wiped a smear of frosting from Lucy's cheek. "Why? I think it sounds perfect. We could even help start the jam with you."

"I'm sorry. I forgot I have plans on Monday. Maybe later in the week?" She brushed a couple of crumbs from her lap.

"Plans? What plans?"

Harriet wasn't going to let this go.

"I may be seeing Will."

Both brows shot up. "Well, well. In that case, we'd hate to intrude. Right, Lucy?"

"Right, Mummy."

"Georgia, you're blushing."

"No, I'm not." She blew a strand of hair from her face. "It's hot in here, that's all. I didn't know late summer could be so muggy in England."

"Uh-huh."

"For goodness' sake."

Harriet leaned in and whispered. "Don't look now but it seems you have another admirer over in the corner, too."

Georgia took a sip of her tea and craned her neck to see what her sister was making a fuss about. A handsome middle-aged man in a pinstriped navy suit averted his eyes and studied his phone. He must have slipped in while the girls were chatting. *So much for me being on surveillance.* He was on his own and appeared to belong on Wall Street or the cover of a magazine rather than in a country village tearoom.

"He's not looking at me." She focused on her teacup.

Harriet chuckled. "Yes, he is. I've been watching him. He's mesmerized. I'm sure he's not a local. We know almost everyone who lives here. Wait. I think he just took a pic of you with his phone. That's a bit much."

Georgia's head snapped up. Cool steel-gray eyes stared back at her. No smile. No emotion whatsoever. A chill crawled up her spine.

He stood, threw cash on the table, and rushed out, the bell jingling his dramatic exit through the door.

"That was weird." Harriet reached across the table and patted Georgia's hand. "Maybe he wasn't photographing you. He could've been taking a selfie."

"Yeah." The cinnamon bun sat like a rock in her stomach.

Lucy inched closer to Georgia and passed a pink crayon. "Color with me, please?"

"Of course, Lucy." *Act natural and perhaps my pulse will return to normal.* "I'll color the princess."

A deafening rev of a car engine outside the window caused all three of them to jump in their seats.

"What on earth?" Georgia's mouth fell open as she watched a vehicle roar down the street and out of sight.

It was a horribly familiar silver sports car.

# Chapter Sixteen

Georgia checked her phone.

*11:00 AM*

She'd been looking forward to this since Will confirmed at church yesterday, and now he and Jack were due to arrive any second. She scrutinized her refection in the full-length gilded mirror in her foyer and wrinkled her nose. Too much? What did one wear blackberry-picking? The sun shone through her living room windows and the humidity was already bordering on uncomfortable. Black shorts and top complimented by a flowy, floral kimono seemed like a good idea when perusing her wardrobe. Maybe she should go for denim shorts and a T-shirt?

The crunch of gravel on her front path alerted her to Will's arrival. Too late to change now. *Since when do I make such a fuss about what to wear?* Before he had a chance to knock, she opened the door wide.

"Hi."

"Morning, Georgia. You look lovely."

He didn't look so bad himself wearing a polo shirt, smart shorts, and dazzling smile.

"Thanks." She peered past him and waved at Jack in the back seat of the SUV. "Did you guys want to come in for a minute or set off right away?"

He turned to his car. "Let's head to the forest. Jack will want to dig into the picnic before long. We should do the fruit-picking while he's amiable."

"Sounds good." Georgia grabbed her bag with camera

stowed inside, locked up behind them, and followed his lead.

"We barely had a chance to chat at church yesterday. Did you get to try the roast beef dinner at the Quail and Plum?"

She laughed. "I did. It was all Harriet promised it would be. The Yorkshire puddings are to die for."

"I hear you." Will opened the passenger door. "I'm glad you had fun. You had a rough start to your arrival in Bramble Downs."

*That's putting it mildly.* Georgia swiveled in her chair and squeezed Jack's bare leg. "Hey, Jack. How are you today?"

He clutched his bunny and rewarded her with a shy smile.

"Thanks for letting me come out with you."

"Dada?"

"I'm right here, buddy." Will jumped in and started the car. "Off we go. Lucy seems to be coping well after her surgery."

"I know. She's such a little trouper."

"The cast bugging her yet?"

"Not too much. She doesn't love it, but Harriet's keeping her occupied most of the time, which sounds exhausting."

He smiled. "I get that."

Georgia settled into her seat. *This is surreal. Out for a picnic with a man and his son... I wonder how Will's feeling about this.*

"I meant to ask, have they heard any news on the woman who tried to take Lucy from the church nursery?" Will glanced at her as he drove. "I'm sure there are plenty of rumors flying around but I can't say I've heard anything positive."

"Actually, yes." She relayed the information Harriet had passed on to her. "I can't help feeling relieved that it was nothing to do with my... predicament."

As they stopped at the end of the road, Will turned to her. "I'm hoping our little outing today might take your mind off your *predicament* for a couple of hours."

"Honestly? That sounds perfect."

Twenty minutes later, Will pulled into a deserted parking area in a clearing and they exited the vehicle.

"This is stunning." Georgia stood with her hands on her hips and inhaled the mixture of pine and something sweet. Was it possible to smell berries in the air?

Will carried Jack in his arms and joined her at the edge of the forest as they admired rolling hills crammed with heather. A sea of pale purple. White fluffy clouds stretched lazily against the turquoise sky, inviting them to savor the moment of rest.

"It's one of my favorite spots for a picnic." He nodded to the wooden table he'd claimed with a red-and-white checkered tablecloth.

Georgia studied his face. Was he reminiscing on times with his deceased wife behind those shades he wore?

"I thought you might like to take some photos while we're here."

She delved into her bag and pulled out her camera. "I don't know if I could ever capture beauty of this magnitude in a single shot, but I'm sure going to try."

"Knock yourself out. When you're done, we'll take you to the best blackberry bushes. They're our secret place, aren't they, Jack?"

Jack nodded.

"Thanks. I won't be long."

"Take your time. I'll get Jack in the carrier backpack. It's easier than running after him and less chance of him getting scratched by brambles."

Georgia let her creative muse take over as she set up each shot with care and found perfect angles to portray what she felt deep inside when she embraced the beauty of creation before her.

She sensed Will's gaze on her and turned. "I'm done for now."

Jack's face peered from behind Will's head.

"Hey, Jack. Do you get to ride on your daddy's back?"

He tugged at his navy baseball cap and rewarded her with a grin that split his face.

Will slid his shades off and squinted at her camera. "Is that a film camera? Haven't seen one of those being used in years."

"It sure is." She passed it to him. "I don't use it often, but there's nothing quite like it. I used to love working with film when I first started in photography. I guess it's like a writer using a fountain pen rather than a keyboard. I dabble in it occasionally."

"Do clients ever ask you to use film rather than digital?" He handed it back to her.

"Rarely. I didn't have an actual darkroom, until now…"

"You have one here?"

She couldn't hide her excitement. "At Bramble Cottage. It's set up in the third bedroom. I can't wait to use it."

"That's pretty cool."

"I think so." She noted Jack squirming in his carrier. "Should we find those berries?"

"Right this way." They wandered over to an area of bushes off the beaten path where they could still keep an eye on the picnic table. "Feast your eyes on these."

As she got closer, her jaw dropped. The bramble bushes were studded with fruit.

"Here." Will plucked the biggest blackberry she'd ever seen and placed it into her open palm. "You definitely need to sample one."

Georgia held the plump, glossy berry the color of ebony in her fingers, and breathed in. Familiar tartness filled her nostrils. "This reminds me of summers here with my grandparents." She popped it in her mouth and closed her eyes.

Sun-baked and grown to perfection, it was pure and comforting. Tangy, rich, sweetness burst in her mouth as she rolled it over her tongue. "This is hands-down the best berry I've tasted in my whole life." She opened her eyes to find Will and Jack both grinning at her. "Wow."

"Glad it exceeded your expectations." Will helped himself to one and passed another to his son.

Georgia watched them both smack their lips with similar mannerisms. *The berry's not the only thing that's exceeded my expectations.*

"You'll want to take some home with you." Will passed her an empty ice-cream pail. "You can make all kinds of delicious treats with blackberries."

She cringed. "You forget my lack of culinary prowess."

He gave that killer half-smile as they stood side-by-side. "You could always put them on ice-cream or add them to a salad. You'll get zero pesticides and one hundred percent natural goodness with these babies. Not to mention all the health benefits packed into each bite."

She picked at the fruit-laden bush and began filling her pail. "I was thinking I might try my hand at blackberry jam."

He pushed his sunglasses up on his head and raised a brow. "Now you're talking. Do you have them growing wild in Vancouver?"

"We do. There are places you pick your own, too. I guess I never think to take time to do it."

"Running a business will do that."

"For sure." She bit her lower lip. "Talking of Vancouver, I heard from my mom…"

As they relieved the bushes of some of their load, Georgia shared the news from her mom—and then told him about the silver sports car's attempt to run her off the road last week.

"You didn't say anything about the car when we were texting." His forehead furrowed. "Did you report it?"

"I didn't want to worry you. The officer made a note of it, I think. Thankfully, no one was hurt and the car was fine."

"But it could have ended badly…"

"It didn't." She lay a hand on his arm and an immediate warmth radiated within.

By the deepening shade of Will's green eyes, he felt it, too.

She continued. "Although I'm fairly certain I saw the sports car again when we were at the tea room. Some guy was acting a little skittish and then drove off in a cloud of dust."

"Georgia, this doesn't sound good." They both stopped fruit-picking and surveyed the area. There was no one in the vicinity.

"Dada?"

Georgia reached up and straightened Jack's hat. "Maybe we should eat now."

"You mean more than berries?" Will tickled his son's legs, resulting in the cutest chuckle. "Sounds good to me. By the time we've eaten our picnic and dropped Miss Georgia home, it'll be time for your nap, Jack."

"Nooo."

As they carried their berry-loot back to the table, Georgia cleared her throat. "Thanks for bringing me here today. It's a really special place."

A muscle popped in his jaw. "I'll be honest, it was a big step for me to ask you to join us, but after our chat last Monday, I feel like you understand a little of where I'm coming from. You're great with Jack and we've dug pretty deep with our conversations already."

"I agree, Will. You make me feel incredibly safe. You're a good listener, too."

"I'll listen anytime." He lowered Jack to the ground and leaned the carrier against the picnic table. "So… I was wondering if you might like to join me for a quick lunch tomorrow."

She bit her lower lip. "No work?"

"My shift doesn't start until the evening and my mom has claimed Jack from midday on. Only if you're free. I don't want to overstep."

Was he serious? "I think I can squeeze a lunch-date in—" *Date? Did I say the word 'date'?* "Umm, not that it's a date." Her cheeks heated. "Gosh. No. What I mean is, I know we're friends and lunch would be lovely."

He failed at hiding a smirk. "Good. A friends' lunch. I like that."

"Me, too. As long as you don't mind hanging out with a woman whose life is currently in tornado-mode."

"Maybe I could use a little tornado. You know you can call me day or night if you're worried. I don't like the sound of this guy with the sports car. It may be nothing but…"

"I know. Trust me, I know."

Georgia dumped her bag and the pail of berries on her doorstep and waved as Will and Jack drove away. She wiped her cheek where little Jack planted a sticky kiss. He was nothing short of adorable. His daddy wasn't so bad, either. *Slow down. Keep it platonic.* Easier said than done.

She gave her head a shake, unlocked the door, and carried everything inside. A smattering of mail lay strewn on the wooden floor and brought a smile to her face. The English letterbox slot in every front door was one of the many curiosities she enjoyed.

Such a personal touch, to have a postman slide mail right into your home.

Kicking off her flip-flops, she dumped her bag and padded to the kitchen, where she deposited the berries in the sink, ready to be rinsed. Her eyes darted to the backdoor. It was still locked. Of course, it was. Would she ever feel at ease after her break-in? Flushed from being out in the midday sun, she poured herself a glass of water and slipped off her kimono.

Will had rushed home in time for Jack's regular nap and as she drained her glass, the fanciful notion of an afternoon nap for herself sounded appealing. When did she ever have time to do that in her regular life? The couch beckoned. She should check her phone first. There could be news from her mom.

As she retrieved her bag from the foyer, she picked up the mail from the floor. *Might as well sift through this while I'm here.* She leaned a hip against the narrow console table and set each item on its surface as she flicked through. Electricity bill. Flier about the village market on Saturday. Random real estate agent letter. Advertisement for hearing aids. Postcard.

*Postcard.* Her vision blurred and she leaned harder against the table. The image was a night shot of Vancouver. Her city on the water. With trembling hands, she turned it over as if in slow motion. A Vancouver postmark. Hauntingly familiar script.

Georgia gasped as she slid all the way down to the floor.

# Chapter Seventeen

WILL SAT AT A COZY TABLE for two in the corner of his favorite village pub, The Pig and Whistle. He had several hours until his Tuesday shift started at the hospital and he'd been looking forward to a quiet lunch with Georgia since their berry-picking outing yesterday. Truth be told, she'd consumed his thoughts since they waved goodbye at her front door.

He took a long swig from a tall glass of water and swirled melting ice cubes. He sensed Georgia was a little distracted from the text message he received from her last night. Not by what she said but by what she didn't say. It was brief. Formal. Maybe she was having second thoughts about their friendship—or whatever this was blossoming into.

"Will?"

He stood as Georgia appeared beside him. The smile fell from his face when he took in her pallor and the quiver of her bottom lip.

"What's wrong?" He helped her to the wooden chair and pushed a full glass of water toward her.

"Thanks." She took a sip and slid her bag under the table by her feet. "Sorry. I'm a little shaken up." She clasped her hands in her lap but couldn't hide the trembling. Will longed to wrap her in comforting arms but returned to his chair, his gaze not leaving hers.

"Do you want me to take you home? We don't have to stay here."

She surveyed the comfortable, half-empty establishment with wide, watery eyes. The gentle lull of muted conversations along with occasional clink of glasses and scrape of crockery was soothing, even to Will's ears. The tempting aromas of savory food wafting from the kitchen made him salivate as he waited for her to reply.

"Actually, I'd like to stay." Her shoulders relaxed. "I need to eat and I'd like to talk. I'm hoping it'll make me feel better on both counts."

"That's fine by me, but please say if you need to leave. What do you want to do first—talk or eat?"

She took another sip from her glass and nodded at the burgundy menu on the table. "Let's order first. I haven't eaten since your lovely picnic. What do you recommend?"

She hadn't eaten for almost twenty-four hours? He focused on the menu. "Everything is delicious here, it depends what you're in the mood for. The fish and chips are fresh, cottage pie is filling, bangers and mash hits the spot if you're starving," he drew his finger down the list, "but I think I'm going with a Ploughman's lunch."

"Remind me what that is exactly?"

He set down the menu. "It's particularly good here. Freshly baked bread, hunks of local cheddar cheese, pork pies, relishes, deviled eggs, pickle, salad, apple slices… they do a platter for two, if you're interested."

She nodded. "Sounds good. That way you can finish what I can't eat."

"Want anything else to drink?"

"Water's fine. Thanks."

Will flagged down the server and placed their order. They'd now have a good ten minutes of uninterrupted time for her to share whatever was on her mind. By the look of her red-rimmed eyes, she hadn't slept much last night and needed to get something off her chest.

"I received a postcard yesterday."

The blurted words took Will by surprise. "You did?"

She wrung her hands on the table and he touched one of them. She was ice-cold.

"It was from Daniel." She peered up through dark lashes.

What? "I don't understand."

She let out a sigh. "Neither do I. He sent it the day before he… died… according to the postmark."

He nodded, willing her to continue. "Okay."

"There's a picture of Vancouver on the front. A night shot. For a second I thought maybe Mom sent it for some reason." She took a moment to compose herself. "But as soon as I turned it over, I knew it was from him."

Will strained to hear every word as her voice fell to a whisper.

"We had this silly code. Back when he used to send me romantic postcards from his travels with work. He said the trouble with postcards was anyone could read what was written. No envelope. So, he developed a code where we used the next letter in the alphabet—which takes a while to both read and write—but anyway, it was our thing."

He reached across the table and gave her hand a gentle squeeze.

"I deciphered the code." Her eyes were pools of pain and fear. "It was a warning." She waited for several seconds. "A warning that someone wants something from Bramble Cottage and will stop at nothing to get it."

Will's stomach clenched. No wonder she looked so undone. "Do you know what he's talking about?"

Georgia clamped her mouth shut and pulled her hands back into her lap. Was she considering how much to share?

"I only want to help, Georgia. Do you want me to go to the police with you? Get some extra security?"

"No." Her answer was firm. "No, I can't involve the police." She blinked back tears. "I don't know everything yet but I'm going to get to the bottom of it." She lifted her chin. "I have to."

Will ran a hand through his hair and tried to keep his voice low. "The police can help. That's what they're here for. If you're in danger…"

"That's just it." She pulled her cardigan tight around her. "It's not only me. Daniel said if I go to the authorities, I'll be putting my family's lives at risk."

Georgia tugged the throw blanket around her shoulders and curled up on her sofa, a steaming mug of tea and a lit lavender candle on the coffee table. Will followed her home after lunch—she'd managed to eat a surprising amount of food—and then set her up with tea before he left for work. She wasn't used to being cared for in this way. It warmed her heart.

He also asked her to keep three promises. She was to call Sophie in Paris and see if she was still willing to fly out earlier than her original date, speak with Harriet and ask if she could stay with her for a few nights, and call Will if she needed him for anything at all. He would check his voicemail periodically throughout his shift.

She stared at her phone. *I hate being the needy one.* Pride often prevented her from reaching out for help, even to family. Now she also had to watch out for them. Make sure they were all safe… even though she didn't know what—or whom—she was up against.

With a groan and a stretch, she reached for the tea and took a sip. Maybe after her calls, she'd have that nap she'd missed yesterday. After recovering from the shock of Daniel's postcard, she'd spent the rest of the day and night pacing, praying, fretting, and trying to figure out exactly what Daniel had been into. She knew it was connected to Paris. That's when everything deteriorated between them at an alarming rate. That envelope addressed to him. The mystery guy with the black beard who stuffed it into her hands. The glimpse of a photograph, which remained with her ever since—no matter how hard she tried to erase it from her memory.

Georgia needed to reread his postcard message. For the hundredth time. She'd scribbled the decoded version on a sheet of paper and stuffed it into her bag. Reaching down, she pulled the bag from the floor to her lap and dug into the zipped compartment.

*Lord, I don't know what's going on. I only know I need you to keep my family safe. Show me what to do, please?*

She unfolded the paper and smoothed it with her fingers. What on earth did Daniel mean?

*GEORGIA—IF SOMETHING HAS HAPPENED TO ME, YOU ARE IN DANGER. YOUR FAMILY COULD BE IN DANGER, TOO, IF YOU INVOLVE THE POLICE. IT'S ALL AT BRAMBLE COTTAGE. DEVELOP THE FILM, READ THE PAPERWORK FOR YOURSELF, THEN TAKE IT ALL TO THE AUTHORITIES. DON'T TRUST ANYONE.*

*I'M SORRY,*

*DANIEL.*

As if he needed to tell her not to trust anyone. Thanks to him, it would be a miracle if she ever trusted another soul again. What was he talking about anyway? A roll of film? He knew she was more than capable of developing film, and she even had her darkroom upstairs, but where *was* this film?

The envelope from Paris came to mind but there had only been a bunch of paperwork and a stack of photographs, as far as she'd been able to make out. To think she'd felt guilty for peeking inside a mere envelope when he was in the midst of a love affair, was laughable now. If only she'd looked further. Asked questions. Not pretended everything was "fine".

Frustrated, she dropped the paper onto the table and finished her tea. Maybe Sophie would remember something from Paris last year. She dialed her sister's number, settled back into the soft cushions, and inhaled the soothing scent of the lavender candle.

"Sophie, it's me. Can I ask you something?"

"Well, hello to you, too. Sure, fire away. I'm walking home from the patisserie, so you'll have to excuse the traffic noise."

"That's early for you to finish, isn't it?"

Car horns and the muted hum of engines sounded in the background. "Not feeling a hundred percent, but go ahead, I can walk and talk."

"That's too bad. You're sick?"

"Stomach ache. So, what's this about?"

Where should she begin? "Well, it's about last summer when Daniel and I were in Paris."

"Sure."

"Remember when that man stopped us outside our hotel on my last day?"

"Yes." Sophie's voice came louder across the miles. "I'd forgotten about him."

*I haven't.* "It was kind of suspicious, wasn't it?"

"He was super creepy. Bushy black beard. He had to be almost seven feet tall."

Goosebumps appeared on her bare arms at the thought of him. "I remember thinking it was weird that he didn't say a single word. Maybe he only spoke French and was worried I would answer him in English, I don't know. I wasn't going to argue with him when he thrust that fat envelope into my hands."

"Did you ever look inside? I totally would've."

Georgia swallowed. "I took a quick peek before I handed it to Daniel. There were papers and photos. I only looked at one picture, but it was enough for me to put it all away and not ask questions. I didn't want to see the rest."

"Why? What was it?"

Georgia closed her eyes at the memory of the vivid image. "It was a photo of Daniel. He held a gun and it was pointed as if he was about to shoot it. Or maybe he had already. I couldn't tell…"

"Wow." Sophie let out a whistle. "That's out of character for Daniel. He was always anti-gun everything, wasn't he?"

"The Daniel I knew. Yes." A chill flowed through Georgia's veins. "It appears he changed."

"And that's all you know?"

"I wasn't sure what to do." She ran her fingers through her hair.

"So, you said nothing?"

"You know me. Non-confrontational to the end." She blinked back tears. "I gave Daniel ample opportunity to talk to me, but he had no idea I'd seen anything. I'm sure of it."

"Ah, sis, how did you keep going with a secret like that between you?"

She brushed a tear from her cheek. "I didn't keep going. Not really. Everything went downhill after that. His work. Our marriage. Any hope of me being a mother."

"Hey, you're stronger than you think."

"Believe me, I have my moments where I'm barely holding it all together. The photo of him with a gun and a crazed look in his eyes." She shuddered. "I thought I'd buried the memory but now knowing what could be under this roof…"

"Umm, Georgia, back up a sec. Why are we talking about all this and what exactly could be under your roof?"

"I had mail yesterday…" Georgia explained the postcard from Daniel.

"I'm flying over." Level-headed as ever, Sophie assured her she would make some calls to rearrange work commitments and find a flight in the next day or so. At least they could be at Bramble Cottage together and maybe locate the film. In the meantime, Georgia was to stay at Harriet's. They both agreed not to mention Daniel's postcard to Harriet or their mom. Both were likely to panic and call the police, regardless. That couldn't happen.

Next, Georgia called Harriet and confessed she was nervous in the cottage, leaving out the details of Daniel's postcard. Without question, Harriet insisted she stay at their home for as long as she needed. Finally, Georgia texted Will to fill him in. All three promises had been kept.

Feeling the weight of a heavy load on her shoulders, she got up and checked both the front and back doors before packing an overnight bag for her stay with her sister, hoping it would be brief. *This is my cottage. My home.*

Before leaving, she made quick work of searching through each and every cupboard, drawer, nook, and cranny that might house a roll of camera film or a stuffed envelope. Nothing. With gritted teeth, she picked up her bags, car keys, and camera, and blew out the candle on the coffee table. The lavender hadn't worked. She was wound up, exhausted, and furious with a man she couldn't even shout at or interrogate.

Because he was dead.

# Chapter Eighteen

"You're not going to believe this." Georgia slammed her coffee mug on the kitchen island and leaned against it, weary to the bone. Sleep had not been forthcoming in Harriet's guest bedroom last night.

"What?" Harriet pulled a baking tray from the oven. "Did you get hold of Sophie?"

"I did." *How am I going to break this gently?* "You know I said she went home from work early yesterday?"

"Uh-huh."

"She's… in the hospital."

"Excuse me, what? I'm her twin. How come I didn't know about this? Is she okay? What's wrong with her?" Harriet clutched the countertop, her face pinched.

"She's going to be fine." Georgia lay a hand over her sister's. "She didn't want to worry you. It's appendicitis."

"No." Harriet's hand flew to her stomach.

"Apparently, she's been having pain for a couple of weeks and thought it was flu."

"She never said anything. She's having surgery?"

"On her way in right now. She promised to call as soon as she's able." Georgia studied her phone. "I hate that she's alone over there."

Harriet was already texting messages. "I know she's got some wonderful friends from church. I've got a couple of their numbers. I'll text them now and make sure she's taken care of. Maybe I can…"

"I hear your wheels turning, but she made me promise you won't jump on a Paris flight."

Harriet's face crumpled. "But…"

Georgia put an arm around her. "I know you two are as close as it gets, but she promised to fly here as soon as she has the go-ahead from her doctor. Maybe a week, if all goes well. She knows you have Lucy, and then there's my drama…"

"Oh." Harriet's frown deepened. "She was supposed to be coming to stay with you at the cottage." She tapped her chin. "Looks like Lucy's going to have her aunt here for a little longer."

"Are you sure? I'll keep out of your hair as much as I can."

"Nonsense. I love having you here."

Harriet set the pan of freshly baked blackberry and apple muffins between them.

"Want to run it by Leo first?" Georgia inhaled the delectable combination of tangy berry and sweet apple. "Wow. They smell amazing."

"Thanks. There's no need to check with Leo. It's not like he's here very often anyway. Work's a beast these days."

Georgia watched her sister. "Everything okay? With Leo, I mean? I don't want to put any extra strain…"

"Help yourself to a muffin." Harriet pushed a small china plate in front of her. "And Leo and I are fine."

"Thanks." She picked one up. Still warm. The first bite made her groan. "Tastes like a perfect autumn day."

"Oh, I like that." Harriet wiped her hands on a towel. "Now it's time for our little princess-with-the-pink-cast to wake up and join us for breakfast. Let's try to have a nice, normal day."

"Sounds good to me." Georgia pasted on a smile but anxiety squeezed her chest. How could she consider normal when her entire life was upside down? She hadn't told Harriet about

Daniel's postcard yet. She was already stressed by the break-in at Bramble Cottage and Lucy's broken arm. Plus, where was Leo? Other than the day after Lucy's accident, he never seemed to be around. Harriet needed him. More than she knew, if Daniel's postcard was anything to go by.

She picked up her mug and sipped the vanilla latte.

Sophie was in the hospital. At least she would be safe in there. Their mom was going to be desperate to fly out yet again…. and somehow, they needed to deter her for as long as possible. Now Georgia had to stay with Harriet and Leo for an undetermined number of nights and it seemed there could be trouble here in paradise.

She longed to call Will, but knew he was working. *Also, he needs time with Jack.* The fact that he would be her first person to call took her by surprise. She had good friends back in Vancouver but only Will could understand the amount of pressure she was under to figure out what was going on with Daniel. To protect her family. To put this behind her and move on.

Her phone dinged on the island granite. A text. Her mouth curved. Will. He was on his break and said he'd been praying for her. She replied with a thank you and an update on Sophie. Prayer as a first resort was something she was still getting used to again after years struggling to control everything herself, but if ever she needed to spend time bringing everything before her Heavenly Father, it was now.

As she heard Lucy and Harriet upstairs, she closed her eyes and poured out her heart.

*"Father, I'm not great at this. I kind of like to be in control myself… You know that. Yet I come before You now and ask for Your help. With everything. I don't understand why I need to see a roll of film, but I have to find it, and soon. My little sister's in*

*surgery—would You comfort her and give the surgeons wisdom? Talking of surgeons... thank You for bringing Will into my life. Even if it's only as a good friend, I'm grateful."*

Who was she trying to fool? God knew her heart.

*"And if it's more than that, I'm going to need some help with my trust issues. Thanks for Your unending patience with me, Amen."*

"Aunty, you saying prayers?"

Georgia chuckled as she opened her eyes and kissed the top of Lucy's head. "Sure am."

"I say prayers." She clasped her hands together and closed her eyes.

"I know. Jesus loves it when we talk to Him."

Harriet attempted to rein them in for breakfast with a fruit platter to balance the muffins.

"Where's Daddy?" Lucy's huge eyes scanned the living room from her seat at the island.

"Work, honey." Harriet turned to Georgia. "Any plans for our nice, normal day?"

Georgia wiped her mouth with a paper napkin. "Yes. I'm going to get some fresh air and take shots of the village market. That happens on Wednesdays, doesn't it?"

Harriet nodded. "I may run into you. I usually pick up my veg and fresh flowers there."

"Cool. I'll pop into the cottage to grab a few extra things as it looks like I could be staying with you a little longer than I'd anticipated."

Harriet raised a brow. "Want some company?"

*Not if I'm going to be hunting for this elusive roll of film that you're not supposed to know about.* "Thanks, but I'll be fine. It's not so bad in daylight, I get a bit jumpy at night. You know."

"Totally. I'd be a nervous wreck."

*Exactly why I have to protect you, little sister.*

Early Friday morning, Georgia called Will from her car on her hands-free device after a nice, normal, uneventful couple of days. Good, in that there were no more scares, but bad, in that she was unable to locate the wretched roll of film or envelope in the cottage. She'd missed Will more than she was ready to admit, but his work schedule had been heavy and she didn't wish to encroach upon the little time he had with Jack.

"Georgia? Good morning. Where are you?"

"Hi, I'm running a couple of errands for Harriet before nipping over to the cottage."

"Still on the hunt for the film?"

"It's driving me nuts. Anyway, how have you been?"

"Work's been a nightmare with unscheduled surgeries. Sorry I haven't been around to help. Why don't you stop by the house? If you have time, I mean."

Georgia focused on the winding road. "Now? I'd love to. If you're sure."

"I'm sure. Jack and I are in the back yard enjoying the sunshine."

"In that case, I'm on my way. See you soon." Georgia beamed at the thought of spending a little time with Will and sweet Jack. The week had been relaxing but frustrating. She'd been unable to concentrate, and even exercising her creative muscles with her camera hadn't helped. The elusive roll of film was all she could think about.

Several minutes later, she pulled into Will's roomy driveway, ready for a welcome distraction. Make that two. She checked her hair in the rearview mirror, grabbed her bag, and headed to the front door. As she was about to ring the bell, her phone chirped a text notification. Sophie promised to call today, so Georgia looked to see if it might be her.

Her stomach dropped. It wasn't Sophie. It was from an unknown number. The message was short and sharp: *IT HAPPENED IN PARIS.*

Will opened the front door wide, Jack at his feet. "We heard your car… hey, what's wrong?"

Georgia held her hand over her mouth. Words wouldn't come.

"Georgia? Come on inside. Do you need to sit?"

She blinked. "No. No, I have to go. I'm so sorry, Will."

She pivoted to leave and Will reached for her arm. With a gentle touch, he turned her back around to face him.

"What's going on? You look like you've seen a ghost." His hands were warm against her skin. "And I'm not sure you should be driving, quite frankly."

"Dada?"

Jack stood between them gazing from one to the other. Will let go of Georgia and swooped up his son.

Georgia sniffled and dumped her phone in her purse. "I hate to be rude but I need to call Sophie. I think best when I'm driving."

His face fell. "Please don't?" He glanced away. "It's just— *I think best when I'm driving*— was word for word the last thing Emma said to me the night when…" He embraced Jack tighter. His sweet baby snuggled into his shoulder.

The comfort offered by son to father made Georgia's eyes water.

"I'm so sorry." She bit her lower lip. "Listen, I promise I'll be careful. I'll take a slow drive to the forest and call Sophie from there."

Jack covered his son's ears. "Are you in danger?"

"No more than usual these days." She shuffled from one foot to the other. "I honestly don't know."

"Why not stay here and make the call? Isn't she still in hospital?"

"She's home today. I really need to go." She pleaded with her eyes. "It's complicated."

He reached out and touched her cheek.

She didn't want to leave.

"Please, be careful. I'm not telling you what to do, but I don't think you should chance going back to the cottage on your own. I have to work in a couple of hours, but I'm off all day tomorrow. Can you hang on until then?"

"Maybe." She squeezed Jack's bare foot in her hand. "I'll call you later."

*Nice and slow. Let him know I'm a cautious driver.* With great care, Georgia eased onto the country road and let out the breath she'd been holding.

The text spooked her. *IT HAPPENED IN PARIS.* Those four words held a sickening reality. One that confirmed her suspicions. The photo. Daniel. The shooting or whatever it was, it must have happened in Paris.

Her fingers clenched the steering wheel.

Daniel made one bad decision to get involved with the wrong people, which then triggered a chain of events—ending in someone being shot. By him? Even killed? It was anyone's guess. She'd been oblivious to it all. Too busy fretting over the fact she couldn't get pregnant.

Ten minutes later, Georgia pulled into a quiet parking area on the edge of the forest and dialed her sister. *Please pick up,*

*Sophie.* With a sudden craving for fresh air, she grabbed her bag and locked the car behind her.

"Georgia?"

Sophie's familiar voice made her exhale. "Hey, sis. How are you feeling?" She paced along a wide pathway as she spoke.

"Not too bad. Happy to be home. I'm not a huge fan of hospitals."

"Me neither. Do you have everything you need at the apartment?"

"Yes. My friends have been so kind. Thanks for the flowers, by the way… they're gorgeous."

"You're welcome. I wish I could be there to help."

"You have your own whirlwind happening. What's the latest? Still no film?"

"No film." Georgia shivered in spite of the warm sun on her shoulders. "I received a text a few minutes ago."

"From whom?"

"An unknown number."

"Strange. What did it say?"

Georgia pinched her eyes shut for a second. "*It happened in Paris.*"

"That's all?"

"Yeah."

Sophie was silent for several seconds. "It has to be connected to your visit here last year. The stuff we talked about before."

"I agree. Now I'm nervous that whoever is messing with my head might be able to track you down, too. You're the one in Paris now." Georgia swallowed the lump in her throat. "How safe is your apartment complex?"

"Fort Knox. Promise. Plus, one of my best friends lives on

the floor below. I'm fine, but I wish we knew what was in the envelope."

"Or on the film. I wonder if Daniel was being blackmailed or if he was doing the blackmailing."

"I don't like the sound of this. Are you sure you can't go to the police?"

"I can't take any chances where you and the rest of our family are concerned."

Sophie took a long sip of something. "Have you been back to the cottage?"

"I was there yesterday. Harriet and Lucy insisted on doing some weeding outside while I continued my search under the guise of cleaning." She sat on a perfect tree stump and watched a young couple stroll hand-in-hand along the path. "I think I'm going to have to tell Harriet everything soon. I hate keeping her in the dark, even if it's for her own good."

"You're not going to the cottage on your own today, are you?"

She nibbled on a thumbnail. "No. No, I think I'll wait until Will can join me tomorrow. I hate to wait, but I don't really want to do this alone—and Harriet has to take care of Lucy."

"Good. That's smart. Keep me posted. My doctor said as long as I rest up I should be able to fly next week."

Georgia smiled. "Sounds good. You need to heal properly though, so don't rush it."

"Maybe by then this will all be figured out."

"That's my prayer. That all of us will be safe." *Please, God. Please.*

# Chapter Nineteen

The next morning, with Leo already at the office and Lucy still in bed, Georgia led Harriet to the sofa. After praying it through, she felt the urge to share about Daniel's postcard and the text message.

"I'm sorry. I should've told you straight away. Only I knew you'd want to go to the police… or Mom."

Harriet's eyes brimmed. "I wouldn't have gone to the police. Not if it would risk the safety of our family. I'm not going to say anything to Mom. There's nothing she can do from the other side of the world anyway. If she let it slip to Uncle Pete…"

"Exactly." Georgia put an arm around her. "Are we good?"

"Other than the obvious danger hovering over you like a storm cloud?" She raised a brow. "We're good. I can help now I know why you're spending so much time *cleaning* at the cottage."

"Thanks." Georgia wound a strand of hair around her fingers. "But I don't know where else to look. I haven't attempted the loft yet, so Will's going to check that out with me this morning."

"You'd think Daniel would've put everything in the safe like a normal human. That's the most obvious place—"

"Excuse me?" Georgia blinked. "Umm, what safe are we talking about here?"

"The one in your darkroom."

"There's no safe in my darkroom."

"Yes, there most definitely is. Daniel had it installed a while back. Eighteen months ago? Said he'd run it by you, and you were good with it as long as it was completely concealed." She squinted. "Tell me he wasn't lying."

Georgia was at a loss for words.

"I'm so sorry. In all fairness, I didn't know you were even searching for anything until five minutes ago."

"It's not your fault, sis." Georgia stood. "Nothing surprises me about Daniel anymore. Lying was his specialty." She clenched her fists. "I'm sorry he went to you behind my back."

"I should've checked. I guess that means it's really well concealed if you didn't even notice it."

"Yeah. Now I'm intrigued. Where exactly is it?"

"In the corner of the darkroom, under the counter behind the white built-in cupboard facade. Press it in and it'll pop open. Super slick."

She shook her head. "I knew nothing about this. Another secret. The film plus the envelope could actually be there. In the safe. Right under my nose."

Harriet narrowed her eyes. "Please don't tell me you're going to Bramble Cottage alone."

"I won't. I promised Sophie I would wait until Will could join me. Although I'm anxious to get this figured out. It's eating me alive. Especially now that I know where this wretched stuff is hidden."

"You will wait for Will though." Harriet's huge eyes were filled with fear. "Right?"

Georgia linked her pinkie with Harriet's. "Promise."

Now she had promised both her sisters and her meeting with Will couldn't come fast enough.

Georgia parked outside Bramble Cottage and checked her phone.

After texting Will about the safe, he'd promised to join her as quickly as he could, and she'd driven straight over. Now she was a little earlier than planned, but Will would arrive soon enough. She tapped her fingernails on the steering wheel and took a deep breath. No. There was no way she was enjoying the view from her car while the evidence was sitting in her safe. *I have a safe.* A wave of anger toward Daniel was followed by a familiar wave of guilt for being angry at a dead person. *I'm going inside.*

She unlocked the front door and scanned the place. She could see most of the downstairs area from the entrance when the kitchen door was open. All was well. She locked the door behind her, kicked off her flip-flops, and headed upstairs. It could get warm in here today, so she wore denim shorts and a gauzy short-sleeved top. Heat rose and she would be upstairs in the darkroom for much of the time. Her pulse raced at what she might find in the safe.

Heading straight into the darkroom, she flicked a switch and light filled the space. A cursory glance confirmed nothing had been disturbed. She was meticulous when it came to her work. Meticulous in every part of her life. Trays, photographic paper, and chemicals stood in their precise spots along the counter. The enlarger took front and center stage, separating wet from dry sides.

There. She dumped her bag on the countertop and scurried to the corner of the room, where a section of white cupboards housed some of her chemicals. The last one. She hadn't even questioned why it didn't have an opening door like the rest of them. She crouched on the floor, pressed it hard, and it sprang open, revealing a small, black safe. *Yes.*

The steel was cool to the touch. She needed to know what was in this secretive box. Next, the combination. There were several possibilities Daniel was in the habit of using, and she tried each one. His birthday, her birthday, his childhood dog's birthday. Nothing. Their wedding day? She tried the six-digit combination using two numbers at a time, turning right, then left, then right again. With each double-digit, a satisfying click sounded. With the final one, she felt the lock release and the door swung open.

Seriously, Daniel? Their wedding day. Like salt in a fresh wound, she groaned as images of the happiest day in her life flashed through her mind. It was supposed to be forever. She pinched the bridge of her nose. Was there such thing as a happily-ever-after? *Deep breaths. I'll never have to deal with him again. Why is forgiveness so hard? The man is gone...*

She inserted her hand and pulled out the familiar padded envelope she last saw in Paris. It was originally addressed to Daniel but now a red line scratched out his name and replaced it with hers. Written in Daniel's handwriting.

She stared at the package, not wanting to see what was inside again, yet knowing she needed to muster the courage. It had been over a year since she held the weight of it in her hands.

She stood, opened the flap, and tipped the entire contents onto the countertop.

*Daniel, what did you do?*

Her phone vibrated in her pocket and she checked the text. Will had been held up but would be there in five minutes. She could wait for him or...

*Might as well make a start.* Georgia glanced over her shoulder even though she was alone. A wad of paperwork, most of it photocopies. A pile of photographs. The mysterious roll of film. *Daniel knew I loved working with film.*

This is what intrigued her most. Who would use an actual

roll rather than some digital application? Maybe professional photographers, purists, and the occasional young, hip enthusiast. Someone keen on photography. Old school. Someone like Georgia…

A rap on the front door made her flinch. Will. She hurried down the stairs, checked the peephole, and welcomed him inside.

"Come in, come in. Sorry, I couldn't wait. You're not going to believe this. The safe in my darkroom? I cracked the combination and found the film."

"Nice." He grinned as he closed the door, followed her back upstairs to the darkroom, and then eyed the roll of film on the counter. "So that's it."

"Yep. That's it."

"What now?"

"I need to develop it. Maybe you could take a look at the stuff inside the envelope?" She winced. "I know it's a big ask."

"Whatever helps." He wiped a bead of sweat from his forehead. "It's boiling in here. Want me to open some windows before we get started?"

"Could you? The last couple of hot days have turned this upstairs area into a furnace."

She started to pull her equipment together with shaky fingers.

Will touched her shoulder. "Hey, are you sure you want to do this now? I'm guessing you need a steady hand."

She gazed into his eyes. "I'm petrified of what I might find, but I need this to be over."

He wrapped her in a hug, and she buried her head in his shoulder and breathed in a mix of fresh laundry and spicy aftershave.

"Let me get some fresh air circulating. That'll help. Then I'll go grab us some water. You take your time."

"Thanks."

He disappeared into the small bathroom and opened up the window with some effort, and then headed into the master bedroom. Her head tilted. Silence. What was he doing in there?

"Georgia." He stood at the doorway of the darkroom with something in his hand.

"What do you have there?" She knew before she finished the question.

Another postcard.

Will's heart squeezed as Georgia stared with unblinking eyes at the postcard in his hand. An image of a framed oil painting in a Parisian gallery. It was beautiful, a stark contrast to the last one left. It didn't lessen the fear of knowing someone was here on Friday or even earlier today, that someone was in her bedroom. Her haven.

Without a word, she took it from him and read the back. *"GUILTY"*. Will recognized the same writing as before. Georgia's face paled.

"Who is doing this?" Her voice was a whisper.

Someone with a very clear message… but why Georgia? Surely, she was guilty of nothing other than being hurt and abandoned by her ex-husband.

Will settled her onto the stool. "Can you sit here while I check we're definitely alone?"

She nodded and stared at the postcard.

Will took determined steps downstairs into the kitchen, noting the backdoor was locked. It was so open-plan down here, he doubted anyone would even attempt to hide, but he searched behind every door and curtain for Georgia's peace of mind. How on earth were these postcards getting inside the cottage, and what could this latest one mean?

She met him at the top of the stairs.

"I think we should sit for a minute." He caught her hand and led her down to the sofa. If she was shaky before, this latest blow could shatter her.

"Make yourself comfortable. I'll get you some water." He kept an eye on her from the kitchen as he filled a glass and then returned to the living room. "There, take a sip."

She swigged half the water and set it on the coffee table.

Will cleared his throat. "So, I'm guessing you don't want to call the police until you've developed the film and figured out what's in this paperwork. I get that, but someone was here again, and they've left you a message." He sat on an armchair and reached over to hold her hand. "Can you tell me what you're thinking?"

She lifted the postcard to her line of vision. "A gallery in Paris. The city of love. Ever been?"

He nodded.

"It was where we spent our honeymoon—and then our final vacation together. Quite the paradox. A year ago, Daniel surprised me with a week there to celebrate our tenth wedding anniversary."

With one finger, she traced the postcard painting of a little blonde-haired girl in a white tutu. She was running through a picturesque field of dandelions, the seeds flying in the air like magical fluff. "I don't know why this picture. Maybe to mock me. The fact it's Paris. That having a child was always my dream. That the City of Lights was supposed to be our special place." Something passed across her face. Regret? Rage? It was hard to tell.

Will squeezed her hand. "Any idea why *guilty* might be the message?"

Her mouth worked but no words came out. She stared at him with fathomless eyes and one huge tear slid down her face.

"I don't know if I can tell you. You wouldn't understand, Will. How could you possibly understand?"

"Because I care."

"Why do you care? Is it because I have nobody else? Do you think I'm incapable of looking after myself?" She stood, her fists clenched. "I'm a lonely loser who failed at marriage and motherhood." She began pacing the length of the living room. "I messed up being a good Christian and came running back to God in desperation when everything else fell apart." She raised her hands in the air. "In fact, my whole life could self-destruct at any moment as I'm discovering what atrocities my ex-husband left me to deal with—and yet here you are."

He let her rant. He sat motionless and took everything she continued to spew.

"The perfect man. Brilliant in every way. Somehow you managed to get tangled up in my ugly web and..." A sob escaped from her throat. "Will, you could get hurt. Or worse. Then there's darling Jack…"

"Come here." He stood and held his arms open. Georgia fell into them.

"I hate that this is becoming a thing, for the record. Me having a meltdown and you being my rescuer." She pulled back and wiped her eyes with the back of her hand. "I'm not good with being out of control. I'll admit, I'm a control freak. Always have been."

"That's when God steps in though, isn't it? When we come to the end of ourselves and remember He's sovereign. He sees all and knows all. It's the only way I've been able to get through the storms in my life." *Lord, help her to know You care.*

"I'm so sorry." She shook her head. "You seem to have everything running like clockwork in your life and I find myself being jealous. I'm a sucker for schedules and planners and no surprises. I forget you lost the love of your life. That she didn't choose to leave like Daniel left me. I can't even imagine. Forgive me?"

He closed his eyes. Yes, Georgia had her secrets and she needed to share them with him so he could help her out of this mess for good. Yet how could he allow her to think his tragic loss was an accident? She'd already been lied to and deceived by one man. He had to tell Georgia the truth if there was even the faintest glimmer of a future relationship for them.

*It's time, Lord.*

# Chapter Twenty

TIME TO SHED THE burden he'd carried for far too long.

"Georgia, I know it's early days and we're only just getting to know one another, but you've been open and honest with me and I need to be transparent with you."

Georgia frowned. "Okay." She perched on one arm of the sofa. "Go ahead."

"You see, I know something about guilt. I can't stand the thought of you thinking I have my whole life tied in a neat little bow." He walked to the window where the first postcard had been taped. Touched the cool glass. "I can assure you, my life's not like that."

"You don't have to explain anything to *me*, of all people." Georgia came up behind him. "I'm sorry if I made you out to be some superhuman. I know we all have our stuff." She put both arms around him from behind and lay her head against his shoulder blade. They fit together perfectly. He closed his eyes. "I'm grateful you're here, Will. I am."

He let out a ragged breath. Now was as good a time as any. "It wasn't an accident."

She froze.

"I'm sorry, what?"

"Emma. My wife. It wasn't an accident."

"Oh."

He was still wrapped in her arms so he spoke out to the sun-filled yard through the window. "I didn't know. In fact, I was utterly clueless." He licked his dry lips. This was the first time he'd attempted to verbalize what happened.

*Lord, give me the words so she doesn't hate me or think less of Emma.*

"You see, she struggled after Jack was born. It was a tough time. Tougher than she imagined, at least." Even as he spoke, the harsh reality of Georgia not being able to even have a baby sank deeper in his chest. She'd shared some of her story with him. How could he expect her to understand?

"Postpartum depression?" Her voice was muffled against his back.

"Yes. I had no idea how severe it was." *Some doctor I am. My own wife…*

Georgia sighed. "It's awful. Harriet had it for a while when Lucy was born."

He nodded. She understood somewhat.

"Unfortunately, Emma was great at masking her symptoms. I'm convinced she knew exactly what the problem was, but tried to plough through without help." He closed his eyes. "Even from me."

"What do you mean? She was a nurse, she must have recognized how serious postpartum depression can be."

"I know it sounds ridiculous. Both of us in medicine. They say we make the worst patients. I think Emma was determined to stay away from medication. She had some issues with drugs as a teen—one of the reasons why she went into nursing actually. That's another story."

"Poor woman."

Will pictured their last Christmas together. Exhausted, anxious, underweight. She said she wanted to lose her pregnancy weight but it was more than that. He knew now. "She never neglected Jack. She may have stopped caring for herself, but she always put Jack first."

"Of course."

Will cleared his throat. "Then one morning, I got home from a shift at the hospital and she asked if I could watch Jack for a couple of hours before I slept. She wanted to go for a drive, it was where she did her best thinking. Maybe walk on the beach to clear her head. I thought it was a marvelous idea—she hadn't wanted to go anywhere in weeks. She'd stopped getting together with friends and hadn't even been to church—and her faith was stronger than mine ever was."

Will turned around and looked at Georgia's face. This was agonizing but he needed to tell her. "So, Emma kissed my cheek and passed me a sleeping Jack along with his bunny. I handed her the car keys and then snuggled down on the sofa with my boy. I watched as she bundled up—it was a chilly winter's morning. I told her to watch for any icy patches. She said she loved us. That was the last time I saw her alive."

Tears brimmed in Georgia's eyes. "What happened?" She rubbed her thumb across Will's hand.

"I was exhausted and ended up sleeping for two hours straight on the sofa with Jack. We didn't move that whole time. Until the doorbell woke us both. It was two police officers. A man and a woman. As soon as I saw them, I knew."

"Emma?"

He nodded. "They came in and told me her car was spotted on the rocks beneath the cliffs at Lulworth Cove. She'd gone through a metal barrier. Plunged right over."

Georgia gasped.

"There was a little ice, no other vehicle tracks, no reason for it to be suspicious. Just a tragic, dreadful accident."

"Will. I'm so, so sorry." She squeezed both his hands. "I don't know what else to say."

His shoulders fell. "We grieved. She didn't have much in the way of family—her mum died when Emma was a teen and her dad was never in the picture. No siblings. Lots of friends. She was a brilliant nurse. A wonderful mother for those first few months. Anyway, it was a bleak period. I took leave from work and my parents stepped in to help. As well as our friends at church."

She wiped a tear from her cheek and clasped his hand again. "But you don't believe it was an accident? How can you be sure?"

He bit down on his lower lip. "She left me a letter."

Georgia's brows rose.

"I didn't find it until months after her death. She intended it that way. She'd made some arrangement at the bank for me to receive a letter on what would have been her twenty-ninth birthday. I read it and burnt it in our fireplace. I figured no one needed to know the truth. Certainly not her little boy. Not her friends. I never claimed anything with life insurance. I thought I could hold the truth tight and live with it…"

"You don't want others to think badly of her, but it wasn't her fault, Will. She was sick."

"And married to a doctor. The ultimate irony."

"Don't." She drew close until their faces were inches apart. "This weight's too heavy to live with. I'm sure she wouldn't want that for you. She needs you to be a wonderful father for Jack— and you are, Will. You're fantastic with him."

"I learned the dangers of being a workaholic the hard way. I didn't know what I had until it was gone. She was gone." He groaned. "In the letter, she was so apologetic. Didn't blame me for not noticing my own wife's pain when I was too busy fixing everyone else's in the operating room. She'd battled depression early in her life and this was too much for her. I should have insisted we see someone and figure out medical treatment for her… I could have saved Emma."

"But she couldn't see beyond the clouds."

"No. She really couldn't. Driving off a cliff was the horrific end result. I couldn't get in a car for weeks after it happened." He shrugged. "That's why I'm obsessed about driving safely now."

"Understandable."

"It breaks my heart when I think of the precious moments she's missing with Jack."

"And with you."

He nodded.

"It's hard." Georgia caressed the side of his face. "Trust me, I know what it's like living with secrets. Lies. It's heavy."

"I don't want to burden you with my stuff. Especially now, but I thought you should know there's no such thing as a perfect life. Not this side of eternity, at least."

She stood on tip toes and kissed his cheek. "I've figured that out all on my own. Thank you for sharing that with me. I know it wasn't easy."

He wrapped her in a hug, their connection deepening with every day. "It feels better having another person know. Now I've laid it out in the open with you, I hope you'll feel comfortable to do the same with me going forward. No matter what we discover. I know this is not going to be good, whatever it is. My story is tragic but it's in the past. Yours is dangerous and very much in the present. You need to trust me."

"I know."

He glanced over at the postcard on the coffee table. "What do we do about that?"

She walked over and picked it up. "I keep thinking he could

have hurt me. Whoever it is that's coming in here. Or worse… but he didn't."

*Yet.* The word popped into Will's mind. "He wants something from you though."

"I know." She slid the postcard into her pocket and drained the last of her water.

"I'm here to help, but I think you need to fill me in on everything so I get the big picture. Are you ready to do that?" He stepped toward her. He'd bared his soul to her, now would she trust him enough to do the same? "Let me in?"

Georgia set the glass down and wrung her hands. Where to begin? Would he think less of her for burying the memory of that photograph of Daniel for a whole year? She could have questioned him. Pushed for answers. Even prevented his death. Who knew what else could have been prevented if only…

Will's phone sounded from his back pocket. "I'm so sorry, that's my on-call phone. Give me a sec?"

"Go ahead." She massaged her temples and watched him as he took his call in the kitchen. A shaft of light pierced through the kitchen window and shone on his face. What was it about Doctor Will Hughes? He made her heart race at the same time as filling her with peace. *Thank you for this… friendship, God. I don't know where we're going with this but it's restoring my faith in—*

"You're not going to believe it." He walked toward her, his brow furrowed.

"You've been called in to the hospital?"

He pocketed his phone. "I'm sorry. There's been a car accident. I'm the surgeon on call."

"Hey, it's not your fault."

His hand brushed her arm, flooding all kinds of warmth through her body. "Lousy timing. I don't know how long I'll be at the hospital, but I want to continue this conversation." His eyes darted toward the staircase. "And look through the evidence with you. I know you want this over with. Is there any way I can persuade you to wait until tomorrow?"

Her shoulders dropped. How much longer could she hang on to get to the bottom of this?

"Please? If I finish work by this evening, I'll call you. Although I don't want to make any promises."

"I understand." As frustrating as the situation was, her pulsating head threatened a migraine and she needed a sharp mind for developing the film. "I think I'll lock the film back in the safe and drive to Harriet's. Rest up and tackle it all tomorrow."

"I can meet you here at midday, after church. I'll let you do your developing while I do some paperwork downstairs. I'll stay out of your hair until you need me."

"What about Jack?"

"I have a sitter I can call on for the afternoon. Will that work?"

"Sounds good. Thanks. Let's hope this is the last night I spend at Harriet's." She picked up her glass and took it to the kitchen. "I love my family but I long to be back here. This is my new home."

"I know. Hang in there."

He waited while she trotted upstairs for her bag and locked everything away in the safe.

"To think that tomorrow we could get to the bottom of this."

She met him in the foyer and slid into her flip-flops. "Have enough evidence sorted out to take to the authorities. Hand it all over to them and go back to my normal life again."

Will reached out and wrapped his arms around her. "I hope that normal life will include me." He whispered the words into her hair.

She squeezed her eyes shut and memorized the feeling of his strength. "I hope so, too."

# Chapter Twenty-One

The migraine hit with a vengeance and Georgia had no choice other than to shut out the vivid, colorful world, and take to her bed. Harriet and Lucy left her in peace as she spent the best part of the weekend in her dark, quiet room.

"Knock, knock." Harriet's voice sounded from behind the door.

Georgia rubbed her eyes and checked her phone on the bedside table. It was almost eight in the morning. How was it already Monday? "Come on in."

"Tea." Harriet carried a steaming mug. "Feeling better?"

Georgia pushed herself up and stretched. "Yes, thank goodness. That was a doozy."

"I remember when you used to get migraines for days back in high school."

"That was rough. I haven't had one in a while… I guess I needed the sleep, too." She peered behind her sister. "Where's Lucy?"

"Having breakfast. I told her to stay quiet until we knew you were up to company." She handed her the mug. "Want anything to eat?"

"Maybe later." Her stomach still felt queasy. "And then I really need to get back to the cottage."

Harriet sat on the end of the bed. "I spoke with Will again last night. You were asleep but he wanted to check on you. Said you might have had another scare at the cottage on Saturday. That it may have triggered your migraine."

"Right." She blew on the tea and took a sip. Harriet always knew when to add sugar. This was one of those times. "There was another postcard. In my bedroom."

Harriet drew her legs up onto the bed. "No."

"I've been thinking about it, dreaming about it, trying to figure out what it all means." She described the picture and the message.

"What do you suppose the relevance is? Why that particular painting?"

Georgia leaned her head back as she explained as much as she knew. The pieces were starting to fall into place. It was all connected. Paris, the black bearded guy, the envelope, but the art? That was still a mystery.

"Why the word *guilty*?" Harriet stroked Georgia's foot through the bedcover. "Does that refer to Daniel?"

"Maybe." Georgia disclosed details of the photograph she'd seen from the envelope in Paris. The incriminating word written on the back of a postcard implied someone else was privy to the secret.

"You mustn't blame yourself, sis. Daniel's dropped you into something beyond dangerous." Harriet pursed her lips. "So why has this all resurfaced a year later?"

"Good question. I think they're after whatever's inside the envelope and the roll of film, not me. They could have hurt me— or worse—by now, if they wanted to."

Harriet shuddered. "But do we even know who *they* are?"

Georgia swigged more tea. "No. I have my suspicions though."

"Such as?"

"That postcard got me thinking. The oil painting. The Parisian gallery. It could be linked with something to do with valuable pieces of art. Maybe theft or even forgeries."

"The art world?"

"It's not Daniel's scene, but if it was a money-maker, he could have been enticed. I know he had contacts in the art world all over Europe from past assignments."

"With his journalist freelancing? That doesn't sound like Daniel's cup of tea."

Georgia's stomach clenched. "We got into a big fight about it one time. He was gone for a whole month and did a write-up on some art gallery chain in France and Italy. I never did see his finished piece… he said the series was cancelled by the magazines, but he'd made some money doing a side-job. I was so busy with my own work, I let it go when he got all defensive."

Harriet's laugh was devoid of humor. "I'll bet his side-job had something to do with the other woman, too."

Georgia groaned. "Vanessa. Probably. What is it they say? Hindsight is twenty-twenty vision. She was on at least one of those assignments."

"I'm sorry." Harriet stood. "None of this is fair on you."

"Or you. They're holding my family over me, and that's the worst part. I would've gone to the police in a heartbeat otherwise."

"So… what now?"

"As I'm feeling human again, I'll shower, get ready, and head back to Bramble Cottage. The answers are there, I know it." She held up a hand. "And before you say anything, I'll call Will as I'm certain he doesn't have a shift this afternoon, so I won't be alone."

"Let me come until he arrives?" Harriet bit her thumbnail.

"I don't want you to bring Lucy into this."

"I can get a friend to watch her…"

Georgia climbed out of bed and kissed her sister's cheek.

"You're the sweetest, you know that, don't you? If you really want to come and you can get a sitter, I'd be grateful for the company. Okay?"

Harriet nodded. "Good." She shrugged one shoulder. "Who knows, maybe her father will even help out? There's breakfast waiting for you whenever you feel up to it."

"Thanks. Tell Lucy I'll be down soon for my cuddle."

Harriet closed the door behind her, and Georgia sank back onto the bed. Attempting to be brave was exhausting. She lay motionless for several seconds as she replayed recent events. Curling into a fetal position, tears flooded her eyes. This was not how it was supposed to be. She had a plan. A fresh start. The cottage. Her photography. Sisters. The possibility of even living here for a while. It was going to be perfect.

*Lord, I don't think I can handle all this. I need You.*

The darkroom beckoned.

Rather than wait on Harriet's arrangements with a sitter, Georgia decided to go on ahead and make a start with the film. It would take a while. She'd checked every room and every window upon arrival. Everything was as it should be. Dreading what she might discover but refusing to put it off a moment longer, she entered the darkroom.

It was her pride and joy. Now it was game time. Hours of research went into making it effective for developing her own prints from film negatives. She unlocked the safe and took out the roll of camera film. She hadn't done any developing for several years, but this was one of her new life goals and she itched to start working in here.

Daniel rolled his eyes every time she mentioned a darkroom at their home in Vancouver, but this? This was all hers. A perfect space to be creative with the craft that was making a comeback for photography enthusiasts. In this case, to reveal truth no matter how painful or how much danger it put her in.

Her left hand made a tight fist as determination pulsed through her. *I will not be chased away from my cottage. A new chapter of my life.* An image of Will in his navy scrubs filled her mind. *Maybe a chance of even trusting someone again...*

Georgia shook her head to concentrate on the issue at hand.

The preparation was laborious, but it had to be perfect. This was all about precision. She'd been so excited about using this space—although this particular project was not what she had in mind.

Everything was ready on the countertop—scissors, a cassette opener, a reel to load the film onto, a tank to develop the negatives in. Check, check, check, check. Plucking an elastic from around her wrist, she pulled her long hair into a ponytail and turned off her phone, making a mental note to turn it back on as soon as she was finished.

Next, she killed the lights.

Pitch black filled the room with heaviness.

*God, I know You're here with me. I need your courage to do this.*

A sense of purpose carried her fingers into a rhythm she thought she'd forgotten from years ago as she cut, unrolled, and loaded the film, feeling her way through each action in the dark. She wound, wrapped, and placed the film in the tank with care, and then tightened the cover.

Flicking the light switch back on gave her a measure of relief, and as her eyes adjusted, she focused on mixing and checking the temperature of the developer liquid before pouring it through a funnel into the tank.

Done. Now to wait. She checked the instructions and set a timer for ten minutes. While she agitated the tank, she glanced over at the safe and thoughts of Daniel crept in. He hadn't always been a jerk. The miscarriages affected him, she realized that after it was too late. She hadn't recognized his grief. He was never any good at showing his true feelings. Then after their fourth loss, he begged her to stop. Said he couldn't watch her go through the devastation again. That's when he checked out.

*Then I was on my own. The appointments, the tests, the tears.*

She emptied and refilled the tank.

*He was there in body, but I'd lost his heart.*

And then his indifference morphed into impatience. Followed by infidelity.

As Georgia took her time rinsing and drying the film, a wave of nausea came over her. What would she see on these negatives? Did she even want to look? It would be easy enough to hand them straight over to the police or even for Will to study them—he wouldn't be traumatized in the same way she would if they were of Daniel with Vanessa, or any other woman come to think of it.

But why would he keep romantic negatives along with the evidence? No, the more she thought about it, the more she realized these were going to be images linked to the illegal business. Or more of him and the gun. Maybe something Daniel could use to blackmail, as leverage, or even insurance?

It didn't help him in the end.

While the fixer liquid worked its magic, she pulled her laptop in front of her and began searching for information on the painting from her latest postcard. There was no title visible, so she didn't hold out much hope on finding the exact piece online. France, Paris, dandelion field, white tutu, tiny ballerina, stolen art—she tried searching everything she could think of. Nothing.

Next, she checked her phone. Harriet was mad because Leo was in a meeting in his home office until this afternoon. She would come over to the cottage as soon as she could. *Poor Harriet.*

With several minutes to spare until the buzzer would sound, Georgia threw her shoulders back and tackled the other job she'd been putting off—a quick peek through the pile of papers from the safe. Will promised to handle it when he arrived but she could make a start. Surely that couldn't be half as traumatic as studying photographs of goodness-knows-what?

She retrieved the envelope and pulled out the pages held together by a thick elastic band. When she flipped it over, the top page was a typed list of art galleries. Some with asterisks. All in France. The next page was similar except with galleries listed in Italy. As she flicked through, she recognized the slant of Daniel's handwriting in the margins. Addresses. Names. Phone numbers.

Her timer buzzed and she let out a cry.

*Calm down, girl.* She needed to be steady while working on this film. She turned her attention to the rinsing stages at the little sink and attempted to focus.

She bit her lip as the moment of truth arrived.

*God, please let this have worked. I can't botch this up now.*

With the greatest of care, she unwound the film from its container. She could see there were black-and-white images. It was hard to decipher details, but she had a magnifying glass close by. Not wanting to damage the wet film, she hung the strip up to dry with clothespins attached top and bottom as it dangled from a length of horizontal twine above the countertop.

"Okay, Daniel. Let's see what was so important it had to be stashed in a safe for the past year and could put my loved ones in danger."

Perched on the edge of the stool, Georgia got as close as possible to the strip while holding the magnifying glass steady and began viewing from the top. *What is that?* She squinted to make out the figures, but they were small. Several people huddled together. Adults.

Frustrated, she went to the next image, and this time she couldn't help but recognize her ex-husband. This was a similar shot to the photo she saw from the envelope last year in Paris. Daniel. A gun. Aimed at something, someone, out of the frame. Heaviness filled her heart.

Her eyes travelled down to the next image. This one was maybe from the same scene only—*surely not*. She squinted and held the magnifier closer. Her breath caught in her throat. She could be wrong, but it looked as if someone was shot and slumped over a desk. Daniel was still holding the gun.

Her pulse throbbed in her ears, but she needed to continue viewing down the row.

*What now?* It appeared to be a graveyard and Daniel held something in his hand… not a gun this time… a shovel?

Goose bumps ran up the length of her arms. Something dark and ugly was playing out in the frames before her. In the following image there were a couple more men with Daniel, their backs to the camera. Their actions indistinguishable.

She moved the magnifying glass down and her eyes bugged as she realized what was being documented here.

*No.*

A body being lowered into a grave.

Bile stung as it rose up her throat.

Daniel and one other guy filling the hole back up with earth.

And then the last frame, a group of them in a cafe raising

their drinks. Were they celebrating their evil deed? Georgia's mouth was bone dry. She may not be able to make out the faces of the men on these tiny squares, but once the pictures were dried and enlarged, she had no doubt they would be identifiable.

So that was it. A murder. An unceremonious burial. Who was this murdered man? He must have been gone at least a year now. Did his family know what happened? She set the magnifier down and wiped at the tears leaking from her eyes.

*Heavenly Father, I don't understand any of this, but I'm so sorry at least one life was taken. Please give me wisdom here. I want to do what's right and I need to see justice served. Daniel's gone now so I suppose it's fallen upon my shoulders...*

She needed to get out of this place. Get some fresh air. Continue when Will or Harriet could join her. Try to erase the disturbing shots now seared on her retinas. Something inside urged her to press on. She had the means to dry these negatives quickly. Make prints, albeit in black and white.

Like a woman possessed, she went through the motions until she had prints large enough to show the heinous crime in action. It was a rush job and her perfection tendencies screamed, but it would suffice.

*Photograph them.*

Yes. As one final precaution, she grabbed her digital camera and snapped each print, trying not to absorb the horror of the images. Because she was thorough, she did the same with her phone camera, too, and then emailed them to herself as a back-up.

Praying they were dry enough, she carefully lay the black-and-white prints on top of the envelope within the safe. Locked it. As an afterthought, she rehung the negative strip on the twine with a clothes pin, like a body from a noose.

When she stopped, her hands trembled and her heart raced.

*Dear God in heaven, will my world ever be right again? I trusted Daniel. I thought I knew him. It seems he was not only capable of cheating on me, he was capable of murder.*

Her stomach roiled. Her head pounded. She shouldn't have eaten breakfast. The mere thought made her heave and she rushed to the bathroom in time. Shaking, she rinsed out her mouth with water from the tap and plodded back to her bedroom, spent.

Georgia flung herself on top of the bed. Tears coursed down her cheeks and turned to guttural sobs as she grieved the death of an unknown man, the actions of the man she once loved more than life, and the realization that she could never trust a man again.

# Chapter Twenty-Two

WILL PACED THE LENGTH OF HIS home office while Jack played with a train track which was set up in the corner. He'd finished the paperwork he needed to do and the sitter was due to arrive soon, but his chest constricted to the point of aching. He was uneasy. Try as he might, he couldn't shake Georgia from his mind.

Last night's phone call with Harriet assured him she was okay and finally getting over the migraine, but when he spoke with Georgia this morning, she insisted on going back to Bramble Cottage early to deal with the wretched roll of film. Alone. She claimed it would be safe in broad daylight and when she refused to wait for him, he had to let it go. He promised to join her there at midday.

He stared through the window and across the lush green fields toward Bramble Cottage. Rain fell in a constant drizzle like misery dripping from the sky. *Who am I to voice my concerns when it comes to Georgia's decisions?* Just a friend. They hadn't known each other long. Yet something clicked deep inside him. An unlatching of sorts. Or maybe a thawing of something he thought forever frozen.

The vacuum sounded from downstairs. The cleaner was a sweet woman from church who came every Monday to keep the house shipshape. If Will was working from home, he and Jack would often retreat to his office upstairs to stay out of her way.

"Shawsha?" Jack held the blue train high in the air as he attempted to pronounce Georgia's name. "Shawsha?"

Will knelt on the rug beside him. "You thinking about Georgia, too, little man?" It appeared so. This Canadian mystery woman swept into their lives like a wonderful whirlwind and now they were both smitten. His head and everything sensible in him cried out to slow down. She could return to Canada in a couple of months if not sooner and leave England in the dust.

His fragile heart was in no condition for another battering. He swore he would never love again after losing Emma. The pain was unbearable, and yet—Georgia. He was drawn to more than her obvious beauty. More than their shared grief. There was something that drew him to her very soul.

*Lord, am I way off track here? Am I making a huge mistake? I feel like she's searching for… something. Answers? Hope? Love?*

As he watched his son fix the train onto the chunky tracks, he recognized his own frown mirrored on Jack's face.

"We're both fixers, aren't we, buddy?"

Jack nodded, not taking his eyes from the job at hand.

Will's phone trilled from his pocket and he pulled it out, hoping it might be Georgia. Close guess, it was Harriet.

"Will? Have you heard from Georgia?" Her words were clipped. Not her usual jovial self at all.

Every nerve in his body went on high alert. "Not for a while. Is something wrong?"

"I've tried to call her but… but she's not picking up." It sounded like she was driving.

"Where are you? Harriet, what's happened?"

"There's a fire. I have to get there. I left Leo at home with Lucy." A car horn honked. "Why won't she pick up her phone?"

*A fire?* "I'm at my house but I can come and help. You may need a doctor. Where's the fire?"

She let out a small sob. "It's at Bramble Cottage."

Stunned, Will scooped Jack from the floor and ran down the stairs. He explained the emergency to the cleaner, who offered to take over babysitting duties for the afternoon, and he left Jack in her capable hands.

Thankful his son was used to him disappearing at short notice but also cringing that it was the norm, Will grabbed his medical bag, jumped into the car, and hightailed it out of the driveway. He tried calling Georgia with his hands-free device, but it went to voicemail. Her Canadian accent and chipper message made his heart beat out of control. Why wasn't she picking up?

The changeable sky was now heavy with charcoal clouds and he prayed for more rain. Torrents of it. Who knew how serious this fire was? He focused on the road and put his foot down with more force than he had in the past eighteen months, his knuckles white as he gripped the steering wheel. Harriet would need him to be calm and professional.

*Please, God, let Georgia be safe.*

As he drove the last stretch of road, he heard sirens. Good. At least the fire brigade was close, maybe even there already. His stomach clenched at the thought of Georgia being scared. The smell of smoke triggered some terrifying memories for her. His heart broke when she told him about her father's tragic death in their house fire when she was a young child.

Almost there, Will turned onto the road leading to Bramble Cottage. Dark plumes drifted up into the sky like ink in water. Police and the fire brigade were there. Good. The neighbors must have called. He screeched to a halt outside the next-door neighbor's place, grabbed his medical bag from the trunk, and sprinted toward Harriet who'd arrived at the edge of the property.

"Harriet? Is she here?" The acrid stench of smoke filled his nostrils.

"Georgia." Harriet sank onto the grass, next to her sister. "You're all right."

Immediate relief flowed through his veins at the sight of her. He joined them, medical bag at the ready.

"I'm fine." Georgia peered up at them both through the drizzling rain, her face streaked with mascara. "I fell asleep and when I woke up I smelled smoke… and I froze… and a fireman… I'm not really sure…"

"Shh." Harriet swallowed Georgia in a hug. "Everything's going to be okay."

Will came around the side of them and checked her pulse. "Have you been seen by a medic yet?"

"I'm good. Really. No smoke inhalation. I went a little crazy when I woke up. The smell." She wiped her eyes with her sleeve. "The fire's in the back yard. I don't know… I think a neighbor called it in when they saw smoke."

Will stood. "I'll go and see what's happening." He waved down the fire chief at the side of the cottage while keeping his distance from the action. He knew better than to get in the way of emergency services.

"Mac, what do you know?"

The chief took a couple of steps toward him, his ruddy face serious. "It looks like foul play on first inspection. Started in the back garden. Several trees have gone up in flames. We can be grateful there's no wind this afternoon and that it didn't reach the cottage structure."

"No damage inside?"

"No. Some smoke. The lads did a run-through and it's clear. Got the owner out straightaway. We'll know more once we've put the embers out completely and can remove some of the debris on the patio. We forced our way through the backdoor with minimal damage, but we needed to check it out. You know how smoke inhalation alone can be serious."

"Of course. Can you let us know when we're good to go inside? I think Georgia will want to grab some of her belongings and make sure everything's in order before she leaves."

"She has somewhere she can stay?"

"Her sister's place."

"I'll give you a shout. It shouldn't be long until I get the all-clear. There's an officer at the front door keeping an eye on things. I'll let him know when she can go inside."

Will thanked him and rushed back to relay the news. A neighbor had given Georgia an umbrella and a bottle of water. Several others hovered at the pavement, no doubt grateful the fire hadn't spread farther onto other properties.

Harriet helped her sister to her feet. "Can we go inside?"

Will glanced back at the cottage. "Soon."

"I'd like Georgia to come home with me, but she'll need her bag."

"I'm right here." Georgia raised her brows.

"Sorry." Harriet winced. "I sound like Mom, don't I?"

"You do, and that's sweet. As much as I love you taking care of me, sis, I'd arranged to see Will this afternoon." She implored him with her chocolate-brown eyes. "Does that still work for you?"

"Of course. I can stay as long as you need. Or bring you back to my house. Whatever you like." He studied her ashen face. "But you should probably sit until you regain your color." He nodded toward a wrought iron bench tucked beneath a plum tree on the front lawn. "Let's wait there. It's pretty sheltered."

They walked across the tiny front lawn in the dwindling drizzle, and the sisters settled on the bench.

Harriet's phone chirped and she checked the screen. "Argh. Leo needs to go back into work for an urgent meeting. I knew it was too good to be true when he said he could help."

"Go." Georgia gave her a hug. "Be with your daughter. Thanks for coming so quickly but there's nothing you can do here and now you know I'm safe."

Harriet nibbled on a thumbnail. "Are you sure? I don't like to leave you so soon after such a shock."

"I'm here. I'm a doctor, remember?" Will tilted his head.

Harriet glanced from Georgia to Will. "There's so much madness going on here. Please, make sure someone's with you at all times until this nightmare is over."

Will nodded. "I'll keep an eye on her. Don't worry."

"Don't let her be alone. Yell if you need me or Leo."

Georgia huffed. "I can still hear you both. I don't need to be looked after. I'm a big girl, you know. A grown woman."

Will nodded. *I'm well aware of that.* He set his medical bag on the bench, thankful it wasn't needed.

Harriet kissed her sister's cheek and mouthed her thanks in his direction.

Will's face flushed at the thought of "having" to look after Georgia. It was no hardship whatsoever.

"You're in good hands." Harriet gazed up at the pale pink cottage. "But don't even think of staying here tonight. Besides everything else, it stinks."

"You don't have to tell *me* that." Georgia grimaced. "I'm so sorry you thought something awful happened." She turned to Will. "Both of you."

Georgia touched his arm. The brief contact sent a current of electricity through his body—how did she do that?

Harriet's eyes pooled. "I'm grateful I was wrong."

Will glanced from Georgia to Bramble Cottage, both unscathed. *Me, too.*

# Chapter Twenty-Three

Georgia patted the bench and Will sat beside her. "I didn't want to say anything to worry Harriet even more, but I developed the film before all this happened."

"You did?" His eyes were wide. "And?"

She stared down at her hands. "It's awful, Will. When I saw the images, I got so… I don't know. Angry. Shocked. Mortified." She bit her lower lip.

"Did you get a chance to read anything?"

She shook her head. "I literally threw up and cried myself to sleep after I saw the negatives."

He took her hand.

"And then I heard banging and there was a faint smell of smoke and a siren and…" She covered her mouth with her other hand. "Do they know how the fire started?"

"Not yet." Will waved at a fire officer and pulled her to her feet. "Seems we have the all-clear to go in. Want me to get your things?"

She straightened her shoulders. "Thanks, but I need to go inside. I want to check the darkroom."

They stepped into the foyer and through to the living area. She scanned the kitchen, amazed and grateful the fire hadn't spread inside. "Everything looks good down here."

"It's going to take a while to get rid of the smoke smell." Will wrinkled his nose.

"It could have been so much worse though."

"True. A spark on your thatched roof would've been disastrous. I'm sure they'll keep an eye on it for a while to be sure it's perfectly safe. Want me to follow you upstairs?"

"Please. I'd like to see every room." *If someone had the guts to light a fire in my yard, they could have come inside, too. It's not like it would be the first time…*

Georgia led the way to her bedroom. "Hopefully, no postcards today." She grimaced.

"That photo's stunning."

A splash of color in an oversized framed photograph above the headboard displayed one of her best pieces of work. A vibrant field of cherry-red poppies taken in France.

Will shook his head. "I feel as if I could reach out and touch those flowers."

"Thanks." Her cheeks heated. Maybe from the compliment, or maybe from their presence in her bedroom… "Let's keep going, shall we?"

She poked her head into the bathroom and then opened the guest bedroom. "Everything seems fine."

Will joined her. "Cute room."

She loved the guest room. Hopefully, Sophie would be sleeping here soon. Knotty pine furniture and cream bedlinen gave it a warm, cozy vibe. A well-worn teddy bear with glass eyes sat on top of the dresser, the only personal element in the room.

"Your bear?" He nudged her arm.

"How did you guess? Rupert's been watching over this room since we were little kids. He was my favorite. Our grandparents bought it for me on our first visit here from Canada. I told Harriet whatever changes we made in the renovations, Rupert was staying."

"I like it." A smile curved his mouth.

Finally, she opened the door to the darkroom. Light spilled in from the hallway, but she flicked a switch to fully illuminate the space. "*No way.*" She walked to the counter and touched the now-empty twine that once held the negatives. "They're gone."

Will walked up behind her. "The negatives were hanging here?"

"Yes." Her heart sank. Not because of the theft—she'd been one step ahead of them there. It was because her home had been violated. Yet again. "I can't believe someone was in here. While I slept. Or in the chaos once the fire started."

Her chin wobbled and Will held her close, his hand rubbing her back and the hint of spicy cologne displacing the smell of smoke.

"I'm sorry the negatives are gone, Georgia."

She sniffled. "No, I made prints. I guess hanging the negatives back up was my version of a red herring. Hoping if they found them, they'd leave me alone."

He pulled back. "Wow. Impressive. You're thorough."

"I am."

"Let's hope it worked."

"Wouldn't that be nice?"

"Are you ready to report anything yet?" His eyes held so much concern, but he understood her dilemma.

"Almost. I want to make sense of the paperwork. At least have some idea what it is I'm reporting. Daniel's message said I should read it before taking everything to the police. It shouldn't take me long, so heaven help me, I'm coming back to finish what I started."

He went to say something and she put up one hand. "Not on my own. I promise." Her head was spinning and she needed to recover first. She grabbed both Will's hands. "I know I keep apologizing but I'm truly sorry for all this."

"You don't have to apologize…"

She looked into his deep green eyes, longing for him to trust her. "Let me assure the police out there that I'm upset about my yard but relieved my home is still standing. Leave it at that."

"For now."

"Yes, for now." She blew out a long, steadying breath. "I'll tell you everything later, I promise. We have a conversation to finish. For now, let's put our acting skills to the test."

His eyes widened. "I don't think I have any."

"Follow my lead." She hurried down the stairs and out through the front door. The two officers in her yard were young— at least it wasn't Officer Parker again. The neighbors dispersed now it was apparent the cottage wasn't going to burn to the ground, and the fire brigade appeared to be almost finished.

"Miss Brooks?" The officer guarding the doorway was ready to ask his questions.

Georgia balked. She was still getting used to her maiden name again. She would answer their questions, it wouldn't be difficult to shed a few tears, and hopefully they would leave her to deal with everything in her own time and be done with this nightmare.

Twenty minutes later, Will joined her in the living room. He'd fixed the back door and borrowed a couple of portable fans from the neighbors. The inside of the cottage was now bearable, although the stale smell of smoke still hung in the air. Georgia shivered as she sat on the sofa and considered how this might have ended in a different scenario.

"Are you chilly?" Will crouched in front of her and touched her bare arm. Her spine tingled.

"No. The smell of smoke plays games with my mind, that's all. It'll soon freshen up in here."

His eyebrows drew together. "I'm not so sure about that. Smoke is a beast to get out of fabrics and furnishings. Would you let me call a friend of mine? He does restoration and clean-up—I'll bet he could have someone over here tomorrow to hurry the process along."

She put her head in her hands. The smoke made her nauseous, but it was the reality of her dire situation that caused her stomach to churn. The thought of involving Will in this fiasco was a big deal. She had to be sure he was willing to know everything. It was going to get ugly. "Why are you here?"

"Excuse me?"

She spoke into her hands. "I know I asked you before why you care, but after this, why are you still here when pretty much everything you've observed about me since we first met should've caused you to run?"

He lifted her chin and stroked her cheek with a tenderness that made her want to cry.

"You want to know why I'm sticking around, Georgia? Honestly? You intrigue me. I know you're hurting. I recognize grief and pain. I suppose the doctor in me longs to make you feel better, healed—but it's more than that."

"It is?" Her cheeks heated.

Will leaned in closer. "I've been in a cocoon of pain myself for the past year and a half. Numb to so many feelings. Other than for my precious boy, of course. I'd forgotten what it felt like to be needed. Challenged." He tilted his head to one side. "Captivated."

Georgia's pulse quickened. What was she doing? How could she put this man in harm's way? She swallowed. "You have no clue what I'm caught up in. I'm not entirely certain myself." She touched the stubble on his jawline and his lips parted a little.

"I'm here for you." His words were a gentle whisper. He closed the space between them and kissed her mouth with a featherlight touch before leaning in deeper.

Georgia's eyes closed of their own volition as time slowed and peace enveloped her. How could this feel so dreamy in the midst of a living nightmare?

He pulled away and his absence caused an ache.

Georgia put her fingers to her lips as she came back down to earth.

Before she could say anything, Will stood and dragged his fingers through his hair. "I'm sorry if I overstepped."

Was he serious? "No, no…"

"I should make the call. You know, to my friend. Does tomorrow work for you? I hope he can send someone over." He turned toward the kitchen and dug the phone from his pocket. "I should check on Jack, too. I-I'll put the kettle on for a cup of tea."

*What just happened?* Georgia slumped back into the comfort of the cushion, her lips still tingling. Why was the answer always a cup of tea in England? Also, what was she supposed to do about the unexpected passion behind that kiss?

# Chapter Twenty-Four



*WHAT HAVE I DONE?*

Will rushed into the kitchen and rested both palms on the cool marble countertop. Head bowed, he took a deep breath. *I kissed her.* He exhaled. *It was spectacular.* Pleasure mingled with guilt. The notion of ever having another woman in his life felt like betrayal to Emma—up until this past week or so. Now, not so much.

*What is it about you, Georgia?* He flicked on the kettle and found two white china mugs on an open shelf and set them down. It felt comfortable—two mugs. He'd missed doing life with a special someone. Was he falling too hard, too soon? It seemed she had enough issues of her own to work through without the complication of a romantic relationship in the mix. There was so much he didn't know about Georgia Brooks. So much he longed to know, to help in her healing.

"Everything okay?" Georgia tucked her long, wavy hair behind her ears as she stood before him, and Will had the sudden urge to run his fingers through the thickness of it.

*God, what is wrong with me?* Maybe praying would help.

"Sure. Yes. Fine." He tapped his fingers on the countertop and met her anxious gaze. If the eyes were a window to the soul, then hers was deeply troubled. "How about you?"

She scrunched her nose. "Honestly, I can't even think with that smell of smoke still in the air."

He sniffed. It was faint now but then her sensitivity to smoke was understandable. "After what just happened, I feel like we've got even more talking to do." He offered a hand. "Why don't we pass on the tea and get out of here?"

Georgia tipped her head back and stared at the ceiling. "What about everything in the darkroom?"

"Is all the important information in the safe?"

She nodded.

"I'm guessing you could leave that until tomorrow. Unless you want me to help now."

"No. You're right." She focused on his hand and took it in her own. "I don't want to stay here a moment longer. I need a clear head to tackle whatever else is in that envelope. I'm asking you one more time—are you positive you want to get involved? I'm giving you an out here."

Will answered by stepping into the space between them and wrapping her in a hug. He felt her tense body relax as he kissed the top of her head.

"I don't need an out. I'm in deep."

They left Georgia's rental car at the cottage and both jumped into Will's vehicle. *At least I can keep her safe at my house.*

Settled into the passenger seat, she cranked the window a little. "Do you think Jack is going to be okay with me crashing your evening at home?"

"I think he'll be delighted to see you again. You have a big fan in Jack. In both of us." He stole a quick peek and caught her blush. "I have to confess, I've been more than worried about you. Now the fire in your back garden—"

She swiveled to face him. "I know. It's getting more bizarre by the minute. I want to tell you about the roll of film."

She went so quiet for a long minute he looked to check if she was still awake.

"Will, I know we're nearly there, but could you pull over for a sec? I'm not feeling so good."

"Of course." Will slowed into a lay-by and ran around to her side.

She flung her passenger door open and leaned her head over her knees. "I need some air."

"Take your time." He took her pulse and coached her breathing.

"Sorry." She straightened and opened her eyes. "I was starting to feel lightheaded there."

"You'll have to do more than that to scare me off. I'm a doctor, remember?"

They both gazed out over fields that looked much like a patchwork quilt, the sound of a tractor rattling in the distance. The rain had stopped but the steel-gray sky didn't look promising.

"Daniel was hopeless when it came to helping with any sort of sickness. Which was quite often."

Will had to ask. "Why?"

Her face fell. "Several pregnancies, and as many miscarriages."

"I'm so sorry." She'd spoken to him of their infertility troubles, but he was unaware of her losses. His heart ached for the woman before him.

"Fainting is also the way my body sometimes reacts to stress." She turned and looked him in the face. "Will, can I be totally honest with you?"

"Always."

She bit her lower lip. "I'm very scared."

"I'd be more concerned if you weren't." He took her hand and led her back to the car, scanning the immediate area as he walked. "Let's get you some tea and you can tell me all about it."

*I'm going to have to tell him everything.* They pulled into Will's driveway and Georgia tugged her leather bag from the floor onto her lap. He'd called his restoration buddy to come over tomorrow and rid Bramble Cottage of any lingering smoke smell. Thank goodness—it had almost been her undoing. Those devastating memories.

Will stopped in front of the house and killed the engine. "Let's go and check on that boy of mine." He exited the SUV and raced around to open her door. So sweet and gentle. He was a healing balm to the onslaught of everything terrible happening around her. Her head pounded but she mustered a smile for Jack.

"Dada." Jack was waving from the front door in the arms of a middle-aged woman with rosy cheeks. "Dada." His squeals melted Georgia's heart.

"Hello, big guy." Will scooped him up and spun him around. "Thank you so much, Caroline. You've been a lifesaver today."

"Not at all, Doctor Hughes. Always happy to stand in for the sitter. You know I love young Jack." Her eyes darted to Georgia. "I hope everything turned out all right."

"It could have been a lot worse. We'll see you next Monday?"

She reached behind the door and picked up a floral tote with a feather duster protruding from the top. "Of course. You have a good evening now."

"Bye." Georgia offered a wave of her fingers and her shoulders relaxed. At least she wouldn't have the awkwardness of having to talk to Will with someone else eavesdropping in the house.

Will lowered his son to the floor and held the door open. "Come on in. Jack, you remember Miss Georgia?"

He held out a pudgy hand. "Shawsha?"

"That's me." She chuckled and allowed him to lead her into his home. Could this little guy be any cuter? A sudden chill swept over her. *I could be putting Jack in danger by coming here.* She glanced down at his blond hair and hesitated. "Wait. I shouldn't be here."

Will came up behind her and whispered into her ear. "We're fine. I have state-of-the-art security—it was a must when I was working nights. Now, why don't you go freshen up in the powder room while I go and change someone's nappy? If you need anything, you'll find all kinds of toiletries in the cupboard under the sink." He ruffled Jack's hair. "Perhaps we'll get your pajamas on while we're at it, hey, Jack?"

Georgia checked her watch. It was almost seven already. "Thanks. I'll call Harriet while you're upstairs—she'll want to know what's going on."

"Good idea." Will picked up Jack and raced up the spiral staircase, leaving little-boy giggles in their wake. The sound of them both laughing faded as they disappeared and Georgia was left standing in the middle of the foyer, frozen. She squeezed her eyes shut and tried to gather her thoughts.

Never would she have dreamed she might be in the house of a caring surgeon with a darling little boy, about to spill her guts about a possible crime her ex-husband was involved in.

According to her five-year life plan, she and Daniel should be living in the outskirts of Vancouver with their two children about now. A girl and a boy. Her photography would have been a satisfying part-time gig she could navigate alongside motherhood. Daniel's journalist career would be soaring, and he would choose to travel less with kids to raise. That was the perfect plan. Where had it all gone so horribly wrong?

The miscarriages. The Paris trip. The lies. The other woman. Now Daniel was dead, and his secret was about to be ripped wide open. She had to share it all with Will before she imploded.

Or before the bad guy decided to take things to the next level and she was silenced for good.

# Chapter Twenty-Five

"HEY, HARRIET, IT'S ME." GEORGIA STOOD in Will's powder room and stared at her reflection in the rectangular mirror. The events of the day had taken their toll. Her eyes were red-rimmed, she was pale, her hair was a post-rain disaster, and her lips were chapped. *Nice.*

"Where are you? Is Will with you?"

"I'm at his house. The smoke was getting to me."

"Good call. I'm sorry I had to take off and leave you like that. Apparently, Leo couldn't miss the finance meeting. Are you all right, sis? I mean the fire… it sure shook me up. Do they have any clue how it was even started?"

Georgia pinched her cheeks in an attempt to regain a little color. "The fire chief didn't find anything obvious to imply it was arson. He said something about the rain washing evidence away, but there was a pile of cigarette butts. Asked if I'd been smoking out there."

"You don't smoke. Come to think of it, I don't think I know many people who do. Curious."

Georgia dug a wide-toothed comb from her bag and smoothed the frizz from her hair. "It's a mystery. I guess it'll remain that way. I'm counting my blessings the cottage is still standing and I only lost a few trees and shrubs."

"I wish they could tell you more. Are you coming back to stay with us tonight?"

"That's why I was phoning. I'd be really grateful. Maybe I could come over in an hour or two?"

"Of course. You know you're welcome to stay as long as you like. I was worried you might change your mind and want to sleep in your smoke-infested home."

"No chance."

"Good. Because until this all gets sorted out, I think you should give Bramble Cottage a wide berth."

The hairs on Georgia's bare arms stood on end at the thought of sleeping there alone. "I think your local police force is going to wish I hadn't arrived."

"It's probably the most excitement they've seen in a while, but I'm concerned for you. More than concerned."

"I'll be careful. Promise."

Harriet let out a long sigh. "I feel so bad. I should have been with you this morning at the cottage. If I'd been there, I may have noticed smoke in the garden."

"Hey, don't you dare blame yourself for anything. I'm the headstrong one who couldn't possibly wait for you or Will."

"Not to mention Leo was being completely uncooperative."

"Is he okay? I've scarcely seen him." Georgia frowned. "And when I have, he's been kind of sullen."

"Moody. I know. He's fine. Don't worry about him. He's the least of our worries."

"You don't need to tell *me* that."

"Right?" Harriet lowered her voice. "I'm sorry to keep on, but I can't get the burnt toast incident out of my head. It has to be someone who knows you well. Or knows Daniel…"

"*Knew* Daniel." Georgia squinted into the mirror, angry he wasn't around to answer her questions. Be held accountable for his actions.

"I can't get used to the fact he's dead."

She clutched the edge of the marble vanity. "There are lots

of unknowns in this, but I'll get to the bottom of it somehow. I want to go home."

"Back to Vancouver?"

"No, to Bramble Cottage." She blinked back tears as frustration vied with fear.

"I like that you think of the cottage as your new home. Your fresh start. You'll be back in there before you know it, sis."

Georgia loosened her grip on the vanity. "This hasn't exactly turned out how I planned. My grand independent adventure as a single woman in a foreign land."

"Not your fault. Besides, it's hardly foreign."

"True. Benefits of dual citizenship. I wanted to give the quiet English country village life a chance, you know? Before deciding whether to settle back in Vancouver or split my time between both."

"I'm sorry your dream home's been tampered with."

Georgia opened the cupboard beneath the sink and found a new toothbrush and toothpaste, as promised. "Me, too. Those lovely trees all burned. Who knows if any of the blackberry bushes survived?" She let out a sigh. "Grandma put so much love into the backyard and now it'll never be the same again."

"We'll figure it out. There's a guy at church who does landscaping. I can ask him to take a look once the burnt foliage has been cleared."

"Thanks. I hadn't thought that far ahead yet. The sooner the smoky debris is gone from the property, the better I'll feel." She balanced the phone under her ear and split open the toothbrush package with some difficulty. "Will's got a guy coming over tomorrow to fumigate or whatever it is they do to get rid of the stench inside the cottage."

"Perfect. So, how come you decided to spend the evening

with our friendly doctor rather than come straight here?" Harriet's voice was thick with sibling taunt.

"He knows I've been at your place a lot. Leo seems to be a little peeved at my presence, which I don't blame him for one bit—"

"Wait, Leo's not peeved at *you*."

"To be fair, having me stay with you guys instead of being in my own cottage wasn't the plan."

"None of this was the plan, but you're family. Leo knows family has priority, so don't give it a second thought."

"Okay, I appreciate that."

Harriet huffed. "Sounds to me like your doctor wants you for himself."

Georgia's lips tingled at the memory of their kiss. "Nonsense. He knew the smoke was too much for me at the cottage and suggested we hang out at his house. Period."

"Did he now?"

Georgia groaned. "Please, don't start. My head is so messed up and I've too much to process to think about Will as anything other than a friend." Ignoring the kiss and the fact her heart beat faster every time he came close. "Plus, I need all the friends I can get."

"*Just* good friends?"

"Yes, we're just good friends." *At least that's all I'm sharing for now.*

"Too bad. I'll get Leo to pick you up about nine. I think we'll all need an early night."

"Thanks. See you later."

Will didn't mean to eavesdrop as he passed the powder room, but those tiled floors allowed sound to carry. He hugged Jack tighter on his way to the kitchen as he replayed Georgia's words.

He was just a friend.

*Of course you are, fool.* Why would some beautiful woman with no ties looking for a fresh start be interested in a boring man with a kid? He was way off with his assumptions on her part. She was vulnerable and he steamrolled in and made a move. Although he hadn't imagined the way she kissed him back…

"Shawsha?"

Will seated Jack in his highchair and kissed the top of his head. "Yes, Miss Georgia's going to have dinner here. How about that?" He tried to sound chipper as he placed a bowl of fishy crackers on Jack's plastic tray. "Here's your gourmet bedtime snack, young man."

"Can I come in?"

Will spun around as Georgia walked toward them, camera in hand.

"Of course." He nodded at the camera. "You really do go everywhere with that."

"Everywhere. Trick of the trade." She held it to her eye and snapped a photo of him and Jack. "I guess it's my comfort. It grounds me."

"Makes sense. You look better. A little color in your cheeks."

"Thanks. I'm feeling a bit more normal. Amazing what brushing your teeth and combing your hair can do."

Jack beamed and held out a soggy cracker.

"Is that for me?" She took it from his hand. "Thank you very much. It's… delicious."

"You don't have to eat it," Will whispered.

"Thanks."

"Everything okay with Harriet?" Will turned on some opera

music for background ambience and opened the fridge to see what culinary delight he could create in a pinch.

"Yes. It's all good. Leo's coming to pick me up later, around nine. Does that work for you?" She leaned her hip against the counter top and set her camera down.

"Perfect. Gives us a couple of hours." *Play it cool.*

"What can I do to help with dinner?"

"I think I can stretch this leftover lasagna between the two of us if you can throw together a salad?"

"Salad is my specialty." She pursed her lips. "Actually, salad is probably the best option to give me. Did I mention I'm a horrible cook?"

Will tried to ignore the effect those dark chocolate eyes had on his heart, and handed her a bag of mixed salad, a red pepper, and half a cucumber. "I find it hard to imagine you're horrible at anything. Do your worst. I'll get this heated up and then I think it'll be bedtime for Jack."

"Sure." She found her way around the kitchen with ease as Will readied Jack's bottle of milk and cleared stray crackers from the floor. He wrestled with thoughts of Emma, the times they cooked together in this space with their shared love of food, and the last time she stood there with desperation in her eyes…

"Hey, Will?"

"Yes?" The overhead pot lights picked up the honey tones in Georgia's rich brown hair. So different from Emma's blonde curls.

"Please, don't let me disturb your bedtime routine with Jack. I know these things are important."

Georgia's smile was almost too much. Now that he had tasted her kiss, those lips were irresistible. *Come on, man. Just friends, remember?* He whipped around to lift Jack from his chair and grabbed the bottle. "Thanks. He's great at going down in his crib, but I'd like to give him his milk first. It's our little ritual—cuddles in the rocking chair with his bottle and his bunny."

"So precious. You go ahead. I can finish off here, as long as you don't mind me helping myself to whatever I can find in order to make this a salad you won't forget."

Will raised a brow. "My stomach's rumbling already. Make yourself at home." As soon as the words left his mouth, he bit his tongue. "What I mean is, you can relax here. I realize it's not your home, but you can make yourself comfortable. That's what friends are for. Use whatever food you can find. There's sparkling water or juice in the fridge. I'll be back soon." *Ugh, could I be any more awkward?*

"Okay." She tilted her head. "I'll do that. Goodnight, Jack." She blew him a kiss.

"Night-night." Jack blew one in return, which Georgia caught in her hand and tucked in her heart.

Will made a swift exit with his son. Even her kisses in the air caused his pulse to quicken.

*That was strange.* Georgia busied herself slicing peppers as she considered the shift in Will's mood. The tender kiss back at Bramble Cottage, his care for her on the drive over, and then the serious frown returned when she walked into the kitchen. Coming home may have caused him to regret the kiss. It may have taken him by surprise as much as it did her. Made him think about his wife. She had triggers of her own that reminded her of Daniel.

Like memories of him cooking for her back when they had eyes only for each other. The kitchen was his domain and she was more than happy to be his sous chef. How had such a sweet marriage turned so sour?

"You're not going to believe this."

Georgia turned at the sound of Will's voice.

"What is it?" She winked at Jack, who was clinging to his bedtime bottle like a life preserver.

"The hospital called, and I'm needed for an emergency surgery. Again." His eyes softened. "I'm so sorry… this doesn't happen very often but apparently, I'm the only surgeon available." He shook his head. "Twice in a week."

She swallowed down the panic that rose from her gut. "Don't worry. You go and do your thing. I can watch Jack." She put down the knife and held out her arms. Jack leaned forward and snuggled in. "I think we'll manage."

Will ran a hand through his hair. "I don't want to leave you alone here, not in light of everything you're dealing with."

*No kidding.* "Isn't it an emergency?"

He nodded. "Yes." He checked his watch and chewed on his lip. She could almost see the turning wheels of his mind devising a plan. "Here's what I can do. I'll phone Rachel, the babysitter, and see if she can come over as soon as possible. She lives close by. Her mom can be my back-up plan."

"Great." *I love that he even has a back-up plan.*

"I'll set the security system for the doors and windows and Rachel knows what to do when she gets here. If you call Leo and ask him to pick you up a little earlier…"

"Yes, yes, go. Some poor child is waiting for you to save them. We'll be fine. I'll put Jack to bed and I already met Rachel at church, so she knows me."

He reached out and rubbed her arm. "I'm truly sorry. I was hoping we could talk. We *need* to talk." His eyes bored into hers. "I'll call you later tonight?"

"Of course. Go be a superhero surgeon. I'll make sure your dinner is back in the fridge for you."

"Thanks for understanding." He planted a kiss on his son's cheek.

*I kind of wish the kiss had been for me.* Georgia cleared her throat. "Go on. We've got this."

He darted around the foyer gathering his keys, wallet, and jacket. "Cheerio." He waved as he slid on his shoes, set the alarm, and left through the front door.

Georgia stood in the welcoming entrance of this stunning home, a baby in her arms, a handsome man caring for her wellbeing… it was almost too surreal. Tears filled her eyes. She couldn't cry in front of Jack.

"Come on, little guy. Let's get you upstairs and settled for the night, shall we?"

He gazed up at her and blinked.

"You are possibly the cutest little one I've ever met. Other than Lucy, but she's my niece so that doesn't count." She chatted as she walked up the staircase. "I think we can handle this bedtime routine. How about you?"

Jack was already supping the milk from his bottle.

"I'm guessing your room is the one with the open door and the nightlight on." She strolled into the nursery and Jack relaxed in her arms. "This is your happy place, isn't it? I can see why."

Beautiful. White and sage green decor gave it a clean, calming feel. A large white crib was situated in one corner with an animal mobile hanging overhead and a white wooden rocker sat on a fluffy area rug by the window.

"Let's sit there for a minute while you finish that yummy milk, shall we?"

After the chaos, Georgia was grateful to be in this cozy, playful space. The room was bathed in gray evening light, so she pulled the curtains across the window in an attempt to make it more sleep conducive. She sank into the rocking chair and took in the painted mural of Noah's Ark and all the animals on one wall, and a large bookcase filled with colorful reading material for children. Had Jack's mom curated all this before she died or had Will been left to make this room a haven for their son?

Jack reached out to the window seat and grabbed his well-loved rabbit.

"I forgot you need Bunny." She folded boy and bunny in her arms and rocked. Her stomach clenched as she yearned for a baby of her own. Mourned the ones she lost. Being here, the memories flooded back. She persuaded Daniel to convert their townhouse guest room into a nursery back when they were trying for a child. With every pregnancy, she would add a little something to the room decor, praying it would be used one day. With each miscarriage, her heart would break a little more as she stared into the empty crib.

*Why, God?* Why had she lost so much? Her babies one after another, her dear dad so many years ago, and even her husband to another woman. A tear snaked down her cheek and she let it fall. She knew better than to believe a baby would have fixed her marriage. If Daniel was going to leave her one day anyway, perhaps it was better there were no children to be hurt in the process. *Still, my heart aches so very much...*

She looked down at Jack. This darling boy would grow up without his mother. He would have no memory of her at all other than stories told by his daddy and those who knew her well. There would be photographs, too—that was one of the appeals of her job. Being able to freeze both special and everyday moments to look back on and remember, was priceless. A pleasure. A privilege.

Jack extracted the bottle from his mouth and held it before her eyes. "Done."

"Good boy." She sniffled and managed a smile. She had become proficient in putting on a brave face. "Let's get you and Bunny to bed, sweetheart."

She stood, carried him over to the crib, and kissed his chubby cheek. He inserted a thumb in his mouth as she lowered him into his bed with Bunny tucked under one arm.

"Goodnight, Jack. Sweet dreams." Georgia pulled a soft blanket up over his tiny form and backed out of the room, leaving the baby to sleep in the soft glow of a nightlight in his familiar surroundings.

*Must be nice.* As she trudged down the staircase, exhaustion weighed heavy. It had been quite the day. Her stomach growled as she padded through the foyer. Food. She needed something to eat, even a little of the salad she was in the midst of preparing. In the kitchen, she carried on where she left off and added sliced red peppers to the greens in the large glass bowl. *Will said to help myself.* She hummed to the familiar classical music playing from the speakers, and discovered some blue cheese in the fridge and a bag of walnuts in the pantry.

She crumbled the cheese, added a generous portion of nuts, and mixed everything together before dumping a portion into a small dish for herself. She turned off the oven as the lasagna hadn't quite made it there before Will left—he could heat some up for himself when he got home.

With a swirl of balsamic dressing, she grabbed a fork and her phone and made her way over to one of the leather sofas. Tucking her legs to one side, she took a bite of her salad and savored the delicious combination of flavors while dialing Harriet's number.

"Hey, sis."

"Hi, Harriet, I'm so sorry to be a pain, but is there any

chance Leo could come for me a little earlier? Will's been called into work for an emergency surgery."

"You're alone?"

"With Jack."

"Shouldn't be a problem. That kind of messed up your plans for the evening, didn't it?"

Georgia speared a pepper with her fork. "The surgeon-life, I suppose. Anyway, the babysitter is coming to take over any minute and I'm happy to hang out here in the meantime. Jack's a dream baby."

Harriet chuckled. "He's so cute. Will's the best dad, isn't he?"

"He is." Warmth spread within her chest at the thought of father and son together.

"I don't like the idea of you being there alone. Leo had to nip into the office, so I'll get him to come straight from there to pick you up. It looks like another storm is rolling in fast. Is it raining there yet?"

The wall of windows didn't lie. "Yes, it just started. Massive raindrops. These summer storms are getting a bit much. I hadn't noticed how dark it was and I've no idea how to operate Will's fancy blinds in here. I feel like I'm in a humungous fish tank. Like I wasn't jittery enough before today."

"Hon, you've been through a lot. When you get here, we can have some ice-cream and talk."

"Sounds good to me." *Although maybe not about everything.* A deep rumble grew outside and Georgia shuddered. "I guess the storm arrived. I'll let you go—see you soon."

"Sure. Stay safe."

Georgia gobbled down the rest of her food as she scrolled through her phone messages. One from her mom checking on her and another from Sophie who was starting to feel up to traveling.

A flash of lightning lit up the room and caused her to drop the fork. *That was intense.* She bent over to retrieve it and as she righted herself, a fleeting shadow at the window caught her eye. Was someone out there? She froze and stared at the space. There was no escaping the view before her. Full-length windows leading to the back patio and yard beyond grew darker as the storm clouds rolled in overhead.

She set the dish and fork on the coffee table in front of her and pulled her knees to her chest without losing eye contact with the windows. Storms didn't usually bother her, in fact, she enjoyed watching them from the comfort of home. Yet this was far from enjoyable as she squinted in order to monitor every sightline in the wall of glass. Was her vivid imagination playing tricks? Tree branches swung low as the wind picked up. It could be a toy blowing across the patio.

Eyes wide, she clutched her phone in both hands and clenched her jaw as another rumble of thunder sounded. *Maybe I should check on Jack.* He wasn't crying, but he would be scared if he woke to this. Her limbs refused to move as she sat transfixed watching for movement outside.

She could almost hear her own heartbeat. *There.* A huge shadow came into view, too dark to make out. Another flash, a scream—her scream—as the shape of a man was illuminated from behind.

Rain-soaked, the figure stood and stared directly at her. Covered in a hooded oilskin coat, he was massive. She screamed again and he flinched. He pulled back his hood and leered.

It was him.

# Chapter Twenty-Six

THE BLACK BEARD. THE SQUINTY, EVIL eyes. Paris guy. Panic set in and Georgia struggled for her next breath. With a mere pane of glass between them, his looming form stood stock still. Her heart pounded. Would he try to break the glass?

He had her full attention. With her gaze transfixed on him, he pointed two fingers toward his own eyes and then back to her. *I'm watching you.* How did she know that was all he intended to do?

*My camera.* Her photographer instinct took over. She should snap a photo of him. The camera was in the kitchen and her legs were like jelly. *My phone.* She fumbled for the camera app. When she looked back at the window, he ducked his head and disappeared into the storm before she could get a shot of him.

Was that it? Was he gone? Scared for herself, for Jack upstairs, and for Rachel when she arrived at the house, Georgia had to be sure he wasn't trying to get inside somehow. Gathering all the courage she could muster, on shaky legs and with phone in hand, she hurried away from the fishbowl and into the kitchen to peek through the side window. Nothing other than rain and trees. She lowered the blind, grateful for a regular window covering.

Next, the foyer. She ran to the front door and peered through the peephole. At the end of Will's driveway, through the sheets of rain she made out a vehicle. Silver. As it sped away, she was certain it was the sports car. Exhale. Okay, so there was a good chance he'd left. He was getting brave. Showing his face like that? Fearless. Maybe he had nothing to lose.

Her index finger hovered above the phone screen. She should call 9-9-9. Daniel's warning rang in her head. Yet if they were watching her, she couldn't take any chances with her family's safety.

She should be okay for now inside Will's house, shouldn't she? He promised the security system was solid. If this guy wanted to attack her, why would he do it here rather than when she was vulnerable in her own cottage? Another scare tactic, no doubt. *I hope that's all it was.*

What if it wasn't? Nausea rose.

*God, am I being foolish to heed Daniel's message?*

The grizzly-man was frightening but he hadn't actually tried to break through the window. He was watching her. Stalking her—like that wasn't horrific enough. She didn't see a weapon. In fact, both his hands were empty as far as she could tell.

*Wait.*

Wait? The small word flitted in her chest like a caged bird as a desire to find the whole truth behind the horrific photographs stirred deep in her soul. Was it the still, small voice she'd heard about? Was it God's whisper?

*Wait.*

It came again. She relaxed her finger to the side of the phone. Yes, waiting was her plan and perhaps it was God's. She would stick with it.

The baby. She needed to check on Jack upstairs. If the storm hadn't disturbed him, her screams may have. A chain hung on the front door as an added precaution, so she hooked that onto the latch for good measure and hurried up the staircase.

No noise came from the nursery, so she crept into the room on tiptoes and peered over the edge of the crib. Jack was sleeping, oblivious to everything happening outside. She padded to the window. A quick look through the curtains showed no movement in the back yard other than straining branches amidst the torrential downpour. Another low rumble of thunder sounded—quieter now as the storm moved on. She closed the curtains tight and checked on Jack again.

So peaceful. The rise and fall of his chest beneath the pale blue onesie so much calmer than her racing pulse. She couldn't resist touching his soft cheek. Was there anything more blissful than a baby sleeping?

A rattling noise sounded from downstairs. The front door. With one last glance at the sleeping child, Georgia dashed to the top of the stairs and waited. She watched in horror as the iron doorknob twisted and the lock clicked. Someone was trying to get inside. What about the state-of-the-art alarm system? Had this maniac come back with a key? He managed to procure one for her cottage, after all.

The phone was still in her hand.

*I'm going to have to call 9-9-9. This is it.*

The door opened an inch but was hampered by the chain. Frantic, Georgia's eyes darted from the phone to the front door. As she went to press the first digit she heard her name being called.

"Will, is that you?" She almost fell down the stairs as she made her way to the door.

"Georgia?"

She lifted the chain and the door flew wide open. Will tumbled into his house, drenched to the skin. Another flash of lightning lit up the trees behind him and Georgia slammed the door shut.

Without thinking, she threw her arms around his neck and clung on for dear life.

"Hey, hey, it's okay. What's wrong? You had the door chain on." He stroked her hair and squeezed her tight.

Sweet relief pumped through her veins.

He pulled back and lifted her chin. "Can you tell me what happened?" His eyes flitted upstairs.

"Jack's fine, he's sleeping. I didn't mean to scare you, but something awful happened, and I put the chain across the door, and I thought you were the man breaking in…" She tried to keep hysterics at bay, but it was proving difficult.

"The man? What man?" Will shed his sopping wet jacket and shoes and clasped her hand in his. "Come, sit with me." He led her to the great room and they sat side-by-side on the sofa. He swiveled round to face her. "Start at the beginning."

Georgia nodded. "There was a man at the window. Over there." She pointed to the patio doors. "I didn't know how to make the blinds work in here so I was eating salad, watching the storm, and he appeared out of nowhere." A shudder ran through her. "He stood there, rain dripping from his coat. One of those long oilskin things. He stared at me while the lightning flashed—it was like a scene from some sick horror movie."

"What?" His voice rose in pitch. "There was a man in my garden? Did he try to get in? Say anything?"

She shook her head as his image came to mind. "Just stood and stared. Pointed to his eyes and then me, like *I'm watching you*, and then he disappeared in an instant before I could snap a photo on my phone."

"You haven't been out there, have you?"

"Is that an actual question?"

"No, no of course you haven't. You were safe inside. The security system would have sounded if he tried to get in through any of the windows or doors."

"That's what I was hoping. I think he left in a silver sports car."

"Sounds familiar."

"I know."

"I should check to see if he left any footprints. Although I think everything will be washed away. The rain's insane out there." He squeezed her hand. "I'm sorry. I should've been here. How long ago did this happen?"

"Not long. Maybe five minutes?"

Will stood and marched over to the windows. The rain continued to pelt the glass but there was no sign of anyone. "I should've dropped you at your sister's place on the way to the hospital."

"But you had an emergency. Please don't blame yourself for any of this, Will." She joined him and looked up into his eyes. "Come to think of it, why are you back so soon?"

The crease deepened between his eyebrows. "I think we need to call the police."

Georgia hesitated. "You know I can't do that."

"I'm sorry, Georgia, but when my son's safety is at risk, I have to do the right thing. When I phoned the hospital to tell them I was a couple of minutes out and they could start prepping for surgery, they had no clue what I was talking about."

Her hand flew to her throat. "What do you mean?"

"Whoever called me earlier with the apparent emergency, wasn't from my hospital." His jaw clenched. "I should've questioned the woman more when she identified herself as a temp. She was so convincing."

*What?* Georgia's knees weakened. So, a woman was involved in this scandal, too. "I don't know what to say."

"At least no one is hurt. We're all okay now."

Georgia's mind flew to Rachel. She could be outside somewhere. "What about the babysitter?"

He paced in front of the windows. "It's fine. I spun my car around and called Rachel on my way home. I'm glad she didn't have to come out in the storm, at least. No one should be out in this."

She couldn't decipher whether he was frustrated with her, or with all that was going on.

"I should never have come here. I didn't want to put you or Jack in danger." She wiped her hands down her cheeks. "I'm sorry."

"Don't blame yourself." Will didn't look at her as he spoke. "I knew I was taking a chance having you here… I really didn't consider I might be called out or that it could put Jack at risk."

Georgia bit her lower lip. "I can't believe he slept through my screaming and the storm raging…" She leaned against the cool window and closed her eyes.

Will stopped pacing. "You're shaking. Ah, what am I thinking? You've had a terrible shock."

He took her in his arms again. That spicy cologne. Could she trust him with all the details? This black beard guy knew where Will lived now. He was involved whether he liked it or not. *What have I done?*

She whispered into his chest as he cradled her head. "I've been nothing but trouble since you laid eyes on me."

"Georgia Brooks, when I first laid eyes on you, I knew I was in trouble anyway. Maybe not in the way you are inferring, but I'm already in deep. In more ways than one."

Her insides melted. Could this man be any sweeter?

"If I can help you out of this situation—whatever it is—I will do everything in my power to protect you. You're a very special woman."

Tears filled her eyes. When was the last time she felt this cherished? She took a step back.

"Am I special enough for you to hold fire on calling the cops? For a day?"

He pursed his lips and shoved both hands in his pockets. "You know I'm the biggest rule-follower out there, don't you? I mean, this will be pushing me to my absolute limit."

"So am I. Trust me, this goes against all my natural tendencies, but I'm trying to keep my family free from danger." Georgia swallowed the lump in her throat. "I feel like I may have only scratched the surface of something ugly and if I can prevent anyone else being hurt—or worse—then I need to get my information perfect and precise. I can't be caught off guard."

"You'll let me help you with that?"

"Yes. I think we could work through the evidence together and then, when we know exactly who it is we're dealing with, we can give it all to the cops and let them handle the rest." Georgia touched the side of his face. "But I realize you have to consider Jack's safety and you barely know me."

Several seconds passed as they stared into one another's eyes, lost in thought.

"Do you think we might remedy that last part?" His eyes bore into hers.

"The 'barely know me' part? Only if you want in on a messed-up divorcée with a stalker and a burnt backyard."

"I think I do." His eyes were the shade of the forest and she was ready to walk right in and explore…

A knock on the front door caused them both to jump.

Will wiped a hand through his damp hair.

"Must be Leo." Georgia bit her lower lip. "An axe murderer doesn't usually knock, does he?"

"An axe murderer?"

She shrugged. "Worst case scenario. It's where I tend to go."

"Glad to see you haven't lost your sense of humor." He pecked her cheek as he walked past and checked the peephole on the front door. "It's Leo. No axe murderer in sight." He opened up. "Hi. Come on in out of the rain."

Georgia grabbed her camera from the kitchen and joined them in the foyer. "Thanks for coming to get me, Leo."

"It's dreadful out there." Leo glanced from her to Will. "But what's going on?" He set his hands on his hips and raised his chin. "I thought you were here alone, Georgia? That was why you needed me to come, no?"

Georgia cleared her throat. Time to take charge and hope Will played along. "It was a false alarm—can you believe it? Now you're here we should leave in case the storm gets any worse."

"I think the worst is over. For tonight at least." Leo clapped Will on the shoulder. "Au revoir. Thanks for taking such good care of my sister-in-law. She's not having a good week. It seems trouble is following her."

Will raised both brows. "Trouble? You mean the fire?"

"Forget it." He turned to Georgia. "Ready?"

Georgia ushered Leo through the door. "Could you get the car started while I get my stuff together? I'll be there in a minute."

"I'll be waiting."

Leo disappeared into the dark evening and Georgia slid on her shoes and jacket.

Will picked up her bag from the floor. "Can we continue this conversation in the morning? I'll wait on notifying the police, but I think we need to put a stop to all this. Tomorrow."

"Yes. I promise. I think I can guarantee you won't have any problem here with me gone. I'm praying I won't put Harriet and her family in danger tonight. I feel like our guy knows he scared me enough for now." *Please, God.*

Will placed a hand on her shoulder. "Make sure no one is following you. I can't imagine there are many people out on a night like this. I only passed a few cars earlier."

"I'll be careful. Tomorrow, I'd like to meet somewhere neutral to talk if that's good with you."

"For sure. Let's get together at ten. My mother's coming to pick up Jack for a sleepover, so I'll be free. I'm all yours for a couple of days."

"Thank you. For everything." She reached up and kissed him square on the mouth. He kissed her back with an intensity that caused every nerve in her body to tingle.

A car horn honked and they separated.

"You going to be okay?" Will picked up her left hand and kissed the back of it.

"I have to be. Sharing the load with you is going to help. You have no idea." So many people were hurting because of Daniel. Because of what she failed to question when she saw that photograph of him a year ago. Because of the danger hovering over her loved ones. Over Will.

"You don't have to carry this alone, Georgia."

"I just want it all to be over."

Because the storm pummeling Bramble Downs outside was nothing compared to the storm that pummeled her guilt-ridden soul.

# Chapter Twenty-Seven

WILL WAVED AS LEO AND GEORGIA drove away in the pouring rain.

*Keep them safe, Lord.*

He locked the front door and jogged upstairs to check on Jack. A quick peek into the crib confirmed that somehow, he'd slept through all the drama downstairs. Will brushed a fine blond lock of hair from his son's forehead and breathed out a sigh of relief. *That's my boy. Safe and sound.*

Satisfied all was well in the nursery, he checked the security app on his phone and returned to the living room. No notifications of anything suspicious. If someone even tried to get in through a window or door, he would have known about it.

*Did Georgia really see someone?* The thought popped into his head. She sounded convinced and something certainly shook her up. She was running on little sleep and a huge amount of stress. Was it possible she thought she saw a figure and her imagination conjured him out of the storm?

Back in the living room, he stood for a moment and observed the shadows in the yard through the massive panes of glass. Throw in some lightning flashes and rumbles of thunder and he could see why Georgia was spooked. Why hadn't he thought to show her the remote control for the blinds? No wonder she was so anxious as she looked out on a raging summer storm from a strange house. If there was a man here, surely there'd be evidence of some kind?

To satisfy his own curiosity, he unlocked the patio doors, slid them open, and poked his head out far enough to see if anything had been disturbed. The torrential downpour drenched the concrete deck beneath the covered area. The patio furniture was intact, although a couple of cushions had blown from their chairs. He would rescue them tomorrow, no point in getting soaked again now.

The timed outdoor lights came on at that moment. He checked his watch. Eight o'clock. The storm brought a darker evening upon them. Too bad the lights weren't on when the intruder made an appearance. If there had been an intruder.

A rumble in his stomach reminded him of the leftover lasagna in the fridge. Not that he had any appetite after the events of the evening, but he should eat something. He was about to shut the doors when an unfamiliar shape caught his eye in the new pool of light. A stone garden gnome. Where had that come from? He'd never seen it before. Wasn't a gnome kind of guy. Could the cleaner have put it there earlier today? Intrigued, he bent down, picked it up, and found something underneath. Paper. No, a postcard.

Adrenaline pumped through his veins as he squinted into the darkness. It had to be another message for Georgia. Her mystery man had been there in the flesh. He grabbed the postcard, hurried inside, and locked the doors. He activated the security system from his phone and with the press of a button on the remote, the wall of blinds purred on their way down to block out the night.

Will set the postcard on the coffee table and perched on the edge of the leather love seat. *Sorry I doubted you, Georgia.* He ran both hands through his damp hair and stared at the picture of an old grave yard. An ancient stone church sat in the background, something typically found in a hundred towns or villages in

England. The church building was blurred out giving main focus to the gravestones. *What on earth does this mean for Georgia?*

Whatever the sentiment behind the postcard, it wasn't good. With the flick of his wrist he turned it over and dropped it back onto the table. There in glaring capital letters was her next message, "GRAVE". The other two postcards were ominous enough, but *grave*? How was he going to tell her about this?

If only he could call the police. That would be the obvious course of action, but with the threat looming large over her family's safety… *Lord, what can I do?* There was no guarantee the stalker hadn't followed her back to Harriet's place.

Leo. He could call Leo. No, text him. Relay caution without giving too much away. He tapped out a message:

*"Leo, hope you got home safe. Worried about Georgia— keep an eye on her? Lock up and take care, friend."*

Will stared at the screen, hoping Leo hadn't turned off his phone.

*"Scared, Will?"*

An odd response.

*"I'm concerned. She's got a lot on her plate."*

*"She knows she can trust me. We're family. You're not."*

What? *"Of course. Goodnight, Leo."*

Taken aback, Will slid the phone in his pocket. If he'd done something to upset his friend, he had no clue what it might be. Didn't he like that he was spending time with Georgia? Too bad.

He rested his elbows on his knees and bowed his head. If only there was some way he could shield her from more fear and pain. Perhaps keeping the postcard until tomorrow would afford her a good night's rest at her sister's place. There was nothing she could do about it tonight, not if she flat-out refused to report any of it.

Will swallowed the lump in his throat. What on earth was she caught up in? He'd only known her for eighteen days—not that he was counting—and yet he felt an inexplicable connection with her, a desperate desire to protect her.

*Since I failed Emma so badly.*

The realization poured over him like the sheets of rain outside. Tears pricked his eyes. When his own wife needed him, he wasn't there to help. He hadn't protected her because he hadn't paid attention. He'd failed her in the worst way. Would the memories haunt him forever? A quick glance at their wedding photograph on the mantel and remorse stabbed his heart.

*Forgiven.*

The word reverberated in his chest with such force that his head jerked up and he expected to see someone in front of him. He wiped sweaty palms on his jeans and scanned the living area. Now who was skittish? His gaze rested on the wedding photograph once more.

*Forgiven.*

This time it was a whisper. Gentle. A caress that touched his very soul and wrapped him in something that felt like love.

"Lord?" His question hung heavy in the air. Of course, it was Him. Will had heard the message of forgiveness a hundred times since Emma's letter came to light. He'd begged forgiveness from God at first, the guilt threatening to consume him. Since then, he'd erected a fence around that part of his heart. A white picket fence, allowing him to function and work and pretend he was coping to the outside world.

*Forgiven.*

He clasped his hands and closed his watery eyes. "Thank you, Father." He no longer needed to punish himself for being a negligent husband to Emma. She had written it wasn't his fault, she'd granted him forgiveness a long time ago. As had God. "I'm forgiven. Truly forgiven." He could stop punishing himself. Live a joy-filled, God-centered life. He inhaled the sweetest breath and let it fill his lungs.

It was time to move on. Be the best father he could be to Jack. Be the man Georgia needed him to be—so she could learn to trust again.

He exhaled and picked up the postcard from the table. He would need to lead with his head rather than his heart if he had any hope of keeping her safe.

And he would do everything in his power to try.

# Chapter Twenty-Eight

GEORGIA BLINKED BACK A BRIGHT SLIVER of sunshine and eased out of a solid night's sleep. The glorious morning was a far cry from the incessant storm of the previous evening. She pulled herself up to a sitting position in the guest bed and attempted to right the crick in her neck.

As promised, Harriet stayed up with her last night and they'd talked over salted caramel ice-cream. Georgia failed to mention the appearance of her mystery man at Will's place yet assured her sister that by the end of today, she would be going to the police.

However, it was something she read before turning out her light that caused Georgia to sleep like a baby in spite of her horrendous day. She'd craved comfort from her Bible and as she flicked through Psalms, she found the verses that stirred her heart back on her first Sunday at Saint Pete's. The words in Psalm 51 that spoke of how God doesn't demand perfection, but rather a broken and contrite heart. It reminded her how she'd always striven to please, to have a perfect life, to be in control. What she really needed was a "heart-shattered life ready for love" as one version put it.

She needed forgiveness and to forgive. Even though she'd tried these past months and hobbled along as if with a limp, she longed to run with the true freedom God promised. She needed her Heavenly Father to step in and take over. To give her the grace to forgive when she couldn't do it in her own strength. Especially to forgive Daniel. Vanessa. Herself.

She'd poured out her heart to God and, even with a grueling day before her as she shared details with Will and studied more evidence, she experienced a peace in her soul. A heaviness lifted. It would be an ongoing process and she wasn't fool enough to think she'd be "fine" now. The pain of betrayal would raise its ugly head time and again, but she was ready to move on. For everyone's sake.

Light filtered through the floral curtains and danced on the knotty planks of hardwood floor. With a hankering for the warmth of sun on her face, Georgia padded over to the leaded window and flung open the curtains. This room had the prettiest vista of the fields that separated Harriet's home from Bramble Cottage. She smiled at the view of cows easing into their day in laid-back village style, and she let out a sigh from deep within. *This*. This is what she had in mind when she envisioned staying in England. Not a stalker and danger and threats and fires.

She pushed open the window and took in gulps of country air. There was a nip to the freshness of the morning that reminded her she was alive and well and needed to get on with her day. Starting with Will.

She touched her lips. Another kiss last night. Since when had she become spontaneous? Will brought out the hope in her somehow, hope that there might be a promising future for her yet. If she could trust another man with her heart.

Her phone trilled on the nightstand and she guessed it was Will.

"Morning." His voice was lower first thing.

"Hi. How are you?"

He hesitated for a moment. "I'm fine, thanks. Did you sleep well?"

"I did, actually. No nightmares even."

"Good. That's great. Listen, my mother picked up Jack for his little getaway and it's rather quiet here. I was wondering if you still wanted to meet up?"

"Of course." She glanced down at her pajamas. "Does ten still work for you? I'll shower here but I need to pick up my car from the cottage. Plus, I'd like to make sure everything's in order over there."

"Do you think you should be at the cottage alone?" His voice oozed concern.

"I won't be alone. I'll get Leo to drop me there and he can wait while I check things out. He offered to help before he heads to a meeting."

"Good."

She heard the swoosh of sliding doors and imagined Will walking out onto his back patio, coffee mug in hand and sunshine on his face. She shuddered at the memory of last night's intruder. "Can we meet in the village somewhere?"

"For sure. Do you know where The Muddy Cup coffee shop is?"

"I can find it. See you there at ten?"

"Perfect. Take care."

She stared at the phone. He sounded different. A little distant. After a night to sleep on it, perhaps he had second thoughts about getting involved. She couldn't blame him.

A boulder wedged itself in her chest. Without knowing it, Will had given her so much already. He showed kindness and genuine care, not to mention how his kisses made her pulse race. Her cheeks heated at the thought.

*Slow down, girl. Protect your heart.* If he decided to go the platonic route, she would respect his decision. He had a son to consider. What did she have to offer him anyway? They could just be friends, right? She needed a friend to help her figure things out. With the plethora of complications in her life at the moment, the notion of a romantic relationship was far from realistic. The question haunted her over and over—could she trust another man after the way Daniel treated her?

*Friends. Maybe it's for the best. Take a step back.*

Yeah, she could at least *try* to talk herself into believing it.

At precisely ten o'clock, a tinkling bell announced Georgia's arrival as she walked into the quaint coffee shop. It was half-full, but Will had claimed a table for two in the corner, nice and secluded. He waved and she walked toward him, ignoring a couple of middle-aged women who watched the rendezvous with interest.

Will stood. "Morning. You look great." He gestured toward the padded chair opposite his. "Can I order you something?"

She tucked her hair behind her ears, glad she chose to wear a cute navy blouse with white skinny jeans. "Thanks. A cappuccino would be awesome."

Georgia settled in at the bistro table while Will went to the counter. The comforting smell of fresh coffee and the hiss of the cappuccino machine helped ease the tension she carried as a constant companion. Her shoulders relaxed as she observed her surroundings. Coffee shops were always her first port of call when traveling, and The Muddy Cup radiated charm.

Black and white mosaic tiles lined the floor adjacent to rough brick walls painted white. Shiny black bistro sets and red leather chairs huddled around low, pine coffee tables giving a cozy-yet-classy vibe. All the staff wore black shirts and smooth jazz played softly in the background. *I could bring a book here and kill a few hours.*

"Here we are. One cappuccino." Will set down a chunky red mug with a perfect heart swirled on top. Best not to read too much into that. "Can I tempt you with any of their pastries? They have phenomenal chocolate eclairs and custard slices."

"I'm good, but thanks. Harriet made me eat omelets this morning."

"Great. Was everything all right at Bramble Cottage?"

She sipped her coffee and nodded. "Thankfully, yes. I didn't stay there long."

"Did Leo hang around while you checked everything out? He didn't leave you on your own?"

"Of course. He even came in and waited in my foyer while I checked every room."

"Did he seem okay to you?"

She squinted. "Why do you ask?"

"I'm worried. He doesn't seem himself these days."

Poor Leo had been run off his feet with work and Lucy's extra care and now Georgia's drama, too. Yet she could tell by Harriet's demeanor that something was off. "He works too hard."

"True. He's away in London a lot. Must be tough on Harriet."

She squirmed. "I mentioned he might want to stay local for a while. I'm worried about their safety, for obvious reasons."

He expelled a ragged breath. "Talking of safety, I have something for you and you're not going to like it." He reached into his inside jacket pocket and pulled out a postcard.

Georgia's mouth gaped and she set her mug on the table with a thud. "Another one?"

"I'm sorry. I found it on the patio after you left last night."

"And you didn't think to call me?" She raised a brow.

"I considered it. I wanted to call the police more."

"You didn't——"

"No. I'm not going to put your family at risk. I texted Leo and asked him to be extra vigilant without giving any details. Which didn't go over well, for the record."

"Do you mind if I see the postcard now?" She couldn't help the sarcasm that slipped out as she lifted her palm.

He handed it over without a word. She felt his eyes on her as she studied the image.

A church graveyard? Her stomach dropped. The images from the roll of film… "Will, do you recognize where this is?"

He shook his head. "Seems pretty generic for England. Do you?"

"No. I don't think so. It could be in France, too." Her fingers trembled as she turned it over. *GRAVE.*

*Of course.* The coffee curdled in her stomach and a lightheadedness swept over her. Daniel's grave? Her grave? Her family's grave?

"Georgia? You've gone awfully pale." He was at her side in an instant. "In through your nose. Out through your mouth. I'll get you some water."

The whitewashed walls wobbled as Georgia tried to focus on the postcard she'd dropped onto the table's surface. Nausea rose from the pit of her stomach. She slowed her breathing although her heart was beating out of her chest. Will put a glass of cold water in one of her hands and she took a sip. Better. He held her hand, no—he was taking her pulse and murmuring something.

More water.

The walls stopped moving and Georgia sat upright.

"There you go. How do you feel now?" Will bent over her, his frown deep.

She turned around, horrified to discover everyone was observing her near-fainting episode.

"Better. Thanks." She took another drink of water and turned her back on the audience. "Sorry about that."

He returned to his chair. "Don't be sorry. Do you know what this postcard means?"

The film shots were too fresh in her memory. She grabbed her bag from the floor and the postcard from the table. "Can we go somewhere private? Maybe a walk? I need some fresh air."

"Great idea." Will stood and drained the last of his coffee. "Do you want me to get them to pour your drink in a cup to go?"

The notion of anything in her stomach made her want to heave. "No, thanks. I'm feeling a little queasy."

Half a dozen pairs of eyes stared them down as he took her elbow and guided her out of the coffee shop.

"We'll be the midweek village gossip, for sure." Will released his hold on her.

"That's the least of my problems." Georgia stuffed the latest postcard into her bag and slung it over one shoulder. "Which way should we go?" The tiny street was double parked with cars but only a handful of shoppers strolled along the pavement.

Will pointed ahead. "If we walk down here a couple of blocks, we'll be at the edge of the forest. There are a few pretty trails we can take if you're sure you don't need to sit."

They passed a small post office with a cherry-red mailbox outside and a carousel display of local postcards. *I never want to receive another postcard again.*

"Watch the puddle." Will ushered her to step to one side of the pavement to avoid the remnants of last night's rainfall. They carried on in silence while Georgia searched for the right words.

She slid the oversized sunglasses down from the top of her

head as the sun made its appearance from behind a smattering of white clouds. She glanced over at Will. His strong build and confident stride eased her angst. She had the urge to reach out and grip his hand in hers. Feel his strength. No, she'd let him make the first move.

"Here we are." His green eyes squinted in the bright light as he slowed his steps. "We can take either of these two paths if you're happy to keep walking."

"Let's head to the left. Keep it to a gentle stroll."

"Sure."

"I'm ready to tell you everything, Will. I'm hoping you can make sense of it all and understand what I'm up against."

"I'm ready to hear it. We can sit if you're still feeling wobbly." Will nodded his head toward an empty picnic table.

"No. Let's keep walking." *I can't look into your eyes when you hear this.*

Will shoved both hands in his pockets as he strolled next to Georgia. Wafts of her delicious floral perfume drifted on the fresh morning air and invaded his senses. Mustn't rush her. She'd share her story in her own time. If they had any hope of developing this budding relationship, honesty would be required from both parties. They'd both learned that the hard way.

"So, this is about Daniel." Her voice was steady. "You already know the police in Vancouver are investigating his death and no longer believe it was a random hit-and-run accident."

"Right."

She pursed her lips. "I'm positive the evidence I have at the cottage is going to expose his murderer."

Will's mouth went dry at the severity of her words. She was in possession of some serious documentation. "Have you figured out why someone would want to kill Daniel?"

Her steps slowed and she checked behind them even though no one was around. Only the rustle of leaves on the tallest trees and the crunch of their footfalls broke the silence.

"I'll know once we dig through the envelope some more." She pulled the strap of her leather bag higher on her shoulder. "He was into some illegal business. The details are still fuzzy, like a jigsaw puzzle with several gaping holes in the middle."

"What kind of illegal business?"

"As far as I can make out, he met some shady acquaintances whilst on an assignment in Europe and somehow got involved in a fraud and theft ring. Stolen works of art from high-end galleries. It seems there's a team with thieves, art restoration experts, the whole enchilada."

He let that settle for a moment. "Do you know what part Daniel played in all this?"

She let out a long sigh. "The only reason I know about any of it is because some bozo handed me a package for Daniel when we were in Paris last summer."

This was crazier than he imagined. They stopped speaking as a cyclist approached from in front and rode past them.

Once he was out of earshot, Georgia cleared her throat. "I knew it was wrong of me to look inside …" A breeze blew tendrils of long, dark hair about her face, obscuring her expression from Will's sightline. Even so, it was obvious she was struggling with these memories.

He reached out his hand and took hers. "I'm here for you. No judgment."

"There was a wad of documents and a pile of photographs."

She pushed her sunglasses up onto her head and he noticed a sheen of unshed tears in her eyes. Difficult as it was, he had to keep quiet and let the story unfold.

She described in detail the photograph she saw of Daniel holding a gun. "In hindsight, I know I should've dug deeper." She turned her head away. "Maybe I could've prevented it going any further. Even saved Daniel's life."

Will didn't rush to reply. Guilt was his specialty and he'd only just learned the power of forgiveness. "Seeing what you did can't have been easy to live with, but neither is this guilt you're carrying. You had no way of knowing what Daniel was getting himself into."

"I know. God's working on my heart when it comes to forgiving myself and Daniel." She looked back at him. "But now I believe there's more."

"Oh?"

"I think… I think Daniel murdered someone."

# Chapter Twenty-Nine

Will's foot froze in mid-stride. "Murdered someone?"

She nodded and he fell back into step beside her, feeling the sudden need to scan the vicinity as they continued into the forest.

"When I developed that roll of film yesterday, I saw some really graphic and disturbing proof I have to figure out…"

How was she handling all this by herself? "I wish I'd been there with you, at the very least."

"Maybe I needed to see it alone first. I've had twenty-four hours to try to wrap my head around it."

He looked down at their entwined fingers. "I want this all to be over. For you and your family to be perfectly safe."

"I want that, too."

He knit his brows together. "Up until last night's visitor at my place with the postcard, I would have suggested the evidence on the roll of film—the negatives they took—was what they wanted all along."

"Same. Seems they want more."

"The whole envelope?"

"Maybe. I feel sick to my stomach. They know I've seen the negatives. There were shots taken in a graveyard. Hence the image on the postcard. I don't know what they're waiting for."

*Lord, we need Your wisdom. I don't want to freak her out, but this is perilous.* "Could they want more paintings, if that's what they're into?"

"Who knows?" She shrugged. "I think blackmail is weaved in somehow. I don't know who else was murdered. There's this guy on the roll of film…" Her voice trailed off.

"You okay?"

She blinked back tears. "I'll show you back at the cottage. This could be so much bigger than we imagine if we're dealing with France and maybe other European countries, too. My mom's in Canada and my other sister's in Paris. Can you see why I can't mess it up by going to the police until I'm ready? I have to believe what Daniel said in his postcard was true. For my family's safety." Her eyes opened wide. "Maybe even yours."

*Jack.* "Right. I need to look out for my son. That much I know."

"Of course."

"I'll ask my parents to hold onto him until we're certain everything's safe. They'll be more than happy to help." He gave her hand a squeeze.

A crack sounded and Georgia gasped. "What was that?"

Will pulled back and checked both ways. They were alone on the path. "It came from behind the hedge toward those trees." He squinted. "Wait, it's a pony. See?"

Above the hedge, a chestnut mane fluttered in the breeze.

"I forgot horses roam wild here." She let out a long sigh. "That's a relief. She's a beauty." The pony moved on unfazed by their presence, the crunch of branches snapping underfoot. "Perhaps we should keep moving though."

Will claimed her hand again and they walked at a decent clip. "We're not far from the village here, but I don't blame you for being nervous. Given what you've told me so far, this group of individuals is incredibly dangerous."

"I'm sure there's more incriminating evidence in my safe. It could put them all away for a long time. I'm surprised they haven't tried harder to remove the whole thing from my darkroom, even though it's well and truly bolted in place."

"I'm not sure that would be possible without some serious demolition."

"Like a fire?"

"Good point." Will struggled to think kind thoughts about this ex-husband. "So, Daniel never hinted at any of this when you were together?"

"Never. After Paris, I gave him every chance to explain the envelope. I didn't push it. Half of me didn't want to know. Not long after that trip, he told me he wanted to separate. I tried to put it all behind me. Leave him to his own devices. I had no idea how serious it was."

The sound of their footsteps crunching on gravel filled the silence as Will processed what she shared. Murder? A possible crime ring? "I'm with you every step of the way, Georgia, but it's a lot to take in…"

She pulled her hand away and picked up the pace with a steady march. "I don't expect you to understand. It sounds ridiculous to my own ears. I should've acted on my suspicions as soon as I saw the photo and knew Daniel was up to something dark."

"Georgia…"

"But I went on with my life as if it didn't happen. I should've done something. I'm as much to blame as he is. *Was.*"

Will ground to a halt. "Georgia, stop."

She turned back, a trail of tears meandered down her flawless cheeks. "It feels like I've been living a great big lie this past year. You must hate me. *I* hate me."

He took her warm face in his hands and kissed her salty tears. "You're the one who's been wronged here. How could I possibly ever hate you?" Pulling her closer, he put a protective arm around her shoulder and they walked on. "I'm worried about you. These people are serious about getting hold of something you've got."

Georgia was quiet for a few beats while he enjoyed her being tucked into his side.

"I know nothing about the art world. It's out of my scope of work and I certainly have no criminal connections. Other than my ex-husband, I suppose."

"We'll figure this out. I need to keep you from danger. Whatever that looks like."

She leaned into his torso while they walked. "You're a good protector."

He'd failed before. "I'll try with everything I've got."

A red squirrel darted across the path in front of them.

"Thank you, Will."

He kissed the top of her head. "For what?"

"For taking a chance on me. For believing me. For making me want to trust you."

Pain for her suffering clawed at his heart. Trust had to be a big issue for someone whose life was turned upside down by betrayal. Yet, somehow, she came out stronger and it drew him like water to a bone-dry soul. She consumed his thoughts... what was happening? So much for leading with his head. He couldn't stop himself from drinking in all things Georgia.

The courage she displayed as a single woman in a foreign country being stalked by a dangerous man was nothing short of impressive. All he wanted to do was put his arms around her and never let go. To soothe her hurt. To protect her from all harm.

"I think we've done the loop." Her voice broke into his musings.

She was correct, they were almost back to where they'd started. "What now?" He checked his watch. "It's almost lunch time."

She looked up and he was held captive by her espresso colored eyes. "The envelope."

"Let's head for the cars. I'll follow you home."

"You realize if they're stalking me, they must know your vehicle by now, too. They've been to your house, Will. Seen it parked outside Bramble Cottage."

"Then we're in this together. All the more reason for me to help."

"That's sweet but I don't think it's necessary for you to literally follow me. I'll see you at the cottage." She moved from beneath his arm so they walked side-by-side at a respectable distance.

Had he overstepped with the protective thing? "Is something wrong?" He lowered his voice.

"Don't want to give the village gossipers too much ammunition, do we?" She winked.

"Right." *Calm down, man. Don't suffocate the poor woman.*

They walked in the sunshine along quiet cobbled streets back to The Muddy Cup. Will saw Georgia to her yellow hatchback and he hurried to the end of the road where his SUV was parked.

"Morning, Doctor. Do you have a minute?" One of the locals he recognized from church called to him from across the street. He cringed. Not the best time for a chat.

Before he had a chance to answer, the elderly woman hobbled toward him with a shopping bag in each hand. She almost pinned him to his vehicle.

"It's my Arthur. He's been on the waiting list for his hip for almost a year now. Could you put a word in, do you think?"

"I'm so sorry. Why don't you have him call me?" He dug a business card from his wallet and tucked it into her shopping bag. "We'll see what we can do."

"Thank you, Doctor. I know it's not your fault. My Arthur can't even help me with the shopping now…"

Will's heart sank as he watched the yellow car disappear at the end of the road. So much for keeping an eye on Georgia. He observed the frail old lady before him and relieved her of both shopping bags. "I'm in a bit of a hurry, but can I give you a lift?"

Her weathered face lit up. "Thank you, Doctor. Wait until my Arthur hears I've been in your lovely car."

After hearing all about Bingo night and Arthur's arthritis, Will deposited his passenger safe and sound at her terraced house along with her groceries, and then headed in the direction of Georgia's cottage. He checked his watch. She would be home by now.

The winding country roads could be tricky for drivers who didn't know the area, but Will appreciated the miles of verdant green fields on either side. Other than the occasional family of donkeys or a wayward cow, the roads were predictable. He opened the sunroof and sucked in the fresh air. He had a lot on his mind.

After living here several years and driving many nightshifts to the hospital, he knew the bends by heart. Of course, he never exceeded the speed limits, but that suited him. He'd seen too many horrific results of traffic accidents to take chances on the road. His heart dropped. *Emma.*

He tightened his grip on the wheel as a car sped toward him and almost ran into him. *Idiot.* Swerving, he managed to stay out of the ditch. *That's exactly why I keep to the speed limit.* Any faster, and he may not have been so fortunate. He glanced in his rearview mirror and saw the back of a silver sports car as it disappeared beyond a hedgerow.

His mouth went dry. A silver sports car.

Without another thought, his sensible foot floored the accelerator.

*Georgia.*

# Chapter Thirty

LORD, PLEASE LET GEORGIA BE SAFE.

Will prayed the words over and over as he focused all his concentration on the road ahead. Perhaps she was back at her cottage already and that sports car was merely a coincidence, someone out on a joyride. No, that had to be *the* silver sports car. His fingers tightened on the steering wheel. *Think of Jack.* He couldn't wrap his own vehicle around a lamppost in haste and leave his son an orphan.

There. A yellow car. Impossible to miss. It was angled toward the hedge on the wrong side of the road at the crest of the hill. He couldn't see what damage was done yet, but forced himself to breathe as he recited his usual mantra when faced with a medical emergency: *Cool. Calm. Collected.*

He screeched to a stop behind her rental car, flicked on his hazard lights, and jumped out to assess the situation.

"Georgia?" The car was wedged into the gulley, muddy from last night's rainstorm. Will's boots squelched as he approached the driver's door. "Georgia?" He kept the rising panic from his voice.

The car door cracked open. "I'm okay. At least, I think I am." Georgia's voice was wobbly and her face, white as chalk. She undid her seatbelt and leaned as if to get out of the car.

"Whoa, hold on a sec. How about you let me take a quick look to make sure you're not injured?" Will opened the door wide. The airbag failed to go off and the car seemed relatively undamaged on first inspection. The impact must have been minimal.

"Really, I'm a bit rattled, that's all." Georgia's huge eyes were glassy but her cheeks were starting to pink up.

"Take a moment to catch your breath and then we'll get you out. Do you hurt anywhere?" He held her face in his hands. There were no visible injuries. She was going to be all right. *Thank You, God. Thank You.*

She followed his instructions and blew out a steady stream of air. "I don't think so. I may have a bruise where the seatbelt caught me across my shoulder but it's nothing a long, hot bath can't fix."

The corners of his mouth curled up as his pulse returned to normal. "Tough cookie, aren't you?"

"I need to get out. Is the car damaged? I can't believe this happened again."

He took both her hands in his. "It was the same car, wasn't it?"

She bit her lip and nodded. "What are the chances?" She tried to smile through the quiver of her chin. "I need to find whatever's in that envelope, Will. Time is clearly of the essence."

"You can say that again." He ground his teeth as he glanced up and down the country road. Nothing. At least the silver car hadn't doubled back. "Let me help you out of here. It's pretty muddy, can I carry you?"

"I guess so."

She was easy to lift as she circled his neck with her arms. Will took several careful steps through the soggy mud, noting how her entire body trembled.

He set her on the gravel. "You steady enough on your feet?"

"I'm good, thanks."

There was not a soul in sight. Somehow… someone was watching her every move. A heaviness settled in the pit of Will's stomach as he surveyed the silent countryside.

"The car looks surprisingly good. I think it fared better than I did." A gentle breeze blew strands of hair across her face and she tucked it behind her ears. "Do you think I can get it out of the mud?"

Was she serious? "It's fairly wedged in there. I think it's best if you don't jump behind a wheel quite yet."

She pursed her lips. "Really?"

"Of course, I'm just a doctor…"

"Right. In that case, I should grab my bag from the passenger seat."

"While you do that, why don't I call for a tow truck? It could take some effort pulling it from the ditch. You can ride with me." He slid his phone from his pocket and peered at her with wide eyes. "Or do you want to report this now?"

She shook her head.

"I know you want to wait, but this is beyond crazy. We could drive to the station this minute and explain everything. Get a police escort back to the cottage to grab whatever it is you need." He ran a hand through his hair. "Georgia, you were run off the road. For the second time."

"I'll go later, but not yet." She clutched his arm. "Please. You know this is about more than my own safety. I have to think of my family. I trusted you with my story—now can you trust my intuition?"

He pulled her into his arms. "Then let's head to Bramble Cottage. Because I'm counting the minutes until this will all be over and everyone's out of danger."

"You and me, both."

He whispered into her hair. "When I saw a silver car—"

"I'm sorry. I know this is killing you. It's excruciating for me, too."

The hum of a vehicle driving up the hill caused them both to turn from their embrace. Will squinted at the car "Hey, is that Leo?"

"Please, don't tell him anything. We have to get to the paperwork as soon as possible. He only needs to know I veered off the road."

"Whatever you say." Strange that Leo would be here at this precise moment. He put a protective arm around Georgia's shaking shoulders and flagged him down.

Leo pulled to a stop behind Will's SUV and jogged toward them. "What happened? Are you guys all right?" He ran to Georgia and kissed both cheeks in his confident French manner.

Will played dumb and let Georgia explain how her car ended up in a ditch on the other side of the road.

"Can I give you a ride, Georgia?"

"Thanks, but I've got it." Will spoke up. "It would be great if you could get this rental picked up though. Maybe the mechanic in the village could take a quick look and make sure no damage was done."

It was hard to decipher Leo's reaction behind his shades. "Sure."

"Thank you so much." Georgia flashed a convincing smile. "I'll get my bag from the car."

"I can fetch that for you…" Leo stepped toward the yellow hatchback.

"No." Georgia's voice was forceful. "Thanks, but it's fine, I can get it."

Leo pulled out his phone as he strolled back to his own car.

Will put a hand on her arm. "Stay here and I'll grab your bag for you. No use in you getting muddy, too."

Georgia lifted her chin. "I'm not afraid of a little mud."

"Are you okay?" Will walked alongside her as she grabbed her bag from the floor of the passenger side of the rental.

"Yes." Her voice was a whisper. "I know I'm being paranoid, but I'm not letting this bag out of my sight for a minute."

Was she second guessing Leo, too? He raised his brows. Or maybe she was worried about her camera. She always carried it around with her and it appeared expensive to his untrained eye. "I get it. That camera is your work."

She slung it over her shoulder and scowled. "No, Will. It's not that. I have shots of the images from the roll of film on here and on my phone. I'm not taking any chances."

Georgia walked into Bramble Cottage and inhaled. The smoky smell had dissipated somewhat, but it still lingered. A reminder someone had been on her property. A shiver ran through her.

Will locked the door behind them. "Shivering could be your body reacting to the shock of your incident back there."

"I'm fine. Anxious to get this over with." She chewed on a thumbnail.

"Let me make tea? This could be a long afternoon."

"Why not? I'm actually getting hungry, but I don't think I should eat until after we go through the photographs."

"I can order something in. Give me the word as soon as you feel up for it. I'm like a camel when it comes to food. I can go considerable stretches between meals."

"How come?"

"Many long surgeries."

"Makes sense." She checked the time on her phone. "What time's your fumigation friend coming?"

"Four. We've got a while before he gets here." Will squeezed her arm as he passed by and headed to the kitchen. "Want me to do a quick scout of the cottage while the kettle's boiling? Put your mind at ease."

"Thanks."

"No problem." He checked the backdoor was locked and followed her up the staircase.

Georgia opened the door to the darkroom and switched on the overhead light.

"Come on in when you're ready. I'll get everything set up."

His footsteps sounded as he walked through the cottage room by room. It was comforting. Heartwarming. As was the clink of her china mugs and the way he whistled in the kitchen while he waited for the tea to steep. The tea he made perfectly for her. A dash of milk, a little sugar. *I could get used to this.*

She rubbed her hands down her cheeks. *Concentrate on the task at hand.* First, the laptop. She grabbed it from its hiding place, fired it up, and cleared the countertop so they could spread everything out.

"Tea?"

His warm voice and that charming English accent was a balm to her soul. "Thanks. You can set the mugs on the counter, if you like."

She could feel Will's eyes on her as she crouched down to unlock the safe. She messed up the combination and tried again. *Focus.* There. A loud click signaled the door could now be opened. She slid the padded envelope out with the enlarged prints on top and placed it on the counter.

"Is this everything?" Will's voice was calm.

"Almost." She emptied the ever-present camera from her bag. "Remember I snapped copies of the film images here." Next, she slipped the phone from her jeans' pocket and added it to the pile. "And here."

"Smart thinking."

"I decided it would be prudent to separate them from the rest of the evidence on the off chance someone was able to get into it. Never say never."

"I thought you said it was impossible?"

"It is, but I'm not taking any risks. Call me paranoid."

He held up both hands with palms facing her. "No. You're not paranoid. Not in the least. I would've done the same."

"Good. Everything's together. Let's get this over with as quickly as possible."

"What is it you want to show me exactly?" He waited for her to take the lead and open the envelope.

"I should explain that I haven't had the courage to study the photographs in the original pile yet. From what I've seen, they're mainly art galleries, paintings, that sort of thing. Some headshots, too."

Will rested his warm hand on hers. "I'll do whatever you need me to do."

"Thanks." *I can do this.* The papers and photos landed on the counter with a thud. "There's a lot here, but it's the images I developed yesterday that I need you to see first."

"You sit on the stool. I'm fine standing."

Georgia was about to argue when he held up a hand. "I've stood for all-night surgeries, trust me, I'm fine. Please, sit."

Perched on the stool, she bit the inside of her cheek, and slid the black-and-white prints in front of him. "Let's start with these. Take your time."

She peered over at the first one.

Will grunted. "Georgia. Is this…?"

"Daniel? Yes. That's the man I was married to."

The close-up of his handsome profile showed him aiming a gun, a grimace on his face.

"I know it's not especially shocking without seeing what was going on in the rest of that room. For me, it hurt my heart to see a gun in the hands of the man I thought I once knew and loved."

"Understandable."

"He'd always been anti-guns and this was more proof I didn't really know him anymore. It was another nail in the coffin of the death of our marriage."

Will nodded. He was taking in every detail of her ex. "I'm guessing it gets worse."

"The next one might look familiar to you."

It was an empty graveyard. Not dissimilar to the image on the postcard she received.

"Most graveyards are creepy. Could be England. Could be France or somewhere else in Europe."

"True. Keep going." She nibbled on a thumbnail and braced herself as she focused on the next print.

His wide eyes met hers. "And that's…"

"A dead body."

# Chapter Thirty-One

WILL'S MOUTH WENT DRY. HE WAS no stranger to blood and even death, but this? This was different… someone taking life, not saving it.

"I should have warned you." Georgia avoided his eyes and stared at her camera on the countertop. "I feel like this image has been seared onto my retinas since yesterday."

He cleared his throat and set down the stack of pictures. This was a wide-angle view of the scene from the first photo. Daniel with a gun in his hand and a dead body slumped over a desk, blood gushing from a bullet wound in his head. Reminiscent of the first postcard she received. "Do you know who the other man is? Or rather, was?"

Her hair fell about her shoulders as she shook her head. "No clue. I don't recognize him, from what I can see at least. You know, I can't help wondering about the photographer."

"What do you mean?"

"Obviously, he wanted proof of this murder for some reason. Maybe he's sadistic and gets his kicks from capturing death. I think it could've been taken by a pro."

"A professional photographer?"

She nodded. "Perfectly centered. Crystal clear. Sick as it sounds, it's a perfect camera shot, and I think whoever snapped this moment was in on the scheme. It's no random quick snap."

"Daniel wasn't expecting to be caught in action." He studied the image. Daniel held the gun as if frozen in place after firing it. The victim, a well-dressed middle-aged man in a dark suit must not have suspected he was about to meet his Maker. "Either this man knew and trusted Daniel, or he didn't notice him coming into the room. I don't see a door from this vantage point so I'm guessing the door was in full view of a person sitting at the desk."

She leaned over the picture and nodded. "Yes. That's logical. So, Daniel and the photographer entered under false pretenses, pulled out a gun and… killed this guy." She massaged her temples. "I don't understand."

"Want me to keep looking through the rest?"

"Yes. Please do. You may catch something I missed. I flicked through with blurred vision after seeing that one."

Poor girl. Who would want to see shots like this of a man she once loved and trusted? "I'm guessing Daniel didn't own a gun at home?"

"No. He wasn't a hunter and had no reason for a gun living in Vancouver." She let out a deflated sigh. "Although what do I know? Our marriage was one big lie in the end."

Will reached over and rubbed her back in a slow circular motion. With his other hand, he placed the images across the counter so they could see them all. There was a close-up of the deceased slumped on his mahogany oversized desk. As if the bullet went through his head.

"I wonder why there are so many photos of specific artwork." Georgia pointed to a cluster of them. "Could these be stolen?"

"Or forgeries."

"True. Although I don't get it. Daniel was never into art. He hated going to galleries and museums. I would have to drag him along to anything like that."

"Money and power can do strange things to a person." This was awkward. Talking about her ex-husband like he was some high-end criminal in the art underworld. Although it appeared he'd shot someone and now he was dead…

Georgia groaned, the corners of her mouth pulled down. "I can't believe how naive I was." She reached for her tea and took a sip.

"It's not your fault. Trust me, I know what it's like to look back and wonder how I missed the obvious. If our loved ones want to hide something from us badly enough, they'll find a way."

She squeezed his hand. At least she knew the truth about his regrets now.

He picked up a photo of three men with Daniel at a graveside. "Any of these other men familiar to you?"

Georgia took it from him and held it closer for inspection. "I'm ninety-nine percent sure that guy kneeling next to Daniel is our black beard dude from last night." A shudder slithered up her spine. "I wish he was standing and then I'd know for sure by his height, but from this angle I would say it's him."

"And the other two?"

"No idea. I'm still wondering who took the photographs and why. He might be the one in a position to blackmail."

"Do you have a magnifying glass? I'd like to be thorough in case our photographer got sloppy somewhere."

She opened a drawer and pulled one out. "Here, try this." She slid a switch along the side and it lit up with LED lights.

"Perfect."

Georgia straightened her back and took another swig of tea. "If you take the gory pics, I'll check through the papers."

Will's stomach turned as he absorbed the reality that a life had been brutally snuffed out in these images. The blood didn't bother him, but the danger did. Especially when it involved Georgia.

One photo caught his eye. The same four men, including Daniel, sat around a table in a cafe. Distinctly Parisian. He peered closer. The back of another young man's head happened to be caught in the shot. *No. It couldn't be.* He looked somewhat like Leo from this angle. There was no way to be sure with a generic black T-shirt and no face to compare, but there was something familiar about the way he leaned against the wall.

"Found anything?"

Will glanced at Georgia, her eyes wide with hope. Dare he even suggest her brother-in-law could be involved?

"Just wondering where this was taken." He set the photograph in front of her and watched for a reaction.

She shrugged one shoulder. "Definitely France. Maybe Paris. Could be any typical cafe you'd find there. I'm guessing it was when we stayed there last summer. Daniel's wearing the collared shirt I bought him for the trip." She dipped her head.

"Right." No mention of Leo. Georgia was a detail girl—alarm bells would've rung if she suspected for a moment Leo was in the frame.

They worked side-by-side in silence for several minutes as they perused the disturbing array of photographs. The room was heating up even with the blackout blind pulled tight and no sunlight allowed entrance. He tugged at his T-shirt collar.

"Sorry it's so hot in here." Georgia picked up the paperwork and fanned her face with it. "Most of this looks like legal jargon to me."

"Could be useful. I don't know what we're searching for but if we can find something concrete to take to the police…"

"You mean other than the photo of a man being shot?"

Will looked up. "We don't know why he was shot or who he was—we're guessing it has something to do with artwork, but it would be helpful to have specifics in writing. Anything promising on first blush?"

Georgia wound a strand of hair around her fingers. "Not really. According to Daniel's message, I need to read through the whole lot. I hope speed-reading counts."

"We'll get through it. Together." There was more to his words than the obvious, and she held his gaze with watery eyes.

"I know." She bit her bottom lip and traced her fingers along his arm. Warmth radiated up to his shoulder and he caught his breath. *How does she do that?*

"Will, if anything happens to me, you have to promise you'll do all you can to protect my family. Tell them the whole thing. I'm worried for Harriet, Sophie, my mom..."

"Hey, you're going to be fine. We're going to the police and you're going to be able to put this behind you and move on." He took both her hands in his. "We have God as our Protector, remember? I've learned the hard way that I can't rely on my own strength."

"Me, too."

"Do you trust Him, Georgia?"

She focused on their clasped hands. "I'm getting there. Trust isn't my forte, in case you haven't noticed."

*Lord, give me the right words here.*

"He's completely trustworthy, you know. One hundred percent. He promises never to leave us. Never to forsake us."

Several seconds passed until she nodded. "You're right. That's huge for me. I need to keep it front and center."

"We both do. We're works in progress."

Georgia mustered a smile.

"You know I'll do everything I can as a mere human to protect you..."

"Thanks. It puts my mind at ease a little to know Harriet and Lucy have Leo to protect them, too…"

Will grunted. It came out louder than he intended.

"What?" She squeezed his arm. "What's wrong?"

"Nothing."

"Will, please tell me. I'm done with being kept in the dark." Her frustration bled through her words. "I need to be able to trust you."

"You can. I promise."

She snatched the photo from the counter and scrutinized it. "Was it something in this one? You've been studying it for a while. What do you see?"

*Here goes nothing.* He pointed to the figure leaning against the wall of the cafe. "Humor me. Does he look familiar at all?"

"It's the back of some guy's head." She leaned in. "Same hair as Leo, I suppose. Please don't tell me you think he could be part of this."

"I'm being thorough, that's all. It's what you asked of me."

She tilted her head. "Leo's your good friend."

"And Daniel was your husband." As soon as the words left his mouth, he regretted the retort.

Georgia's mouth dropped open and silence hung between them like a ghost.

*Idiot. Why did I have to hit her where it hurt the most?* "I'm so sorry. That was uncalled for. I only meant we can't always really know a person—"

She stood, her cheeks flushed. "I'm well aware of that." Her eyes brimmed. "If being betrayed by my husband wasn't bad enough… now you're suggesting I can't trust my family…"

Will held up his palms. "I'm sorry. I shouldn't have said anything about Leo."

"I need to think." She ran her fingers through her hair. "And I need some space."

"Please, let me help you?"

She paced across the room to the door. "I have to figure out who I can trust, Will. Clearly, I'm not the best judge of character."

*What have I done?* "You can trust me, Georgia."

She folded her arms across her chest. "Please, go." The words came out as a broken whisper.

"Whoa, slow down there." His chest squeezed at the notion of her continuing on alone. He stepped toward her as if approaching a timorous deer. "*Your* life is in danger. There's no way on earth I'm going to desert you."

"You're not deserting me." She turned and headed toward the staircase. "I'm telling you to leave."

*What?* "Let's talk about this, shall we?" He followed her down the stairs.

"I'm sorry, but I don't have the luxury of time to sit and discuss my feelings and my poor judgement. There are murderers out there and I need to get them put away for a very long time. I can assure you my sister's husband is not one of them."

Exasperated, Will raised his voice a notch. "You're a *target*, Georgia, you know that, don't you? They have a guy here in town who knows exactly where you live. He's been in your house, for crying out loud. You have something they want and they aren't going to back down until they get it."

"That's a chance I'm willing to take. I care about you, Will, but you've shown me I'm not ready to let anyone else in yet." She stopped in the foyer and turned to him, tears in her chocolate-brown eyes. "If you want to help keep me safe, pray for me?"

He shook his head. "This is absurd. If you won't call the police for protection, I'm going to wait outside in my car. I have nowhere else to go. I hate to break this to you, Georgia, but I've fallen hard for you. When you're feeling up to it, come and get me and we can carry on here together." He was nothing if not patient. He could wait this out.

He picked up his jacket and closed the space between them. When she didn't step away, he ran the back of his fingers down her soft cheek and memorized every detail of her beautiful face.

"Please, be careful, Georgia." *I think I'm falling in love with you.*

# Chapter Thirty-Two

GEORGIA CLOSED THE DOOR BEHIND WILL and locked it. She leaned her forehead against the cool sheen of wood and let tears of frustration fall. *What have I done?* Was that the end before it had even begun? A sob rose in her throat at the thought of not having this man in her life. How had this happened in such a short period of time? She'd sworn off men and was supposed to be giving her heart chance to heal after Daniel's betrayal.

Her phone chirped from her jeans pocket and she checked the screen. A text from Will.

*"I'm not going anywhere. Ordering pizza—you've got to eat. I'll leave it on your doorstep. I'm in my car outside if you want company."*

Georgia wiped her wet cheeks with the back of her hand and pocketed the phone. Of course, he wasn't going to leave her alone. He was giving her the space she'd asked for. Did she overreact? The idea of Leo betraying her triggered the searing pain Daniel inflicted not too long ago. It was still fresh. Still burned.

She trudged back up the staircase and entered the darkroom alone. The subtle hint of Will's spicy aftershave hung in the stifling air. She glanced at the array of photographs littering her countertop, and picked up the one taken in the Paris coffee shop with the guy who looked somewhat similar to Leo. *It couldn't be him. Could it?*

She eased onto the stool. No way could she call Harriet or show her the photo. She'd be brokenhearted that Georgia would even consider he was involved. No, she had to keep all this private for now. Plough on until she was at the point where she could go to the authorities. It had to be tonight.

*I need to focus.* Noting it was almost two o'clock, she silenced her phone, set it next to the photographs, and buried her head in her hands. "God, I don't know what to do here. I'm scared for my family and for Will. How did I get into this mess and more to the point—how do I get out of it?"

For a moment she sat there, eyes closed, in the quiet. There was no audible voice yet a quickening in her chest gave her a sudden urge to move. Without a second thought, she rose to her feet, picked up her camera, and proceeded to photograph each page of the paperwork, just as she had done with the prints yesterday. If any of this was stolen or destroyed, she would still have evidence on her camera.

And heaven help anyone who tried to snatch her camera from her.

To be extra cautious, she doubled up and snapped everything with the camera on her phone, too. As she turned over each document and scrap of paper, she scanned it for any glaring red flags. A tough assignment when she wasn't sure what she was looking for.

*I want to get this over with. Please let there be something I can take straight to the police to explain all this...*

With only a few more to snap, she checked how much power was left in her laptop. Once she finished photographing, she would download the images as another safeguard. It was low, so she grabbed the charger, plugged it in, and resumed her work.

Bank documents recording extraordinary amounts of money. Names of museums and art galleries and pieces of art she didn't recognize but guessed were precious. Funds changing hands. Daniel's handwriting with directions and street names in England, Paris, and even Vancouver.

She struggled to hold her hands steady as she depressed the shutter over each one and did her best version of speed-reading. It must all be important to someone who knew about art and crime, but nothing specific jumped out to her—until the very last sheet of paper. Daniel's handwriting again.

Her eyes widened when she saw it was actually written to her. Why was it buried at the bottom? She snapped a photograph and picked it up with unsteady fingers. It was dated September of last year. Must have been after the Paris trip when he came to England for "business".

*"Dear Georgia,*

*If you're reading this, I guess nothing has gone as I planned. Perhaps I'm not even around anymore. First of all, I want to say how desperately sorry I am. You were never supposed to get caught up in this. I hoped you would focus on building a new life for yourself at home in Canada and let the cottage go."*

Georgia ground her teeth. The nerve. He knew how much this cottage meant to her—it was part of her family history.

*"If this envelope hasn't been tampered with, you'll see some pretty horrific images. I'm not going to try to explain—suffice to say, I got involved in the surprisingly dark underbelly of the world of art in Europe, with no clue how deep it would pull me in.*

*Remember the assignment I had in Germany two years ago? It's where I met Vanessa, and that's where I got greedy. She had contacts and they needed fresh blood to take over their operations. We were the new team and I soon realized it was big. Dangerous. You were so engrossed in your quest to be a mother—*

*our paths were heading in very separate trajectories even before I fell for Vanessa."*

The words blurred as tears filled Georgia's eyes and she pressed one hand to her heart. No wonder Daniel was less than supportive in her "quest to be a mother." She presumed they were building a family together when he was off to the next thing. The next woman. Was Vanessa a photographer? *The* photographer? Georgia always presumed she was a journalist, same as Daniel. She blinked and continued reading.

*"I don't expect you to understand or forgive me but I do need to give you details on where one particular piece of art is stashed away. It's my nest egg. My security. It was worth one man's life, maybe more by now. If they've done away with me then I can only imagine—and I hate to even put it in writing—Vanessa has double-crossed me."*

Was Georgia supposed to feel sorry for him? Not a chance…

*"She will come for the painting eventually. The men in the photographs are powerful and there's no way to know if she's with them or against them. Be very careful. You need to get out of the cottage. Now. Take everything from the safe. Take the piece of art. Go to the authorities. They will return it to the rightful owner.*

*It wasn't until after we did away with the original team leader, a prominent banker in Paris, that I discovered the story behind the art. You know I'm a sucker for story. This piece, "The Dandelion Dance" needs to be returned. A family in France is mourning not only the death of their sick child but also the loss of this piece of art, their last healthy memory of her, captured by a master artist before he died of old age. It's priceless in the art world—but to them, it's sentimental more than monetary. They need to have it hanging in their home again. They need to see their little girl. I've taped the details to the back of the painting."*

She gasped. "This is crazy. Where did you put it, Daniel?"

*"It's in the master bedroom of Bramble Cottage. I slipped the painting in behind our poppy photo above the bed. It was always my favorite shot."*

Her eyes darted to their bedroom. *Her* bedroom. Every hair stood on end. She'd been sleeping beneath some priceless masterpiece? She had to get out now. With the art. Will was waiting outside, and they could take everything straight to the police. She stood as she read the final paragraph.

*"And there are more paintings. Safely stashed in a warehouse at the coast. The key is in your special tree. So, there you have it—my confession. I know your heart and I'm sure you'll do the right thing. When you read the story behind "The Dandelion Dance" painting, you'll know why even in my darkest moments, I couldn't bring myself to send a thing of beauty into the ugliness of the black market. I hope it's not too late.*

*You're a special woman, Georgia. I hope you'll find love again with someone smarter than me who can see you for who you really are. Brave and beautiful.*

*Love,*
*Daniel."*

It took several seconds for the words to sink in. Daniel was dead. She was in danger. Some family needed their precious piece of history restored to them. Something about a key in her special tree?

She could be free of all this in a matter of hours. Minutes even, if the police believed her and took everything seriously.

*Please, God, let this all work out and make these people pay for what they've done.*

Her hands shook as she vacillated with what to do first. *Think.*

The pile of papers and the photographs, everything she needed to show as evidence, she stuffed back into the envelope—except the last page. For some reason, she needed to keep that letter close. She took a shot of it, but it was so… personal. She folded it up and stuffed it into the back pocket of her jeans.

As much as she itched to see the art behind her framed photograph, it made sense to go and explain everything to Will first. Apologize for sending him away. He was only trying to protect her, wasn't he? They could discuss Leo once they'd talked to the police. *This is bigger than my trust issues. The end is in sight.* Thank goodness Will hadn't actually left her alone. He could help maneuver the huge frame down the narrow staircase—it had to be four feet tall and three feet wide.

With no time to download onto her laptop, she stuffed her camera and the full envelope into her leather bag and slipped it over her shoulder. The sound of footsteps on the stairs made her heart race. Will. She would show him the letter, they could take everything to the police, and maybe, just maybe, there would be a way forward for them after all, as long as she hadn't blown it with her temper. The last words in Daniel's letter rang in her head. *"I truly hope you'll find love again…"*

She stepped out to the hallway to greet him. Wait. How did he get back inside the cottage?

Black shaggy hair. Black beard. Eyes of pure evil. *Lord, please, no…*

# Chapter Thirty-Three

GEORGIA FROZE AND HER BAG SLID to the wooden floor, the contents scattering between her and the man. He eyed the bulging envelope and bent to retrieve it. Adrenaline kicked in and Georgia thrust her knee into his face. A crack. He barely flinched. Her body shuddered as a trickle of blood oozed from his bulbous nose. He rose to full height and tucked the envelope inside his jacket.

*Run.*

Run where? He blocked the cramped hallway and there was nowhere to go. A whimper escaped her lips as she tried to ram her way past him alongside the wall. It was hopeless. Without a word, he produced a dark hood from his pocket and covered her head before she could move. In the next breath, he threw her over one strong shoulder. Her muffled screams were rendered useless as the behemoth trundled down the stairs, carrying her like a sack of potatoes.

Her teeth rattled with the jolt of each step, and the stench of sweat and something acidic on the fabric of the hood made her gag. She punched and kicked but nothing slowed his pace as she sensed him leave the cottage through the back door in the kitchen.

Will. Where was Will? Surely, he would see them leave? She tried to calculate where he was taking her. Through the backyard? There was a gate tucked among the hedgerows at the rear. It was almost hidden until the fire ravaged the surrounding fruit trees. She recognized the sound of the latch and the creak of old hinges as they passed through it. Her heart sank.

Will would be none the wiser as he kept vigil at the front of Bramble Cottage.

*Perfect.* Will managed to pull in a favor from the local pizza place for an extra speedy delivery. He was a regular customer, partial to indulging in take-out after a long hospital shift. Not only was his stomach rumbling at the thought of the comfort food, but this would also be an ideal excuse to check on Georgia. She hadn't replied to his earlier text, but at least he knew she was safe.

The delivery boy pulled up outside Bramble Cottage and Will rewarded him with a generous tip. Who could resist Antonio's crumbled beef and feta cheese pizza with Alfredo sauce?

The large box was warm, and the tantalizing aroma of cheeses and herbs filled his senses as he took long strides toward the front door.

*Lord, please soften her heart and give me wisdom so we can talk everything through. We both need You so desperately...*

He used the brass door knocker to announce his presence and took a step back. The lack of a modern doorbell made the cottage all the more charming. When she failed to answer, his shoulders dropped. *What if I really have blown it with that comment about her ex?* So much for the kind, compassionate doctor. What was he thinking? She was still reeling from the devastation of being betrayed by Daniel. To even suggest a family member might be involved… Yes, they needed to talk. He sniffed the enticing savory flavors permeating the box in his hands. They also needed to eat.

Will knocked louder this time. Three sharp raps. *That should do it.* Even locked away in her darkroom, she couldn't fail to notice his insistence.

Still nothing. Will chewed his lip. She may need more time. He could wait a while longer in his car with the pizza. Give her space.

*She needs you.*

That still small voice. Will didn't move a muscle in case there was more. He didn't want to miss anything. After several seconds of silence, he balanced the pizza box with one hand and dug in a pocket for his phone. Dread settled in his chest.

Will tapped her number on speed dial and glared at the screen. "Come on." It went through and started ringing. He pressed his ear to the front door in hope of hearing the ringtone from inside. Nothing. Finally, it went to her voicemail. She could be giving him the deep freeze, but somehow, that didn't seem Georgia's style. He needed to check on her.

The smell of pizza now soured his stomach, so he set it on the cobbled path and turned over all the large stones near the front door. He knew Harriet always kept a spare key under a clay pot by the entrance of her own home, so there was a chance she did the same here. For Georgia. Although after the break-ins… surely, they were being more cautious.

They were indeed. No keys in sight. He banged on the wooden door again, this time not holding back. The lack of movement from inside caused his gut to clench. Something was off. He jogged around the cottage to the backdoor. He'd checked that it was locked earlier but it was worth a try.

The door hung wide open. Will's jaw dropped. One thing he knew—this wasn't Georgia's doing. She was upstairs intent on finding answers to the mystery. An intruder could be in the cottage even now and there was a good possibility Will could walk straight into the fray—but how could he not?

"Georgia?" He shouted as he rushed into the kitchen. "Are

you here?" Nothing looked out of place downstairs as he surveyed the rooms and took the staircase three steps at a time. "Georgia?"

He reached the hallway. The doors were open. A glance into the master showed nothing out of place. When he turned to check the darkroom, his heart hammered in his chest. Georgia's leather bag was on the floor, the contents sprawled across the wide wooden planks. Including her camera. She'd been taken.

"No." He poked his head into the spare bedroom, the bathroom, and finally the darkroom before running full pelt back down the staircase and out through the kitchen door. Where was she? At the end of the garden, a small iron gate swung on its hinges. How had he never noticed that before? He hurried through and then stopped. A narrow hedge-lined alley separated this row of cottages from those behind. It was deserted. They'd gone.

He sprinted back to the cottage and headed straight upstairs, where he fell to his knees beside the bag and took quick inventory. Her camera, phone, lipstick, wallet, passport—at least they didn't have plans to take her far. As soon as the thought took root, it was chased by the possibility that they may have plans to take her only as far as necessary. She could have seen too much.

"Oh, Lord." He shook his head in an attempt to think clearly. Her phone had been silenced, and he saw his number along with Sophie's as recent calls. What to do? Go straight to the police? Everything in him screamed to get help. This was an emergency of epic proportion. He couldn't get her imploring eyes out of his mind when she'd begged him to leave the police out of it for her family's sake. Until they had all the evidence and the authorities could act upon it. *The evidence.*

He jumped up and hurried into the darkroom. The safe was open and empty. Everything was gone except her laptop. The photographs, the paperwork, even the envelope. He ran a hand through his hair and collapsed onto the stool.

They had her. With the evidence. All that was left behind were her phone and camera. He eyed the camera through the doorway, still on the floor in the hallway. Perhaps…

He picked it up from the floor and set it on the countertop. Georgia the photographer. She photographed everything important to her. She'd mentioned snapping shots of the images from the roll of film yesterday. Maybe she took some of the paperwork before she was snatched.

With the strewn bag in the hallway, it appeared she was on her way out when she'd been intercepted. He picked up the camera, thankful it was her digital. It was a lot fancier than any camera he'd ever used, but he switched it on and found the viewing button. Nothing. He pressed every button he could find. It was dead. What now?

Her phone vibrated with another call from Sophie. He went to answer, then stopped. What if the photos were on her phone, too? Yes. He scrolled through the images. It appeared she'd documented every page as well as every photograph from the envelope. Even if her captors had the physical envelope as proof in their hands, they'd never know she had copies. Unless they made her talk. A chill of terror climbed each bone in his spine as he imagined what they might do to get the truth from her. They'd killed her ex-husband. Unless they needed her alive for some reason.

"God, help me know what to do. Georgia's life is on the line." There were two choices—call the police now and attempt to explain everything, or skim through the images and figure out where she might be. Then he could call them en route and let them take over. Which would be quicker?

*She needs you.*

He blew out the breath he'd been holding and wiped his hands down his face. Drawing on his training and experience of staying composed under pressure, he focused on the life-and-death task at hand and studied each document image on the phone in search of something, anything that might offer a clue as to where Georgia might be at this moment.

*Keep her safe, God.*

*Be her Protector.*

*Let her know You're with her right now.*

# Chapter Thirty-Four

*"GOD, HELP ME. PLEASE."* GEORGIA FOCUSED on her breathing, her eyes shut tight against the reality of her current predicament. She was in the trunk of a car and the dank, carpeted insides of her tomb were closing in. Fast. *God, help me.* She fought rising nausea as the stale air filled her senses. *God, help me.* Gulping oxygen and choking back sobs, panic rose from the pit of her stomach. *Please…*

She lay in a fetal position, hood still in place, with wrists bound by zip straps behind her back, making it almost impossible to move in the cramped space. From what she could feel, the trunk was empty. Other than her body.

Where were they taking her? When she'd been bound and bundled into the trunk by Black Beard, she heard two additional voices, one male and the other female. It was three against one. Perhaps she could appeal to her fellow female. Although what kind of woman would involve herself in something like this? Vanessa. It had to be. Her chest tightened and she gasped the dwindling stuffy air. How much oxygen did she have left in this trunk?

One of her captors drove in a different vehicle and she was certain it was the ominous silver sports car. She was no car buff but it had that same roar. Obnoxious. Fast. Now as she heard him rev the engine behind this sturdier vehicle, terror set in. She swallowed saliva and screamed again. It seemed useless as they were driving, but she refused to accept defeat, even with the odds stacked against her. For some unknown reason, they still needed her alive, that much was certain.

Her throat was raw and she craved water. Damp carpet was all she could smell through the fabric of the hood, and a headache worked its way up her neck and pounded with every bump they encountered. The straps around her wrists dug into the tender parts of her skin as she wriggled. It was useless. She knew there was such a thing as a release mechanism inside a trunk but without being able to see and with her hands behind her, what could she do? Her legs were free but what good was that when she was trapped inside the—

Her head rammed into one side of the trunk's interior as the car swerved a sharp left and then continued over rougher terrain. They couldn't have been traveling for more than ten minutes but it felt like an eternity. The sports car was still behind them, its driver most likely cursing the uneven ground. Pothole after pothole…

They pulled to a sudden stop.

Georgia waited for their next move, every nerve screaming.

Her hearing was on high alert as all three captors got out of their vehicles and slammed doors before trudging on gravel to meet up outside the trunk.

*God, if this is my time, please be with my loved ones I leave behind. My dear sisters and my mom. Help Will. Don't let him blame himself for this…*

Their muffled voices revealed snippets of words as she strained to hear her fate. Something about the cottage and fire.

*NO. Please don't let them burn down Bramble Cottage.* Her family's heritage, their memories, not to mention the valuable painting which still hung in the master bedroom. Will—was he still keeping watch outside like a devoted soldier? He couldn't get caught in the crosshairs of this. He had his sweet boy to raise.

The door to the trunk popped open and a gust of fresh air rushed inside. Georgia drew in ragged breaths, relief pumping through her veins. Until she considered what could be next.

"Get her out, Gabriel." A woman's voice.

Georgia recoiled and then thrashed as she was manhandled out of the trunk and pulled to her feet. Her head swam for several seconds as pinpricks of light shone through the fabric of her hood. It offered a shard of hope. Light. God. He was here with her.

"Nolan, take that ridiculous thing off her head."

She gasped as it was snatched from her, yanking her hair at the roots. Her eyes squinted as they adjusted to daylight. Should she look at them? Wouldn't they kill her if she could identify them? *I guess they don't plan to let me live.* Her ears thrummed as blood rushed to her head. *Is this really the end, Lord?*

She swallowed down bile and squinted from the familiar bearded face she'd already seen too often, Gabriel apparently, to another male. The silver sports car driver from the tearoom. Brown leather jacket. Shades. A disgusting leer on his face. Nolan.

Next, she turned to the woman. Her mouth went dry.

"Vanessa." Georgia's eyes narrowed. They'd only met in-person once before. She clenched her teeth and bit back the foul flurry of words she may have once spewed. Not now. Even in this moment, she felt a trickle of God's forgiveness flow through her. *Give me strength, Lord.*

The attractive brunette raised a brow. "Unfortunate circumstances to meet again."

Georgia stared her in the eye without blinking. "Why are you doing this?"

Vanessa put one hand on a narrow hip and smiled with

scarlet lips. "Daniel always said you were too trusting. So naive. You still don't have a clue, darling, do you?"

Georgia attempted to keep her voice even in spite of her trembling body. "So, Daniel's suspicions were right. You double-crossed him. Did you kill him, too?"

She held up one perfectly manicured finger. "I'd never actually murder anyone. I get others to do my dirty work. Daniel was a sweetheart and helped me out with that when the need arose." She shrugged. "I merely document everything. For my own protection."

The photographer. "Why film?"

"I'm an old-fashioned girl at heart." She batted her eyelashes. "I didn't want those spectacular shots getting into the hands of just anyone."

"Yet they found their way into my hands."

"Unfortunate for you, I'd say."

Georgia lifted her chin. "Or unfortunate for you. Daniel knew full well I could develop the film. How did you brainwash him to shoot someone?"

"It wasn't difficult. I used my womanly wiles and the promise of power. Plus, a boatload of cash."

Both men snickered at this. They appeared to be equally as enamored with Vanessa. In fact, Gabriel seemed to melt in her presence, giving off puppy dog vibes rather than his usual Pit Bull persona.

Georgia gritted her teeth. She would not show them how petrified she was. "What are you going to do with me?" She scanned the secluded area. Trees and more trees. They were at the edge of a familiar patch of the forest. "Why are we here?"

"So many questions." Vanessa's nasal voice grated on Georgia's every nerve. "Obviously, you have something we want.

Don't try to feign innocence. Daniel told me he put everything in the blasted safe in that twee pink cottage of yours."

Georgia clenched her bound fists. "The documents and the prints are in that envelope." She jutted her head toward Gabriel. "Take them and go. I don't know what you want from me."

The man called Nolan stepped up until he stood inches from her. "You don't recognize where we are, love? This delightful little clearing isn't ringing any bells for you from yesteryear?"

She broke away from his steel-gray eyes and turned in a circle. They were parked off the beaten track and she could hear the gentle trickle of a brook above the thudding of her heart. Yes, she knew precisely where she was.

"Come on, we know there's a key here somewhere." Vanessa elbowed Nolan to one side and was in Georgia's face.

*The key is in your tree.* Daniel's letter to her was jumbled in her mind. He meant the secret tree from her childhood. It had to be. She'd shown him once, but that was maybe ten years ago. How did these thugs know about it?

"I don't know what you mean."

Her feigned innocence was rewarded with a slap across the face from Vanessa. Her ears rang and her skin smarted as she licked her lips and tasted blood.

"Listen, we don't have time for this." Vanessa raised her voice. "Your ex was my lover, remember? We shared everything. I mean *everything.*" She curled her lip. "Including your insecurities with fire and the smell of burning and your idyllic childhood holidays in the forest. He told me about your silly secret tree where you hid treasures with your sisters. Pathetic."

Georgia closed her eyes. Had Daniel mocked her entire life when he was with this awful woman? *How could he?* Rage grew in her belly and heat rose up her neck. *Then he got what he deserved, after all.* She squirmed as that thought was followed by regret. *Sorry, Lord. I'm struggling here.*

"And I know it's in this vicinity. I discovered a crude map in his belongings. I also know he stashed the most valuable piece of art separately."

*Interesting.* "But you don't know where exactly?" Georgia smirked with a hint of smugness. "Daniel didn't quite share everything with you then."

A vein pulsed in Vanessa's forehead. "That's my nest egg and you *will* lead us to it."

Vanessa well and truly double-crossed Daniel. Or maybe he'd double-crossed her. Regardless, they were both greedy and now Georgia held the key. Literally.

"So, yes, we need you." Nolan forced his way between the women. He kissed Georgia's cheek and she shuddered. "Such a waste of a beautiful woman." Sickly, strong aftershave filled the air between them as his eyes travelled the length of her, and when she followed his gaze, she realized one of her blouse buttons had popped off during the struggle. There was not a thing she could do about it with her hands behind her back.

Gabriel laughed. It was the first time he'd made a sound. It was deep and menacing. Georgia pictured an ogre from her childhood storybooks. *I have to stall them.* If they found the key and then the painting in her master bedroom, she would be superfluous.

Will. Would he think to check on her or give her the alone-time she requested? Even if he got into the cottage through the backdoor, would her strewn bag on the floor and the empty darkroom give him any clues? He might find her camera or phone and check the recent photos. It was a stretch, but he was smart. Or he may go straight to the police. At this point, at least her family was safe.

*Please, Lord, let him find the photograph of the letter… and help him to figure this out?*

In the meantime, she needed a plan. Fast. In order to save her own life. Not to mention Will's if he happened to still be at the cottage when they returned for the painting or to torch the place.

She eyed a grassy patch to her left, and with a convincing sigh, collapsed into a heap on the ground.

"What's wrong with her? Did she faint?"

*Yes, I believe that's exactly what I did.*

# Chapter Thirty-Five

WILL WIPED A BEAD OF SWEAT from the back of his neck. This was more stressful than any all-night surgery he'd pulled. Every minute counted. He'd scanned through a series of printouts with maps and addresses until he came across a handwritten letter. It had to be something useful. He swiped to the end of the letter and saw it was from Daniel. Gritting his teeth, he went back to the beginning and read every word.

He reread it. A key in her tree? What on earth did that mean?

And the framed photograph in her bedroom was the one of poppies he'd noticed. There was a masterpiece hidden behind it?

He jumped from the stool and strode to Georgia's bedroom. Exercising as much care as possible, he lowered the frame from the wall and rested it on her bed, face down. Sure enough, it was obvious something had been tampered with and the backing was re-taped. There was no time to check it out.

He had to find Georgia.

Back to the key in the tree. What tree? He peered through the bedroom window and looked out into the backyard. The charred remains of a plum tree and an oak flanked the space along with a variety of shrubs. Why would her captors take her if the key was in her own backyard? It didn't make sense.

He paced back to the darkroom. Georgia's phone lit up with a call. It was Sophie. He answered in the hopes she might be able to shed some light.

"Sophie?"

"Who is this?"

"Sorry, it's Will. A friend of Georgia's."

"Of course." He heard the smile.

"Listen, I know this is going to freak you out, but I have an emergency."

"Georgia? Is she okay?"

He blinked. "I hope so. She's been… taken."

"Taken? Like kidnapped?"

Will tried to explain as swiftly as possible with his calm doctor voice but the facts were horrific no matter how composed he sounded.

"I'm hoping you can help."

"Of course. Tell me what I can do."

"Does Georgia have a tree that's special to her?"

"A tree?" Sophie gave a soft gasp. "I wonder… we had this special tree we used to play at in the New Forest when we visited our grandparents."

"Would it be a good place to hide a key?"

"Yes. Yes, we hid our stuff there all the time as kids. That has to be it. Harriet could show you…"

He needed details. Now. "There's no time to involve Harriet." Not to mention he was unsure about Leo. "How can I find this tree?"

"I'll figure it out and send coordinates to this cell phone number. If you can head in the general direction of Oak Grove… do you know it?"

"Yes. Yes, I know it." He threw the camera into the safe, locked it, and hurried to the master bedroom. "I can be there in ten minutes. Maybe sooner." He wedged the phone between his ear and shoulder, and gingerly lifted the framed artwork.

"Then go, Will. Keep me posted."

"On my way."

"Hurry. Help her. I'll be praying."

"Thanks." *I need it.*

Georgia gave the performance of her life as she regained consciousness after "fainting". With bound hands, her left shoulder took the brunt of the fall and would be badly bruised, but the faint only bought her a couple of minutes. Vanessa was not a compassionate woman.

"Get her up on her feet, will you?" The men grabbed an arm each and pulled Georgia to a standing position. "We need that tree. Now."

"I'm not moving until you untie my wrists."

"You don't give the orders." Vanessa got right in her face.

"You need me."

"We're not going to untie you, lady." Gabriel spoke with a French accent. Interesting.

"Then tie my wrists in front. My shoulders feel like their dislocating."

Vanessa whipped her head toward him. "Do it, Gabriel. Quickly. I can't have her whining."

He dug his free hand into his coat pocket and brandished a knife. He flicked it open with a flourish and worked on the straps. It was then that Georgia remembered she had Daniel's letter tucked in the back pocket of her white jeans. *Oh, please let me have pushed it in deep enough to not show.* If they found the letter, they would know where the masterpiece was located in the cottage.

Gabriel grunted and her wrists came free. She rolled her shoulders and then gasped as he pulled her hands together in front of her and re-strapped them in one smooth move. He'd done this before. At least he hadn't seen the letter.

"Now let's move, princess." Vanessa flicked her long hair

behind her and surveyed the area. "I suggest you start remembering the location of your tree. Before I lose my patience."

"I haven't been here in forever…"

"Gabriel, hurry her up, will you?"

He touched the tip of the blade against Georgia's neck. A tiny trickle of liquid escaped down to her collarbone. She swallowed. He wasn't playing games.

She tried not to move but every part of her trembled. "You'll have to take that away if you want me to walk." Her voice was barely a whisper.

"Fine." Gabriel positioned the knife to one side where she could see it, but at least she wouldn't be cut with every footstep. "*Allez.* Go."

Georgia was flanked by the men and Vanessa followed as they marched away from the clearing into a more densely wooded space. With every footfall, wisps of memories blew through her mind like a gentle breeze. Foraging for treasure with her little sisters and stashing it in the hollow. Her grandparents keeping watch from a nearby picnic blanket. Her daddy playing hide-and-seek before he was lost too soon in the dreadful fire.

She pushed down the ache that rose in her chest.

Years later, as newlyweds, she brought Daniel here and opened her heart to him. Shared deep secrets and sweet nostalgia.

And then he betrayed her.

Georgia's blood boiled at the thought of Daniel and Vanessa together as they planned to tarnish her childhood memories with their illegal activities. This forest had always been magical to her and now she was being held hostage. The wetness of her bloody neck made her weak at the knees.

Would she breathe her last right here?

Possibly.

Poetic in some ways, but she wasn't ready to give in yet. The next chapter of her life beckoned.

There, up ahead she spotted the tree. An ancient oak. It was bigger than all the others surrounding it. Perfect in its balance of full branches still laden with leaves. The late afternoon sun shone through the canopy giving the woodlands a chartreuse hue—yellowish, almost enchanted.

"It's pretty."

Even Vanessa was taken with this perfect place. Georgia slowed her steps as she neared the oak. They might take the key, cut their losses, and forgo the painting at the cottage. That would mean killing her here.

*God, please send help. Will's smart. Show him what to do.*

"Which tree?" Vanessa twirled in the carpet of fallen leaves. "Let me guess." She walked to the correct one. There was no denying it was the most magnificent of all. "Where do I need to look? Where would Daniel have hidden the key?"

Gabriel shoved Georgia over to Vanessa and the women circled the trunk.

"Hurry. We still have to collect my painting after this."

Georgia flexed her sore wrists. "And only I know where it's hidden."

"And you *will* take us to it."

Georgia raised a brow. "So you can kill me afterwards?"

Vanessa ran a hand down the gnarly bark of the tree. "I've no desire to kill anyone else. All I've ever wanted is this stash of art. To start fresh. Bury my wretched past. Try again." She brushed her hands together. "You'll be free to go after this is over."

A ripple of hope took Georgia by surprise. "How do I know you're telling the truth?"

"Because if you ever so much as think of reporting any of it, your family will be held responsible." She glared with eyes so cold, Georgia shivered. "Trust me, you don't want that on your conscience."

So, they had no intention of leaving her dead body here in the forest. That was encouraging. She would take her sweet time with the tree. There were various hollows and they would check each and every one.

"I haven't been here in years. It would be easier if my fingers were free…"

"Shut up." Vanessa folded her arms across her chest. "Tell my men exactly where they need to get their fingernails dirty." She inspected one of her own. "I'm not grubbing around in the filth."

Georgia bit back a retort. She remembered a few smaller tree trunk cubbies they used for storing goods and nodded her head to indicate the placements. "No, left a bit. There. Try that."

She had both men delving into cavernous spaces, some filled with bugs, the rest empty.

Nolan was not impressed. He squeezed her arm with his filthy fingers leaving dirt smudges on her flesh and bruises beneath. "Come on, quit playing us like a fiddle, lady. Last chance before I'm forced to decide what I want to do with you." His eyes roamed to her exposed skin.

Georgia shuddered. "The last place I can think of is around the other side, about half way up."

Gabriel was there in a flash. "There's nothing. She lies."

"No, no, I'm not lying. There's a trapdoor kind of thing. It's probably covered with moss." Her dad made it especially for her when she was four years old. She blinked back tears.

Gabriel used his meaty paws to locate the tiny door and yanked the moss from it. "I have the door."

"Open it." Vanessa stood at his side, her hands clasped like a child lost in wonder on Christmas morning. Or the devil waiting for some poor soul to fall.

Georgia held her breath. All three of them had their full attention on the tree. *It's now or never.*

She turned on her heels and sprinted as fast as her legs would carry her. She knew these trees, and even with her hands bound in front of her, she was able to pick up her pace.

Three seconds and her captors realized what she'd done. Shouts. Confusion. Orders. Jubilation over finding the key turned to rage at the thought of her escaping. The crunch of leaves from behind urged Georgia to run faster. She couldn't slip, it would mean a face-plant she wouldn't be able to recover from in time. He'd be on her.

Without looking, she knew it was Gabriel. She couldn't imagine the others running in their designer footwear. Long strides, slower, steadier. His heavy panting gaining on her.

In her peripheral vision, she spotted something. A pony? One of the wild ones who called the forest home. White with caramel-colored splotches. She screamed at it and as she hoped, the creature reared and caused a fuss in her pursuer's path.

He cursed behind her as she sped past the clearing where their vehicles were parked. No time to check for keys left in ignitions. She couldn't stop now. Instead, she darted to the right where the embankment fell away toward the stream. It was her best hope of losing Gabriel. This was her childhood stomping ground. A slender advantage. She'd find refuge in the thick undergrowth—if she didn't trip up and tumble headfirst.

This was no time for second guessing.

It was focus or fall.

# Chapter Thirty-Six



"Come on, Sophie."

Will squinted at the winding road as he sped toward Oak Grove—and hopefully, Georgia.

"I need those coordinates."

A quick glance at Georgia's phone, mounted on the air vent. Nothing. *I have to know where I'm going. Now.*

Chaos and confusion clouded his mind. He needed clarity. At least his clipped, disjointed phone call to Officer Parker gave him hope. They were dispatching two police cars to the area. Five minutes behind him. They had to make it in time.

*I know you're with me, God. Please protect Georgia until help arrives.*

The phone pinged. Sophie. As soon as he arrived at the grove, he would check the message. Find the tree and find Georgia—if his hunch was correct. Of course, her kidnapper would be there, too. Presumably, the man who'd been following her. *How do I balance protecting Georgia and surviving for my son?* Will gulped. At least Jack was with his grandparents.

*Lord, you know my limits. This feels like a David and Goliath situation here. Just watch over Georgia and lead me to her. Bring me back home for my son.*

The police could deal with the rest.

He gripped the steering wheel until his knuckles turned white. Georgia. He'd failed to protect her. The intensity of his feelings caused his pulse to race. Adrenaline, fear, protection, love. They coursed through him in unison. He checked his rearview mirror. The priceless piece of art rested along the length of the folded backseat and into the trunk area.

The car in front slowed to a stop and Will hammered on the brakes. *What now?* He opened the window and craned his neck to see what was happening to create a standstill in the trickle of traffic. *Really?* Donkeys in the road. Country living. He dragged his fingers through his hair and honked on the car horn, which earned him an unfriendly gesture from the driver in the vehicle ahead of him.

*Argh.* He took the stationary seconds to check Sophie's text message. The snippet of a map showed precisely where he had to go. Not much farther. *I can figure this out.* He looked up. Donkeys were back in the field, cars were on the move, so he rounded the bend and flew down a clear stretch of road until he reached the turning for Oak Grove.

Heart pounding, he started along the pitted lane. *I haven't thought this through.* He slowed to recheck Sophie's coordinates. He was close. The lane continued on, rougher and narrower. Not many cars would venture along there. Decision time—wait for the police to arrive or to head in alone. Officer Parker told him to wait. His heart told him otherwise.

*Go to her.*

The words echoed deep in his soul. If God thought it was the right thing to do… but what about being safe for Jack? The little boy couldn't lose another parent.

*Go to her.*

He clenched his teeth. "God help me." With no time to evaluate the situation, Will pressed his foot on the accelerator and sped toward the grove, his SUV bouncing and rattling over the rutted surface.

Eyes peeled, he spotted two vehicles parked up ahead. He slowed to a stop. Two? Outnumbered. A quick glance at the GPS confirmed he was almost at the tree's location.

*Where are you, Georgia?*

"What now, Lord?" He spoke the words aloud, desperate for God to hear him. There was nowhere to hide his car. They were sure to have heard him already. Think fast. Buy time until the police arrive.

With one hand, he smashed on the car horn, and then turned up the radio full blast and pushed the buttons to open all the windows as he continued on toward the clearing. *I'll be a distraction if nothing else.* The closer he approached, the faster his pulse raced.

A gun shot.

*Georgia.*

His heart sank. The hollow noise reverberated through the forest even above the commotion he was creating.

Directly ahead, a woman stood with hands on her hips and stared straight at him. Brunette, but definitely not Georgia. One of the vehicles was a silver sports car—not a coincidence. How many kidnappers were here?

Keep driving.

A man ran into the clearing. The glint of a gun. The woman pointed a finger at Will.

Another shot.

Followed by the shattering of glass as his windshield caved in.

# Chapter Thirty-Seven

A GUNSHOT? GEORGIA LET OUT A strangled cry. Almost lost her footing. The blanket of leaves covering the ground was slippery with moss, and tree roots rose gnarly like prominent veins in an ancient hand.

*I'm okay.*

It was loud, close—but perhaps not close enough. As she trotted in a side-step down the embankment, she remembered Nolan was the one with a gun. He could be following behind Gabriel. Unless he stayed with Vanessa. Gabriel's lumbering footsteps still echoed behind her. By the sound of his labored breaths and grunts, he was struggling to keep up.

Mountain goat versus wooly mammoth.

She inclined her ear as she ran. Was that music?

Shooting. Shouting. Shattering.

Georgia couldn't afford to slow or turn around, so continued down toward the stream and deeper into foliage. She yelped as twigs snagged her blouse and poked her skin. Her left shoulder stung but with her hands tied, there was no way to see if it was bleeding. Every breath was loud in her ears. Sweat ran rivulets down her back. More yelling in the distance. Revving of car engines. Would they leave without Gabriel?

As the small river came into view, the ground evened out a little. She attempted to flick long strands of hair from her vision and chanced a quick glance behind. Where was he? Either he'd been hit by a bullet, given up on her and headed back to the others, or was struggling to keep up with her—which was wishful thinking.

Her tentative plan was to double back to Oak Grove. Hide out in the forest until help arrived. *If* help arrived. Maybe Vanessa would cut her losses and take the key…she must know where the storage place was. Forget about the painting in the cottage. Trust Georgia would stay quiet with the threat hanging over her family.

Another peek behind. Still no Gabriel. She turned right at the stream. Could the other two have gone already? With or without him?

It was worth taking a chance.

Jogging along the edge, she was still protected by thick bushes. She knew if she followed along it would lead her back up the embankment to her tree.

The sparkling water flowing alongside looked enticing as her tongue stuck to the roof of her mouth, but she couldn't stop now. If both their cars were gone, she had to warn Will. Vanessa might head back to Bramble Cottage, where he could still be standing guard. If they'd gone and the coast was clear, she could run as far as the main road. Maybe flag someone down.

Thighs burning, going uphill proved challenging with her hands bound in front of her. She dug her wrists into the damp earth on the steeper sections and pressed on until she recognized the perimeter of the clearing up ahead where her tree stood. Wiping her face with the back of her hands, she leaned over her knees and caught her breath. Quiet. Only the flutter of leaves and a distant chorus of birdsong.

*What now, Lord?* Surely, they were long gone from the tree. Vanessa had the key and no reason to stay—unless she was bent on torturing Georgia for the location of the masterpiece. She shivered, in spite of her burning cheeks and sweat running down her back. Keep moving.

She crouched down and wove her way between thick tree

trunks. She was close. Leaves changed from dull green to the familiar golden yellow of her ancient oak. She froze. Someone was there. A leg poked out from behind the gray bark as if resting against it. That boot. She recognized it and gasped.

"Will?"

A groan sounded from the tree and she sprinted toward it.

"Will?"

He leaned against the gnarly trunk, head in hands, a plethora of cuts covering his lower arms. "I… I found your tree." He lifted his head in slow motion. "You're safe?"

She kneeled before him and touched his hair, which was peppered with shards of glass. "I am. Will, what happened to you?"

His bright green eyes popped against the pallor of his face. A goose egg lump formed on one side of his forehead and was already bruising. His fingers covered a nasty gash on his head. "Georgia?" He blinked. "Are you injured? I heard a gunshot. Thought you'd been hit." He squinted and studied the blood trickle on her neck.

"Wasn't me. This is just a nick. What about you? Your head's bleeding. A lot. Tell me how I can help."

He grimaced. "They shot my windscreen out. I smashed a tree. Hit my head. Concussion. Cuts. I'll be fine. Can't stop everything from spinning."

"Stay still." Her eyes swept the area. Nothing but trees.

"They left. Both vehicles are gone. We're out of danger."

Georgia bit her lip. "Do you think so?" It was peaceful. Light dappled through the leaves as if offering speckles of hope. "I was so scared. I'm sorry. For so much…"

"Shh." He writhed with every word. This man was in pain. "Police are coming."

The hand he pressed against his head wound wasn't stopping the blood flow. It oozed through his fingers and down his arm.

"Will, I need to bandage your head." If only her hands were free. "Do you have a knife or something?"

"In… in my car. My medical bag." He went to stand and fell back in place.

"Whoa." Georgia stood. "I know you're the doc but my legs are fine. Is your car in the clearing where the others were parked? I can find that."

"Yes."

The faint wail of emergency sirens pricked her ears. "Sounds like police are en route. Hopefully, an ambulance, too."

Will's eyes cleared. "I called from the car. Told them to follow those two vehicles. I thought you might be in one of them."

"Oh." Her face fell. As much as she wanted Vanessa and her men to be caught, Will needed medical attention now.

"They're sending help here, too. It… it's okay. Won't be long." He slumped harder against the trunk.

"I'm not waiting. I'll go fetch your bag. You can tell me what to do." She turned to run for the car.

"Georgia, stop." He pointed to her. "You… you've been shot."

Blood rushed from her face. "I have? Where?"

"Back of your arm." He sat up straighter with considerable effort. "Come closer?"

"I can hardly feel my arms anymore." She peered down and adjusted her gaping blouse.

"A… a bullet grazed your shoulder. You'll need stitches."

She raised a brow. "You and me, both."

Will groaned and closed his eyes.

"I'll be back."

She took one last look at her brave surgeon, battered and bloodied. *Please let him make a full recovery, God. Patients need him. Jack needs him.* She swallowed. *I need him.*

She pivoted and raced to his car, praying her adrenaline would last a little longer, relieved Jack hadn't lost his daddy today.

As she approached the parking lot with legs now resembling wet noodles, Will's vehicle was the only one in sight. The front had indeed collided with a tree and was in even worse shape than Will. She stopped at the trunk of the car and depressed the button. The use of her muscles triggered a shot of pain up her wounded arm. She grimaced and jumped back as the trunk popped open.

*What on earth?* Her mouth gaped as she saw the framed picture from her master bedroom. Make that the hidden masterpiece. It was here. Will must have figured it all out. Her lips curved into a smile. *He's brilliant.*

The medical bag was squished in the corner, but she managed to pick it up. The trunk would have to stay open—no way could she reach up with her tied hands.

Exhausted and aware of warm blood now trickling down the back of her arm, she took one more glance at the art in the trunk, satisfied it would soon be on its way home to the rightful owner. *We'll all be home soon.* A sprinkling of serenity washed over her.

"Stop right there."

She shrieked and spun around at the familiar sound of the French accent.

*NO.*

# Chapter Thirty-Eight

Georgia dropped the medical bag to the ground, her heart kicking against the walls of her chest.

"Nice to see you again." Gabriel was sweatier and dirtier than before. He hadn't fared well in their chase.

He nodded toward Will's car. "What have we here? Something precious in a frame?" His gold tooth glinted as he grinned, as did the blade in his hand.

She could let him take the art and leave in Will's car. If it still worked. Be done with him. Yet who was to say he wouldn't come back and kill her in her sleep? Or her family? Even if the other two were caught, Gabriel could slip away. Return later.

"I can't let you take it." The bravado in her voice surprised them both. "This is valuable not only in money, but it's part of a family's heritage."

He spat on the gravel.

She had to keep talking. Stall as long as possible. "Family means everything to me. Daniel knew I would do the right thing. It has to be returned to its owner."

"Foolish."

He grabbed her good arm and she let out a chilling scream.

"I don't need your permission, lady. I need the car keys."

"Why? Did your friends leave without you?"

That earned her a backhanded blow across the face. Her ears rung and black spots danced before her eyes. She regained her balance.

He raised the knife in front of her.

She flinched.

"Let's see if your doctor comes to save you if we start cutting those pretty cheeks of yours, shall we?"

Georgia's entire body quaked as she stood her ground.

"Give. Me. The. Keys."

Her eyes darted toward her ancient oak and Will.

"Ah. Your doctor has them, no? Let's go and see if he will exchange his keys for his lady."

He took another step closer and she backed up. "Don't touch me."

He grabbed a handful of hair and yanked her head closer to his.

She let out a cry as garlic and sweat assaulted her senses.

"Don't tell me what to do. Let's go."

He released her hair and she glanced down at the medical bag.

"Forget it. Neither one of you will be needing that."

More sirens in the distance. Help was on the way. They must be heading here. *Please, hurry.*

Gabriel scowled. "Come." He grabbed her upper arm—just below her wound. Fire radiated from her shoulder and nausea rose from her stomach as he marched her back to the tree.

*God, please help. Help Will. Help me.* She shot up desperate prayers with every step until they arrived at her tree.

Will? He'd disappeared. For a crazy second, she thought perhaps she'd imagined he was there in the first place—until she noticed a patch of flattened grass where he'd been sitting… and a dark pool of blood.

"Where is he?" Gabriel squeezed her injured arm.

"I… I don't know." Tears dripped from her face. The pain was excruciating, but sirens were closing in.

Gabriel swore.

Georgia looked up at him. "Listen, you've been double-crossed. Trust me, I know what it's like to be betrayed. Take the high road, Gabriel. Come clean. Give yourself up. There's always hope for a future."

He squinted at her like she was insane, and then he growled. He scanned the thick forest surrounding them. "You have three seconds to give me the keys or I cut her throat." He brandished the knife in mid-air to prove his point.

She held her breath. *Please have a plan here, Will.*

*Thud.* Gabriel dropped the knife to the ground. His hands flew to his face. He crumbled to his knees.

Georgia blinked and then rammed into him with all her might, tipping his bulk to one side. She let out a cry as her shoulder smarted. The knife. Teeth gritted, she plucked it from the pine needle carpet and fumbled with bound hands to get a decent hold.

"Will?" Where was he?

She stood over Gabriel, the knife poised awkwardly like a dagger in her shaky fingers. The hole in his forehead was perfectly round but too big for a bullet. What happened? She didn't dare take her eyes from his still form.

"Will?"

Gabriel was breathing but stunned. He could recover and pounce on her any second. *Please God, where is Will?*

One of Gabriel's eyes opened.

"Don't move a muscle. Don't tempt me. I'll take out every ounce of my frustration on you with this knife. So help me, I will."

Gabriel said nothing. His eye glazed over and closed as he expelled a soft moan and his head flopped to one side. He was out cold.

The sirens. She'd blocked the drone out, but now they were close. Several of them.

"Georgia?"

She spun in the direction of Will's voice.

He stumbled toward her, his one hand still covering the head wound. "Georgia… you're okay."

A roar filled the air and Gabriel barreled into them, slamming both Georgia and Will onto the dirt. The knife flew into the foliage and Georgia scrambled to retrieve it while Gabriel focused on Will.

Where was the knife? She blinked back tears and clawed at the bushes, catching glimpses over her shoulder of Will as he attempted to block haphazard blows, crushed under the other man's weight. Could Gabriel even see what he was doing? As flesh pounded flesh, Georgia gave up on the knife and scoured the area for another weapon. Anything. A branch had fallen from her tree. She picked it up. Lifted it high in the air. Smashed it over Gabriel's head.

Silence.

Seconds stretched until the man fell.

She dropped the branch and stood, chest heaving.

"Police. Stay where you are."

Three officers ran into the clearing wielding batons.

"Where's Will Hughes?"

"Me. I made the call." Will pulled himself to a sitting position and pointed to Gabriel. "You need to apprehend that man now before he wakes up."

Georgia's hands flew to her mouth. Everything ached, her head pounded, but when Will's eyes found hers, peace washed over her like a waterfall.

"Come here." He held out his blood-stained hands.

She covered the ground between them and sank to her knees, falling into his outstretched arms.

"Georgia... oh, Georgia. Thank you, Lord." He whispered her name over and over as they clung to each other until two paramedics pulled them apart.

Will cleared his throat. "I'm Doctor Will Hughes." His voice was weak. "This is Georgia Brooks. She has a bullet wound graze. Left upper arm near shoulder. I have… concussion, in case I pass out on you."

Georgia lifted her chin. "I'm fine. Give him the gurney. I'm perfectly capable of walking by his side."

Will scowled but he was in no position to argue. His knees buckled when he attempted to stand. "By my side…?" He raised a brow as the paramedics helped him onto the gurney and bound his head. "I do like the sound of that."

"I hope it's not the concussion talking." She squeezed his hand as they moved in the direction of the ambulance.

"What happened to this guy?" A fresh-faced officer pointed at Gabriel as he was loaded onto a second gurney.

"I threw a stone at his head." Will touched his own and grimaced. "It was a matter of life and death."

"And I smashed him with a branch from my tree." Georgia looked up at the old oak, its protective branches hovering over them like a mother hen over her chicks.

"I love your tree." Will's eyes were closed but his mouth curved into a smile.

Georgia relived the last few minutes in her mind and shook her head. "Wait. You threw a stone?"

"All I had."

"Like… David and Goliath?"

"Like a cricket pro. The bowling practice paid off." He wriggled his right hand, still covered in dark blood. "Actually, it was all God. I could barely see straight."

They reached the ambulance and were carefully loaded inside. Georgia's heart-rate returned to near-normal as she sat next to the gurney. They were safe.

"Do you think they'll catch the other two?" She bit her lip. "I would love to be able to put this behind us."

"Us?" His eyes were greener than the forest as he gazed into hers.

"Yes. Us."

Will reached up and touched her wet cheek with a tenderness that promised a future filled with love and kindness.

She hadn't even noticed she was crying.

These were cleansing tears. Tears of sweet relief, washing away betrayal and pain and fear. Making room for trust and hope and joy…

# Epilogue

"Everyone, smile."

For once, Georgia was in front of the camera, together with her beloved family. Given recent events, they'd postponed the twins' thirtieth birthday party for another month, but now they were all together. Healthy. Happy. No longer in danger.

Georgia's heart swelled while she attempted to memorize this precious moment. An arm around her mom and a twin on either side of them, the ladies posed as Will snapped a series of photographs. She hugged Sophie and then Harriet. "Happy belated birthday, both of you. I'm beyond blessed to have you two in my life. Especially now."

"I'm so glad you're staying longer in England." Harriet squeezed her hand. "Lucy's already planning to meet you here for tea every single week."

The entire Brambles and Berries tearoom had been transformed into party mode by their mother. Pink and silver bunting and matching balloons hung in a riot of festive celebration, and one long table laden with food and fresh flowers ran down the center of the room. It was bookended by two elaborately decorated cakes. One pink and one silver. Their mom never made the twins share a birthday cake.

Georgia grinned. "Mom, you did a fabulous makeover for this party."

"It's her thing." Sophie caressed the pink petals surrounding the photo booth. "Remember our over-the-top birthday parties when we were kids?"

"I can hear you, girls." Their mother accepted the camera from Will and put a hand on her hip. "You might recall this is how I earned a living and kept you all in food and clothing."

Georgia wrapped her mom in a hug. "And we love you for it." She pulled back. "I'm going to miss you, Mom."

"Not as much as I'll miss you, sweetheart." She cupped her daughter's face in one hand. "But I think you've made the right decision. A six-month trial period living here seems like the smart thing to do."

"Thanks." She studied her pale pink stilettos. "I'm looking forward to settling into Bramble Cottage without the drama. You know it could end up being longer than six months..."

"I know. I also realize Vancouver holds a lot of tough memories for you, and you have some beautiful new ones to make here."

Georgia peered over at Will, who left the ladies to their chatter and was now leaning against the brick wall, observing the party with his trademark half-smile.

"Sweetheart, you deserve your happily-ever-after."

"Maybe."

"You do. A mother knows these things." She squeezed Georgia's hand and then directed her attention toward Harriet and Sophie. "You all know how much my momma-heart is bursting right now, don't you?" She gathered them all together for a group hug. "My little women. I'm so proud of all three of you. So grateful God kept us all safe. Please, let's not leave it too long until we're all together again?"

They stepped back watery-eyed, beaming with gratitude. This day could have looked very differently, and they all knew it.

"Now, let's just have the birthday girls for a photo." Her mom was having way too much fun with all her family in one place. "Say, 'thirty'!"

"*Mom.*" Harriet and Sophie whined in unison. Neither were particularly enamored with entering a new decade, but they humored her with identical stunning smiles.

Georgia joined Will over at the leaded window, where the late afternoon sun lit the tips of his brown hair. He was almost back to his usual healthy, handsome self again—his head had been stitched and only a few of the deeper glass cuts on his arms and chin were yet to fully heal.

"Hey, beautiful."

He kissed her cheek and her face flushed. This would take some getting used to. Especially in front of her family.

"Did I tell you how gorgeous you look today?"

"You did, actually." She took one of his hands and gave it a squeeze. Her pink, fitted dress was a good choice with its floaty sleeves covering fading scars. "But feel free to tell me again."

"I'd be happy to tell you every single day."

She gazed up into his eyes and was lost in those deep emerald pools.

"Not to mention, you're incredibly brave—the mastermind, in fact, behind the solving of the 'Masterpiece Murders.'"

She chuckled. "I've never been called brave, but I do like the sound of that. Although…" She bit her lower lip and glanced away.

"Although what?"

"'Masterpiece Murders'? The press make it sound so sensationalized with that label. I guess it doesn't sit well with me. A ring of criminals, including my ex-husband, left so much pain and carnage, all in the name of greed."

"I know, but they're facing the consequences now."

Will lowered his head and kissed her cheek. "I'm so proud of you."

"Who'd have thought our tough Goliath guy would squeal like a piglet and throw the whole lot of them under the bus." Georgia shuddered. "It's such a relief knowing they're all caught and are going to spend a very long time behind bars. My family has nothing to worry about anymore."

"Shawsha?"

Her heart warmed at Jack's little-boy voice and she crouched down to his level. "Hey, Jack. Have you had cake by any chance?" The smear of cream on his cheek was a giveaway.

"Cake." He peeked up at his daddy with adoring eyes. "Cake?"

"I think you've had enough, buddy. High tea and little boys are an interesting combination."

Lucy skipped over, her arm no longer in a bright pink cast, and grabbed Jack by the hand. "Come, Jack. Photos."

He followed her lead and they trotted back to Georgia's mom.

"Aren't they the cutest kids you've ever seen?" Will shook his head. "I think they'll always be the best of friends."

Georgia blinked back tears. When would talk of children and babies stop hurting so much? Would the desperate longing to have a child of her own ever fade?

"Hey, what is it?" Will lifted her chin. "We agreed to be open and honest if we want to build a future together. You know you can tell me anything."

The past few weeks, they'd taken their relationship slowly. They were both a little fragile and knew they'd been through a traumatic event. Yet there was no doubt they were both falling for each other more every day. Conversations were getting deeper. Like this one.

"This is very forward to even ask, but how do you feel about not being able to have any more biological children, Will?" *I have to know if it's a deal-breaker for you.*

He put a protective arm around her shoulder. "I feel blessed that God saw fit to give me Jack. If He ever asked me to adopt more, I would be up for it, but I'm content to leave it in His hands."

Good answer. "I like that."

As Harriet waltzed over to them, a vision of grace and beauty, her dazzling smile didn't quite reach her eyes. They held a hint of sorrow. Pain even.

"How are you two faring over here?"

"We're both great. How's the birthday girl?" Georgia lowered her voice. "Is everything okay?"

Harriet raised a shoulder. "Leo had to leave, but nothing's going to spoil our birthday party. We haven't all been together as a family in forever."

"He left already?" Will scoured the room. "I didn't get a chance to chat with him."

"He had a flight to Paris."

"When he knew it was your birthday party?" Georgia's hackles raised. "What was so important?"

"Work. Something. Please let me enjoy this special afternoon with my people?" Harriet set her mask of happiness back in place. "I'll call you tomorrow and we'll chat. I should go check on Lucy." She scurried off before Georgia had opportunity to press her further.

"That doesn't sound good." She watched her sister fuss over the children at the photo booth. "I hope everything's okay between her and Leo." *Lord, please help them work out whatever the issue is...*

"I'll try to call him in the morning. See what's going on."

"He's been noticeably absent since our incident." Georgia pleaded with her eyes. "You don't still think he could have had anything to do with it, do you? Not Leo."

Will pressed another kiss on her forehead. "No. He explained about that photo. The café is a favorite haunt of his when he's in Paris, and he often meets clients there. Even Harriet confirmed that."

"I know. I get it. Daniel spent a lot of time in Europe on assignments back then and he didn't get on particularly well with Leo, so it makes sense that Leo never mentioned running into him on occasion."

Will let out a sigh. "I don't know what's up with my friend these days, but I feel bad suspecting he could have been involved."

"You were trying to be objective."

Will shook his head. "I was wrong though. He's going through something, but he's a good man."

"Who's a good man?" Sophie pulled them toward the food table. "Because if you know of any, please tell me. Mom's putting the heavies on again."

Georgia grabbed Will's arm. "Sorry, I'm afraid I've claimed the very best man."

"So, what's up?" Sophie's forehead creased.

"I'm a bit worried about Harriet, that's all."

"Me, too, actually. Something's off between her and Leo." Sophie crossed her arms over her chest. "I get that he was ticked when his name came up after he was caught in that photograph. Talk about wrong place at the wrong time. I thought he was cool with everything now though."

Georgia nibbled on a thumbnail. "I really hope he's not blaming Harriet for any of this. I have a feeling they were already going through a sticky patch."

Sophie squeezed Georgia's hand. "Try not to worry, sis. I'll talk with Harriet later tonight. She's been so excited for this party, I don't want to put a damper on it. Have you guys eaten yet?"

The table was piled high with a delectable selection of fancy iced cakes, triangular cucumber sandwiches, and plump scones with blackberry jam and clotted cream.

Will eyed the selection. "Did you make the scones?"

"I did." Sophie blushed.

He let out a low whistle. "Impressive."

Georgia nudged her sister's arm. "I happen to know how amazing these scones are. She's famous for them in Paris."

Will chuckled. "In that case, I'm digging in."

Sophie tilted her head. "As a matter of fact, my latest specialty has taken off quite well in Paris, too. I'd love the chance to give it a whirl here in England."

"Awesome. What are you working your magic with now?"

"Well, as my latest writing project is a romance manuscript and I'm thinking all things love, I thought I'd try my hand at wedding cakes." She looked from Georgia to Will. "I'm taking orders, just so you know."

Georgia gasped, and her sister darted away with a chuckle toward a gathering of friends who arrived at the tearoom entrance.

"Good grief." Georgia handed Will a floral china plate. "Sophie's extra sassy since her surgery. It's like they removed her filter along with her appendix. Sorry."

"I'm not." One side of his mouth turned up in a way that made her pulse race. "I think it's worth bearing in mind. Don't you?"

Wedding cakes? Her heart hammered in her chest. Dare she hope? She closed her eyes.

One day at a time.

"Georgia? I'm sorry. I didn't mean to push things—"

"Oh, I think it's definitely worth bearing in mind." She lifted herself on tiptoes and kissed him square on the lips. "It may be my sisters' birthday, but I feel like you're the greatest gift I could ask for."

"Shawsha."

Jack pulled on the hem of Georgia's dress. "Photo."

"Hey, I didn't know you could say that word, Jack. It's one of my favorites, you know."

"What did you say, buddy?" Will set his plate on the table and squatted down next to his son. "Say it again for Daddy?"

"Photo." He glanced from Will to Georgia. "Dada, Shawsha, Jack-jack. Photo."

Georgia threw her head back and laughed. "Oh my goodness, you're so smart. You want us all in a photo?"

Jack nodded.

"Let's do it." Georgia grabbed Will with one hand and Jack with the other, and almost walked on air over to the photo booth area.

Her mom was still on camera duty and gave her daughter a wink. "Don't you three make a perfect picture?"

Will picked up Jack and put his other arm around Georgia.

"Everyone, smile."

Will leaned in toward her ear and whispered the words she'd been longing to hear right as the picture was snapped.

"I love you, Georgia."

In that moment, hope flooded her soul as love was captured in frame.

# Author Note

"Going through the motions doesn't please you,
a flawless performance is nothing to you.
I learned God-worship
when my pride was shattered.
Heart-shattered lives ready for love
don't for a moment escape God's notice."
Psalm 51:16-17 (MSG)

**"Though our feelings come and go, God's love for us does not." C.S. Lewis**

Thank you, dear reader, for taking time to join Georgia Brooks as she navigates her first nail-biting weeks in the not-so-sleepy English village of Bramble Downs.

Like any author, all my published books are precious to me in some way or another—they are my book-babies! *Captured in Frame* is my sixth romantic suspense, but she's the first one set in jolly old England, and I was absolutely thrilled to go back to my English roots. Born, bred, and living the first half of my life in the UK before emigrating to Canada, it was only a matter of time before I tiptoed over the pond into an English series.

Many of my stories are inspired by setting, and this book is no exception. It was a typical rainy, chilly January evening in 2019, and I was staying with my sister Heidi and her family at their vicarage in a quaint little village in the English countryside. Apparently, I have now lived outside the UK long enough to refer to English things as "quaint"!

The whole experience had been utterly delightful complete with donkeys in narrow country lanes, sounds of church bells in the air, rows of Wellington boots, scrumptious Sunday lunches at the village pub… but that particular evening, as my sister and I relaxed in their cozy living room, it came to me. There he was, plain as day—the soaking wet, grizzly, bearded man in the hooded oilskin coat staring straight at us through the French doors.

Of course, this was my overactive imagination at play, and I had to assure poor Heidi that all was well in real life, yet this scenario was the split-second that ignited my story into flame. Turmoil in tranquility. Notes were scribbled and copious photos were snapped during my brief time in that village, and then I returned home to Canada, where I was in the midst of another romantic suspense series being published. Yet I couldn't shake my English story, and so in the "quieter time" of 2020, I dug out my notes and delved into Bramble Downs.

In case you're curious, Bramble Downs is a fictitious version of my sister's village, and I took great joy in naming it as a nod to "Brambly Hedge", a beautiful collection of children's books by Jill Barklem, which holds a special place in my heart. As a side note, my sister and her family have since moved on from that original village—but I can assure you it was in no way related to any grizzly man in an oilskin coat!

To balance out the somewhat stressful suspense elements in my writing process, I enjoy going deep in creating compelling characters with relatable issues, always some heart-stopping-yet-heartwarming romance, and exploring unique struggles in their faith journeys.

Truly, my ultimate desire in writing these fiction books is to encourage and inspire you in your REAL life with stories of hope, leaving no shadow of doubt that you are loved by God. Always.

If you have enjoyed Georgia's story in *Captured in Frame*, be sure to look out for the next book in this Bite of Betrayal series… it's Sophie's story in *The Final Word*, coming in 2025!

You can contact me and find details on all my books, blog, writing coaching, and my free monthly newsletter at: www.laurathomasauthor.com


Books by Laura Thomas:

(Bite of Betrayal Series)
Captured in Frame

(Flight to Freedom Series)
The Glass Bottom Boat
The Lighthouse Baby
The Orphan Beach
The Christmas Cabin
Snow Globe Secrets

(Tears Trilogy)
Tears to Dancing
Tears of a Princess
Tears, Fears, and Fame

The Candle Maker
Pearls for the Bride

www.ingramcontent.com/pod-product-compliance
Lightning Source LLC
Chambersburg PA
CBHW071218210726
48293CB00002B/485